Wild Bird

Also by Wendelin Van Draanen

How I Survived Being a Girl
Flipped
Swear to Howdy
Runaway
Confessions of a Serial Kisser
The Running Dream
The Secret Life of Lincoln Jones

The Sammy Keyes Mysteries

Sammy Keyes and the Hotel Thief
Sammy Keyes and the Skeleton Man
Sammy Keyes and the Sisters of Mercy
Sammy Keyes and the Runaway Elf
Sammy Keyes and the Curse of Moustache Mary
Sammy Keyes and the Hollywood Mummy
Sammy Keyes and the Search for Snake Eyes
Sammy Keyes and the Art of Deception
Sammy Keyes and the Psycho Kitty Queen
Sammy Keyes and the Dead Giveaway
Sammy Keyes and the Wild Things
Sammy Keyes and the Cold Hard Cash
Sammy Keyes and the Wedding Crasher
Sammy Keyes and the Night of Skulls
Sammy Keyes and the Power of Justice Jack
Sammy Keyes and the Showdown in Sin City
Sammy Keyes and the Killer Cruise
Sammy Keyes and the Kiss Goodbye

Wild Bird

Wendelin Van Draanen

ALFRED A. KNOPF
New York

THANK YOU

I am grateful to the parents and teens who trusted me with their pain, to the Utah desert for its incomparable beauty and humbling lessons, and to Shanan Anderson of the Southern Paiute Nation for her guidance and insights. Any mistakes are my own.

—WENDELIN VAN DRAANEN

THIS IS A BORZOI BOOK PUBLISHED BY ALFRED A. KNOPF

Visit us on the Web! randomhouseteens.com

Educators and librarians, for a variety of teaching tools, visit us at RHTeachersLibrarians.com

Library of Congress Cataloging-in-Publication Data is available upon request.

ISBN 978-1-101-94044-0 (trade) — ISBN 978-1-101-94045-7 (lib. bdg.) — ISBN 978-1-101-94046-4 (ebook)

The text of this book is set in 11.5-point Apolline Regular.

Printed in the United States of America
September 2017
10 9 8 7 6 5 4 3 2 1

First Edition

for Elizabeth

1

"Wren . . ."

My name is floating around me. Bouncing on the clouds in my mind.

"Wren . . . wake up, Wren."

Everything's cocoony. Drifty. The clouds are so soft.

"Wren, come on. It's time to go."

Go? Go where? Who said that? I don't recognize his voice. I look around my cloud, but it's dark. Like a storm is coming.

Then thunder begins to roll. "Wren!"

I pull in, hunker down. Why is he on my cloud? "Go away," I mumble through the rocks in my mouth. I need a drink. Maybe if I licked the cloud . . .

"She's totally wasted, Mom."

Wait. That was Anabella. What's she doing on my cloud?

She was definitely not invited.

The narc.

I can't see her either, though. And now the cloud is rocking. Rocking and spinning.

"Go back to bed," my mother whispers.

My mother? No! Not her, too!

A new voice struggles into the darkness. A small, sleepy voice. "What's going on?"

It's Mo! My little buddy, my Mowgli, my Mo-bro! He can be on my cloud. Anytime! But . . . no . . . wait. First I have to hide some things. Quick. I need to hide some things.

"Take Morris and get back to bed!" my mother hisses.

"I can't believe you're doing this," Anabella says.

"Take your brother and go!" my father commands.

My father?

Why am I even on this cloud? It's so crowded now. And dark. And rolling with thunder.

"Wren! Wake up!"

Who *is* that?

Light stabs my eyes as I peel them open. A man comes into focus. He's large. Standing over me. Wearing dark blue. With gold-embroidered shoulder patches.

A . . . a *cop*?

I sit up a little.

Yes, a cop.

He starts swaying. But . . . no, it's not him swaying. It's me. Or my bed. I grab for my trash can and puke.

My mind runs to Nico as my guts come up. Did he get busted? Is that why there's a cop here? Did they connect the dots?

I try to play it cool as I wipe off my mouth. "Sorry. Flu."

That line's always worked before. But this is a cop, not my parents. And he's got that look.

4

He's not buying.

The clock digits are a bloody red: 3:47 a.m. "What happened?" I ask my doorway parents. "Why is he here?"

"It's for your own good," my father says. His voice sounds icy. Hard. A freezer door slamming shut.

"Can you walk?" the cop asks.

I muster a sneer. "Of course I can walk!"

"Then get up and get dressed." He hands me jeans and a hoodie. "You're coming with me."

"What? Why?" I look over, and one of my doorway parents has disappeared. "Mom!" I call. I can hear her crying her way down the hall. "Mom! What is going on!"

She doesn't answer me. Nobody answers me. I'm shaky and cold and my head is pounding. There are handcuffs on the cop's belt. I've heard they hurt, so I pull on the jeans and yank the hoodie on over the T-shirt I slept in. I feel haphazard. On the verge of puking again. And then I notice that my phone's gone.

Full-on panic floods over me. I scramble around inside the covers, under my pillow.

"We've got your phone," my father says.

I am so busted.

"Use the bathroom," the cop tells me. "You'll be in the car awhile."

When I come out, my father hands a duffel to the cop and turns to me. His lips are tight white threads across his face. "We've tried everything, Wren."

"So you're turning me over to the cops? MOM!" I scream past him. "MOM!"

The cop grips my arm, and when I struggle to get free, he wrestles me down the hallway. I can hear my mother crying in the kitchen. "MOM!" I shriek. "WHAT IS GOING ON? HELP ME!"

My brother's voice seeps through Anabella's door, high-pitched and desperate. "We have to help Wren!"

"Mowgli!" I call out. "Mo-bro, help me!"

"Are you really that selfish?" my dad says, his words singeing the space between us.

"Why are you doing this to me?" I ask as the cop drags me through the house. We pass by the living room, pass by the piano, and now I'm crying.

"Because we're at our wits' end," my father says. "We've run out of options."

Then the cop's saying, "We'll be in touch, Mr. Clemmens," and I'm being hauled outside.

"Daddy, please!" I cry.

The door closes in my face.

"I'LL BE BETTER! I PROMISE!"

But I'm talking to wood.

Dead, heartless wood.

2

The cop maneuvers me off the porch and out toward the street, where a black SUV is waiting. It has no police-force markings. Just sleek black, with tinted windows.

"You an undercover narc?" I ask.

"You worried about that?" he says. "At fourteen?"

"Just answer me!"

"Get in." He opens the door and points me to the far-back seats.

There's a woman behind the wheel. Blue uniform, gold patches, sunglasses.

In the middle of the night, she's wearing sunglasses.

"Mornin', sunshine," she says, grinning over her shoulder at me.

I want to tell her to shut up, but I climb in back, hoping she'll give me some answers. "Where we going?"

"Joel didn't tell you?" she asks, looking at me through the rearview mirror.

So the narc has a name. Joel. "You just told me more than I've gotten out of anybody this whole time."

"Ah," she says, and eyes Joel over her glasses. "Classified?"

"Need-to-know basis," he says, shutting the door and sitting in the middle row. "And what *you* need to know is she's coming off a high and hungover bad."

She hands him a barf bag, which gets relayed back to me. "You're stuck in what you're wearing for at least twelve," she says through the mirror. "So I wouldn't mess 'em up if I were you."

"Twelve? Twelve what?"

"Hours, honey." She puts the SUV in drive and pulls forward. "You're in for a long day."

"Twelve hours! Where are we going?"

She glances in the mirror. "To LAX."

"To the *airport*?" I lunge for the door, but Joel swats me back.

"See?" he tells the driver. "She didn't need to know that." Then he turns on me like a big, angry bear. "Let's get something straight," he growls. "You're in my legal custody. I'm allowed to restrain you by force. I've dealt with a lot bigger and badder than you, and I'm not in the mood for attitude, runners, or whining. If you want to be handcuffed, just try that again. If not, sit down, strap in, and shut up."

He stares me down, and it doesn't take long. I slink back, feeling sick, but in a totally different way.

My parents turned over legal custody?

Like, disowned me?

I look out the window. We've already left our neighborhood and are speeding along Culver. The street is eerie without the usual traffic. It's misty nighttime, but there are so many lights along the road, it's like daylight. We drive past block after block of curving sidewalks lined with hedges and trees and long-leafed plants. Perfectly trimmed, always. When we moved here, that seemed nice. There weren't chain-link fences or alleyways scattered with trash. Everything was clean and green. And there was *room*. But we've been living here over three years, and I still get turned around when I go more than a few blocks. Every neighborhood looks the same.

We stop at a red light near Nico's street, and I think about making a dive for it again. Joel's sitting sideways, and I can see that his eyes are closed. . . . The driver's looking straight ahead waiting for the light to change. . . . If I can get out, I can ditch them, easy. But . . . would Nico even help me? He's told me more than once that if I bring trouble, I'm gone.

Suddenly Joel sticks his leg out. "Down, girl," he snarls, eyes still closed. "Don't make me cuff you."

How can he know what I'm thinking? I slump back, feeling way out of my league.

We ramp up to the I-5 freeway and head north, all five lanes to ourselves. I'm paying attention, trying to memorize how to get back to the neighborhood if I can get away.

I recognize the Costco turnoff, which normally takes twenty minutes of stop-and-go traffic to get to, and before I can believe it, we're long gone, passing signs for Disneyland.

My heart hurts, thinking about Disneyland. Thinking about my brother. He's never been Morris Lee Clemmens IV to me. He's always been Mo, Mo-bro, or Mowgli.

My little *Jungle Book* buddy.

What are they telling him about me?

Will he believe them?

And how could they do this to me? My own parents!

We fly past Disneyland, leave it behind. I hold my head. My heart aches. I can't seem to breathe.

How could they do this to me?

3

I cry myself to sleep in the back of the SUV and wake up confused all over again when we get to the airport. The clock in the dash says 5:12. At first I'm not sure if that's a.m. or p.m., or where I am.

Then it all comes back.

The world spins as I climb out behind Joel. I have to stop, catch my breath. My head feels like it's splitting in two.

There are cars double-parked, dropping people off, but we're third from the curb getting honked at. "Come on," Joel says, grabbing me. He's got my duffel in one hand and a messenger bag strapped across his chest.

"Please," I beg him. "I've got to barf."

He shuts the door and drags me along between bumpers. "Do it at the curb."

I try, but nothing comes up. "Do you have aspirin?" I ask as he pulls me through a door marked Terminal 5.

"You said you had the flu."

"Yeah, and my head is about to explode!"

He gives me a smirk. "Ever heard of Reye's syndrome? No aspirin for kids with flu symptoms."

A surge of hatred twists through me. "Let go!"

"Cooperate, and I will."

"Let me have my duffel!"

"Cooperate, and I will."

"I'm *sick*, you idiot!"

"I'm no idiot, Wren. Now, move it."

Inside, the place is huge. Counters seem to go for miles in both directions, with mazes for lines set up in front of all of them.

We don't go up to a counter. Instead, Joel makes a beeline to big screens announcing DEPARTURES. The cities are listed in alphabetical order, and he seems to be scanning the "S" cities—Seattle, Sioux Falls, Spokane, St. Louis . . .

"Please tell me where we're going," I beg, and I'm suddenly weirdly panicked. "Are you coming with me?" There's a huge lump in my throat, making my voice sound weak.

Scared.

Which I am.

He looks down from the board, and for a second there seems to be a little break in the armor. "Yeah," he says, "I'm coming with you."

Then we're off again, walking way too fast to a line that goes way too slow, back and forth, back and forth, like we're waiting to get on a Disneyland ride instead of through security. He gets us past a uniformed guy sitting at a podium by showing him some paperwork, but he probably didn't even need to. His shoulder patches say it all—he's in charge, I'm in trouble.

Once we're through security, we walk down corridors that seem to go on forever. Especially since every step is a jolt of pain in my head. "Can I please get something to drink?" I finally ask. "I'm dying."

He takes me over to a water fountain. "Drink."

"Really? *Really?*" What I need is an energy drink. I nod at my duffel, clutched in his hand. "Is there money in there?"

"Not one red cent." He points to the fountain. "Drink. And not too much. No bathroom break until we're on the plane."

"You've got to be kidding me!"

"Drink. Or don't. Your choice."

I take a few sips.

It doesn't help a thing.

We walk and walk and walk some more, and finally he pulls over to an area marked B-54. There's a counter with an electronic board behind it that says

Flight 4746

SALT LAKE CITY

On Time

I squint at him. "Salt Lake City?"

He motions to two seats in the waiting area and hands over the duffel. "There's a letter inside. You might want to read it."

4

The envelope is sealed. My name is typed across the front of it. I recognize the Lucida Handwriting font, my mother's favorite.

I tear it open, unfold two typed pages "handwritten" by Lucida.

The letter begins: *My Precious Baby Bird.*

"I am *not* a baby bird!" I cry.

Joel's right next to me, focused on his phone. "Then quit chirping like one."

I fold the letter up. I don't need to read it. I already know what's in it—how she just doesn't understand what's happened to me. How we used to be so close. How she wants her baby bird back. Besides, it's typed. Something about that really bugs me.

"You don't want to know where you're going?" Joel says as I start to chuck the letter in a trash can. He's still looking at his phone, flicking through messages.

I tell him exactly where *he* can go.

He gives a little shrug. "Not until I deliver you."

I spin back. "Deliver me? To whom?"

"Nice grammar," he says, looking up with a grin. Then he shrugs and goes back to his phone. "I guess if you really wanted to know, you'd read the letter."

"How would you know what's in my letter?"

He pats his messenger bag. "Got a copy in your file."

"My *file*?"

"Mm-hmm."

"Why is there a *file* on me? Who had time to make a *file*?"

He flicks through his phone. "Maybe you should read the letter."

"Maybe you should just *tell* me!"

He shakes his head. "You can read the letter or find out when we land in Salt Lake. Up to you."

I stare at him flicking through his phone. I really, really don't want to read the letter. I really, really just want someone to tell me what's going on. But finally I break down, sit down, and read. And just like I thought, I hear all about what a disappointment I am and how nobody understands what's happened to me, and how they've tried everything—counseling, therapists, surefire behavior modification techniques that have backfired instead, how my antagonistic attitude is ruining our perfect family, and how "little Morris" is in danger of my evil influence. Then she goes into this awful metaphor about icebergs and the *Titanic* and listening to the pings of radar and being desperate to do something before it's too late to "turn this ship around."

On page two—indicated by a tidy "2" precisely centered

in the footer in case I couldn't figure it out—I finally learn what this means:

They've "enrolled" me in a wilderness therapy program.

"That's it?" I blurt out, and I'm suddenly smiling. "I'm going to camp?"

Joel smiles back, but it's a wily smile. Like maybe I don't know what I'm talking about.

"It says so right here," I tell him, pointing to that part. But then I see something else. "Eight weeks?" I gasp. "Are you serious? Eight weeks?"

He nods. "Sounds about right."

"What about school? It'll be almost over in eight weeks! What are they going to do—hold me back?"

"Looks like you were headed that direction anyway."

"What? How would you know?"

He pats the messenger bag.

"That's in my file? The *school* is in on this?" I feel weirdly embarrassed. "I was going to pull those grades up," I tell him. "No way I was going to flunk my freshman year."

A woman behind the B-54 gate counter announces that it's time for our flight to board. Joel grabs my arm and steers me into a corral that says Group 3.

"How is eight weeks in the woods going to change anything?" I ask him.

He starts to say something but checks himself. "You've got the window seat," he says. "Try to enjoy the views."

But once we're in the air, the sun hurts my eyes so bad that I pull down the window cover and close my eyes instead. And I'm mostly asleep when the coffee cart rolls by. "I want some!" I call, because it's already going past.

"You want coffee?" the flight attendant asks, not sure what a kid would want with that.

"Yes!"

"Cream and sugar?"

"Yes!"

Joel frowns but lets it slide. "Give her a ginger ale, too, would you?"

The coffee helps my head, but not my stomach. So I sip the ginger ale and eat half of a pack of the saltines that Joel has in his bag.

Like he knew I'd need them.

Something about that bothers me more than I can explain, so I lean my head against the window, close my eyes, and block it out.

Who cares, right?

Who cares.

5

I think a lot about my mother's letter on the flight. I try to sleep, but I can't get comfortable. Plus, the coffee's kicked in, so my mind keeps going back to it.

Something about her letter tweaks me, and hard. If I was home right now, I'd be yelling stuff at her to tweak her back. That's always easy. And she'd deserve it. I mean, what kind of lame parent is she? Just because she can't handle me, she has me hauled off in the middle of the night, removed from her precious house like a criminal? I thought this had to do with Nico, but I was sweating that for nothing. It's about her *stuff,* and the precious family unit and how I've messed everything up. She can't deal, so she gets rid of me? What kind of mother does that? What kind of *parents* do that? I mean, hello, Dad? Where have *you* been the past four years? Besides detailing your precious new Prius every single Saturday.

Joel doesn't say a word to me the whole time. He eats some powerhouse sandwich with sprouts sticking out everywhere, drinks tomato juice, and reads. I can't stomach anything but the saltines, and seeing him chow down is gross. I shoot hate at him extra hard, but it doesn't seem to faze him.

When I have to use the bathroom, he follows me, then waits outside the door for me to come out. Everyone watches us coming down the aisle. I can hear them wondering what my deal is. One old lady's staring so hard, I tell her, "Mind your own business!" which makes her jerk away like I've hit her.

Stupid nosy hag.

Then I'm back in my seat, trapped by Joel and his annoying eating and reading.

When we land, Joel sends a text, then escorts me off the plane without letting me in on anything. The airport's not nearly as big as LAX, and it doesn't take long to get to baggage claim. Not that I have anything to claim.

"We're looking for a woman in army-green pants and a red bandanna," Joel says, hawkeyeing the place.

"Her?" I ask, pointing to a woman in army-green pants and a red bandanna.

"Michelle!" he calls out, waving like a goofball. Then he grins at me like the sun's just come up on a God-given glorious day. "End of the line for me, kiddo."

Much as I hate him, I'm weirdly not ready to hear this. "You're leaving?"

"Got an eleven-fifteen out. No time to dawdle." He leads me over to Michelle. "Here she is, one Wren Clemmens."

"Perfect," Michelle says, smiling at me. She looks like she's in her late twenties, and her teeth are like candied gum soldiers standing at attention. There are tattered straps of cord around her wrist, with dried berries strung through, and a red bandanna wrapped around her head.

I notice her feet.

Hiking boots.

Good for the mountains, maybe, but bad for speed. Plus, her pants have lots of dorky, weighted-down pockets. And nowhere on her do I see handcuffs.

"Welcome to Utah," she says to me. Then she asks Joel, "Stat report?"

He hands over a folder—my file—and says, "Threw up at oh-four-hundred, clearly wasted—suspect drugs with alcohol. Coffee with sugar and cream at oh-eight-thirty, followed by ginger ale and a sleeve of saltines. Complaints of headache and nausea."

Michelle nods. "I'll bet." She eyes me. "The altitude's not going to help that any. You'll probably feel pukey for a couple of days while you detox and get used to thinner air."

Detox? The word floors me. Do they think I need *rehab*?

She's already turned back to Joel, asking, "Anything else?"

"She slept on and off. Thirty minutes in the car and another thirty on the plane. Used the bathroom at oh-nine-fifty."

I feel like a stupid kid, being picked up at day care.

"Okay," Michelle says. "I think we're set. Have a good flight back."

He gives her a little salute, tells me, "Good luck, Wren," and takes off.

"Ready?" Michelle asks, and when I nod, she small-talks me toward the exit, chitter-chatter, chitter-chatter.

I hate her already, but it doesn't matter. I'm keeping an eye on Joel as he hurries away.

Chitter-chatter, chitter-chatter.

We're almost at the door.

Chitter-chatter, chitter-chatter.

Move it, I tell Joel in my head. *Faster.* He turns a corner and is . . . *gone.*

And just like that, I take off running.

6

My plan is to get out the door.

That's it.

I drop the duffel because I don't need it slowing me down, and it doesn't have much in it anyway. Undies, a brush, and hygiene stuff is all I saw when I took out the letter—things I can shoplift if I need them, no problem.

I do make it out the door. And about twenty yards down the street. But then some guy in army-green pants grabs me and wraps my arms behind my back so fast and hard I squeal.

"Help!" I shout. "I'm being abducted!"

"Nice vocabulary," he says in my ear.

"HELP!"

People look, but they don't do anything.

"HELP!"

He snaps cuffs on me, ratchets them down until they hurt, then holds a big walkie-talkie up to his mouth and says, "Got her."

"Thanks" comes crackling back.

Michelle.

The guy who's nabbed me has such a deep, glowing tan that it looks like the sun's shining from inside him. His hair's in a thick brown man-bun with little kinky waves breaking free here and there. And he's strong. Really strong. "I'm John," he says, muscling me forward. "Welcome to Utah."

"Great," I grumble, and let him steer me to a—how creative—black SUV.

John hoists me into the middle seat, where he takes off the cuffs and causes more pain with cheerful introductions. "You've already met Michelle."

"Hi again," she says from the driver's seat.

"That's Nash, riding shotgun."

"Hey," Nash calls back.

"And Dax," John says, hitching a thumb at the guy in the backseat. "Just in from Chicago."

Dax is looking bloodshot. Mad, dirty, and bloodshot.

And about eighteen.

"Meet Wren," John says to nobody in particular.

"Wren," Dax snorts. "A real *wren*-egade, huh?"

"Shut up," I tell him over the seat.

He's looking more evil than mad now. "Da doo wren-wren-wren, da doo wren-wren."

I squint at him. "What?"

"Looks like Dax is waking up," Nash says over the seats as Michelle pulls into traffic.

Dax doesn't bother to explain the doo wren-wren thing. Instead, he starts singing, "Wren, wren, wren 'til her daddy takes the T-bird awaaaaay."

"Knock it off!" I shout back at him.

"Wait," he says, like he didn't even hear me. "It's fun, not run." He slumps back. "Whatever. Beach Boys are lame."

"I have to camp with *him*?" I ask with a squint.

"Uh, no," Michelle says. "He's just your in-flight entertainment."

"Can I switch the channel?" I ask.

John snickers, which gives me a strange little jolt of happiness. "Not until we get to the field office."

"You can wren, but you cannot hide," Dax says, giving me a creeper look.

"Gross."

"Seen yourself lately, little bird?"

I flip around in my seat and try to whack him, but John yanks me back. "Cuffs?" he asks.

"Cuff his mouth!" I shout.

Dax is the one who snickers this time. "Such an angry bird."

"Shut up!"

"Stop taking the bait," John says under his breath. "He'll leave you alone."

"No he won't! *You* try living with my name! You'll see— it's the stupidest name ever!"

"Are you kidding me?" Michelle says. "I think it's an awesome name. Wrens are beautiful, delicate birds, with an incredible bubbly song. We had one nest at our house a few years ago. It was a joy to wake up to."

"You sound just like my mother," I grumble. Then I close my eyes and turn away, trying to block all of them, all of *it*, out.

7

I didn't used to hate my life or my name. Back in elementary school, they seemed okay. I went to a school where most of us had known each other since we could remember. People were used to my name, and even though I wasn't a *fan* of it, I didn't hate it.

Then my dad got a new job, and we moved. And instead of going to sixth grade at the school I'd gone to since kindergarten, I got thrown in with the wolves of a huge middle school in a sprawling city south of Los Angeles where I knew nobody but my family. I had to start all over, and my name got stupid reactions or had to be explained again and again and again.

"Anabella will help you adjust," my mom assured me. "You'll meet new people, experience new things. . . . It's an exciting time! Give it a few weeks—you'll love it."

But Anabella was in the eighth-grade wing and too busy making her own new friends to worry about me. Outgoing and really pretty, she was instantly popular.

I do look like my sister. But I'm the knockoff version of the designer model—the cloth doesn't hang right, the stripes don't quite match.

Teachers at my old school always began the year excited to see me. "Oh! You're Anabella's sister!" they'd say, expecting someone polite and attentive; someone who would raise her hand with correct answers.

I used to try to live up to that.

I used to try hard.

But I always felt like I was chasing my sister's shadow. Like I could never actually touch what she was.

And then we moved and my friends were gone and I had no one to sit with at lunch. Anabella and I may have been in different wings, but I'd see her in the lunch quad swarmed by new friends, and it finally sank in that she really didn't want me around.

It also sank in that, as much as I tried, I would never live up to what she was. She would always be ahead of me. Always come in first. Always fit her name, like I fit mine.

After a month of feeling alone and hating my new school, I ran into this girl in one of the Wing-6 bathrooms. "Hey," she said, giving me the once-over. She was at the mirror, busy with an eyeliner pencil.

"Hey," I said back.

"What's your name? Haven't seen you before."

"I'm invisible, that's why."

She laughed and really looked at me. "I've got magical powers then, 'cause I can see you fine." I went inside a stall and relieved myself, and when I came out, she said, "I'm Meadow, by the way."

"Shut up," I said, washing up at the sink.

"I know, right?"

"I'm serious. Shut up."

"Whatever."

But as I was drying my hands, I wondered if she might *not* be making fun of my name. So I said, "I just don't like people messin' with me because of my name."

"Your name? I don't even know your name! Why would I ask what your name was if I already knew it?" She went back to working the eyeliner. "Just get out of here, would ya?"

"It's Wren," I said.

She turned to face me. "Seriously?"

"Like I said, shut up."

"Like the bird?"

"Like the stupid bird."

"Ohmygod!" she squealed, throwing her arms around me.

I laughed. "So your name's really Meadow?"

"Yes!" She started bouncing up and down. "This is so awesome! This is meant to be! We are totally going to be best friends!"

I laughed too, and for the first time since we'd moved, I felt a surge of happiness.

"This is un-freakin'-believable," she giggled. "Meadow and Wren, best of friends. Even rhymes!"

"Right, huh?" I laughed.

"We should celebrate!" she said, then pulled out a joint and a lighter. I felt the happy bubbles inside me pop, saw warning lights flash through my brain. But with a flick of her thumb, she brought fire to life. "You're cool with this, right?"

I was afraid to say yes.

I was more afraid to say no.

8

We get on Utah's Interstate 15, heading south. It's a freeway like any other freeway. On-ramps, off-ramps, too many cars. If you believe the signs, Las Vegas is in the direction we're going, only four hundred miles away.

I'm trying to pay attention to our route, although I don't know why. Where would I go if I could escape? That didn't matter when I ran at the airport, but for some reason it does now. Maybe it's being on the freeway. Running seems so hopeless.

I'm mad about everything. About being kidnapped. About not getting to say goodbye to Nico or Biggy or even Meadow. About my parents. About Anabella—the narc. About my having no phone and no money and not being allowed to make any calls or even text anyone. I'm twitchy without my phone, and I'm mad about being trapped in an SUV with three hippie-dippie camp counselors and a strung-out thug whose sense of humor stinks as bad as he does.

But I'm also kind of distracted. Out my window, up on the mountaintops, there's snow.

Lots of really white snow.

I've never seen real snow before. The closest I've come is the white stuff on top of the Matterhorn ride at Disneyland. When I was six, I thought it was real. I also thought the ride was scary.

One of the snowcapped mountains looks a little like the Matterhorn to me. It feels scary, too. But why? I'm not six anymore. And we're not even heading toward the mountain. Still, it's like the ride I'm on now has nothing to hold on to. And it feels like a *real* Abominable Snowman is lurking right around the corner.

"Lots of snow sports around here," John says, totally invading my thinking. His arm shoots across my face as he points. "Right up there is Park City—it's fabulous."

I squint at him. "Fabulous? What guy says 'fabulous'?"

Dax leans forward, invading from behind. "I think it would be *fabulous* if we could quiet the monster in my stomach."

"Hungry?" John asks.

Dax pats him on the shoulder. "Dude, you broke the code."

"Are we stopping at the usual place for their last supper?" John calls up front.

"That's the plan," Michelle says via the rearview mirror.

Fifteen minutes later, we're pulling into a Burger King drive-thru. "Hungry or not, get something," Michelle tells us. "We've got a three-hour drive ahead of us, and then it'll be a whole new kind of cuisine for the next eight weeks."

John snickers. "Cuisine. Nice."

"Sounds *fabulous*," Dax grumbles.

I'm still feeling queasy, but I order a burger anyway. I can take a hint.

Dax gets cut off after his fourth item and starts whining like a little kid. "Dude. You said it was our last supper. Come on!"

After the food comes piling through the window, Michelle pulls around to the front of the building and Dax and I get escorted inside one at a time to take a "potty break."

"We won't be stopping again until we reach base camp," Michelle says. "If we're going to get in the field before dark, we have to hustle."

I'm not sure exactly what that means, but I don't care, either. I do my business, get back in the SUV, and, after we're on the interstate again, eat what I can, then close my eyes. The snowy mountains are behind us now, my head still hurts, and I'm so, *so* tired.

9

I wake up to the sound of snoring. It sputters to a stop as I sit up.

"Thank the Lord," John says, eyeing me, and there's a chorus of "Amen!" from Michelle and Nash up front. I check behind me, looking for someone else to blame, but Dax is out cold, sleeping like a baby.

Out the window, the earth is flat. Flat and dry and covered with low, dusty, gray shrubs. We fly past a sign in the shape of a beehive with the number 24 inside it. "Where are we?" I ask, feeling like we've landed on some alien planet.

"We're getting close," John tells me. "Another half hour?"

"But . . ." I strain to look farther ahead, and then across John out the other side. The same dusty gray shrubs go for miles in every direction. "Where's the forest?"

The hippie-dippie counselors grin at each other. "You're lookin' at it," John says. "This is our version of wilderness."

We zoom by a patch of wicked-looking plants—spindly arms with needles everywhere. "We're camping in the *desert*?"

"Beautiful time of year for it," Michelle says through the mirror.

I pinch a look at her. "Oh, I can see that!"

She laughs. "Seriously. You've come at a great time. Spring in the desert is beyond compare."

I watch the pathetic excuse for landscape zoom by, and the pit of my stomach knots up. "Do my parents know this?" I ask. I sound whiny, but I need to know.

I really need to know.

"They do," Michelle tells me.

So that's it. I suspected it before, but now it's an indisputable fact.

My parents hate me.

Beehive-24 has one skinny lane in each direction. There's not much traffic. Big surprise. We're in the middle of godforsaken nowhere.

"So what happens next?" I ask.

John nods. "We stop at the clinic, where you'll get your physical, then head over to base camp, where we'll issue you your gear. Then it's out to the wild, where we'll meet up with the Grizzlies."

"There are *grizzlies* out here?"

He laughs. "That's the name of your group. You're joining the Grizzly Girls. There's six in the group right now. We do staggered starts, so you'll be the newbie."

"Lucky number seven," Michelle says.

"And the only Rabbit," Nash adds, like he's so excited for me. "Everyone starts at Rabbit. You advance to Coyote, then Elk, then Falcon. By the time you earn Falcon, you'll be ready to fly."

Dork.

Hippie-dippie shrub-hugging dork.

"So I'm a rabbit among grizzlies," I mutter. "Great."

"Actually," John says, "you're a Rabbit who is *also* a Grizzly."

From behind us, Dax says, "That's a rad image."

I turn around. "When'd you wake up?"

"Back at spring in the desert being fabulous." He stretches out his neck. "So what am I?"

From the front seat, Nash calls, "You'll be on Rabbit in Snake."

"Yum, if you're the snake," he says. He sits back, then springs forward again. "I'm guessing Snake is the superbads?" He sounds so calm. Like none of this is new.

"Adjudicated, yep," Nash calls back.

"What's that?" I ask John.

Dax answers for him. "Judge assigned me. It was this or jail." He snorts. "I ain't no dummy."

But then he looks out the window and gets quiet. I look, too, and know exactly what he's thinking.

This *is* jail.

We are prisoners, but instead of being locked up in small cells with bars, we're trapped in the wide open, surrounded by thorns and dry endless desert.

10

There *is* something worse than flat land with low gray shrubs for as far as the eye can see: pathetic shacks collapsing in the middle of flat land with low gray scrubs for as far as the eye can see.

Maybe the Middle of Nothingness, Utah, is considered a town, but it's more like a rotting corral battered by tumbleweeds.

The sides of the road into town slope off into shallow ditches. No sidewalks. No curbs. No clean and green. Just worn, cracked asphalt fading into dirt.

A mangy coyote trots alongside the road like a thirsty desert wolf. It glances at us as we pass and keeps right on trucking. Its eyes look sharp and dangerous, and they flash almost golden in the sunlight.

"Dude," Dax says, watching it too. I can't tell what kind of "dude" it is, good or bad, and I don't ask.

After the shacks on the outskirts of town, we drive by a few houses and some more boarded-up buildings. There's a market with a post office sign, and a fire station that's half burned down.

A real confidence booster.

But for all the things this tumbleweed town doesn't have, what it *does* have is two pristine churches, right across the street from each other.

Dax notices too, because he says, "We must be in God's country."

"They take their prayers seriously around here," John tells him.

Dax snorts. "I can see why."

He actually gets a smile out of me for that one.

"Okay, guys," Michelle says, pulling up to a brick building with a faded blue sign announcing CLINIC. "We'll get your physicals here, go next door for supplies, then head out to the field. Daylight's burning, so please cooperate with the procedures regardless of how lame or invasive you think they are. You don't want to be hiking in the dark."

My heart starts beating weirdly fast as I stand up, and walking to the clinic door gets me totally winded. Dax doesn't look much better. "We're at seven thousand feet," John says, reading us. "You're both used to something near sea level. It's going to take a couple of days to acclimate."

Inside the clinic, Nash and John take Dax one way, and Michelle takes me another. We go down a short hallway, and Michelle taps a knuckle on a half-open door. Inside, I can see a woman in a lab coat behind a desk. She stands and smiles. "Come in, come in."

"This is Wren Clemmens," Michelle says. "Wren, this is Dr. Kumar."

"Right on time!" Dr. Kumar says.

Her voice singsongs. A happy bubbling brook. I'm not in the mood for singsongy doctors. I growl at her without making a sound.

She points me to a chair. "Have a seat, won't you?"

I've been sitting all day, but the silent growl exhausted me, so I sit.

I'm just so *tired.*

Michelle takes a seat in the corner as Dr. Kumar perches on the front edge of her desk, facing me. "I'm going to do a basic exam," Dr. Kumar singsongs. "Blood pressure, temperature, that sort of thing."

I let her, and it's no big deal.

Then she sits behind her desk and turns her dark eyes on me. "So. Tell me about your recent drug and alcohol use."

She says it with a smile. Like she's my friend. Like of course I use drugs and alcohol.

"I don't do drugs," I tell her. "And I only drink . . . once in a while."

She crosses her arms and keeps her eyes on me. "Wren," she says softly, "this program won't work if you can't be honest."

I force myself to not look away. I've been in this exact situation with my parents because of Anabella—the narc. I know how to stick to my story.

"Fine," she says, pushing back from the desk. "You'll have a therapist in the field helping you come to grips with that."

Her singsongy voice is not so friendly anymore, but *Fine?* That's it? No cross-examination? I watch her as she walks around the desk and toward the door. No calling me a prevaricator?

She opens the door with a tight smile. "Michelle will take you to the supply room."

Well, that was easy! "Thanks," I tell her, and she gives me that tight-lipped look and a nod. I know she thinks I'm a liar, but what do I care?

We walk over to the building next door, and Michelle gets another woman to go with us down to the supply room. Once we're inside it, Michelle locks the door. It's a sliding bolt lock, too. Metal on metal. *Sssss-clink.*

All of a sudden, I'm noticing that the second woman's got some beef to her. Bench-press beef. Like, Olympics, hello?

I look from her to Michelle as I back up. "What is this?"

"It's for privacy," Michelle says.

I look around at the tall rows of shelves that hold camping stuff. "Uh . . . why do we need privacy?"

Michelle shoves a cardboard box at me. "Because you need to strip out of everything you're wearing and put it in this box."

"Here? Now? In front of you?"

"Sorry, but yes."

"That's not exactly *private.*"

"We're more concerned about Dax or the male staff walking in unexpectedly."

"So . . . but . . . *why?*"

"We need to make sure you're not carrying anything into the field."

I still don't get what she's talking about. "Like?"

"Drugs." She frowns at me. "Even though you don't use them. Right, right, I know."

"But—"

"You need to turn over what you're wearing. We'll issue you clothes for in the field—everyone starts with the same equipment. Now, please. Let's get this over with."

The other woman gets busy at the shelves, and by the time I've stripped down to my underwear, she's handing over stacks of clothes. I can see T-shirts, a sweatshirt, a jacket, socks, a pair of hiking boots, and pants with big, dorky pockets and zip-off legs just like Michelle's, only sand tan instead of army green.

"Those come off too," Michelle says about my underwear.

"You've got to be kidding."

I just stare at her until the beefy woman says, "Get with the program, kid."

She's scary and she's moving toward me.

I strip.

"Now squat," Michelle tells me, "and cough."

"What?"

"Squat and cough!" the beefy woman snaps. "And cough hard."

"Why?"

"Wren, it's part of procedure," Michelle says.

But the beefy woman explains. "Users get creative with the way they smuggle stuff in. Not that you're a user, right, we get that."

"It's procedure," Michelle says. "We have to do it."

It's cold and I'm standing there in front of a nature hugger and an iron pumper feeling very . . . vulnerable. And since they're between me and the door and I'm *naked*, I can't exactly ditch it out of there. So I squat and I cough. And I cough again, harder. And again, even harder. And when they're sure

I'm not smuggling anything, I take the clothes they give me and get dressed.

"What are you going to do with that?" I ask the beefy woman, because she's walking away with my box of clothes.

"We'll label it and tape it closed. You'll get it back when you're done with the program." She unlocks the door, but before she leaves, she turns to tell me one more thing. "Also, if you decide to run, we'll use it to have tracker dogs pick up your scent. Don't want you dying out there in the desert."

I watch her go, and it finally hits home.

I've just put on my prison clothes.

11

Michelle, John, and Nash try to teach Dax and me how to make packs out of thick blue tarps. Besides what was packed in our duffels, they've given us all sorts of stuff—clothes, a small, metal "billypot" for cooking, toilet paper, wet wipes, sunblock, a plastic bag bursting with "curriculum materials," food, and other random things. We're supposed to magically fold everything inside the tarp and wrap it up with a parachute cord. And once we've made this big blue blob, we're supposed to strap a sleeping bag and ground pad to it and attach seat belt straps so we can carry the whole mess on our backs.

Seat belt straps. Which look like they've been cut out of wrecked cars! The whole thing's stupid, and three tries later, it doesn't even come close to working. The yippy-hippies keep giving us instructions, making us try again, telling us that creating balance in our packs will create balance in our lives.

What a crock.

Dax hasn't said a word since the physicals. He looks pretty

dorky in his prison clothes, but I'm sure he's thinking the same thing about me. His backpack bundle is a disaster, all lopsided and falling apart. But then, so is mine.

"Try again," Michelle tells us. "You can't have it coming apart on the trail."

It takes two more tries, but finally our backpacks are good enough and we're told to "circle up" right there on the cement floor. Then the three of them tell the two of us The Rules.

It's a really long list.

We have to say "I understand" after every single one.

Pretty high up on the list is "No profanity," followed by an annoying explanation about cussing being a form of masking emotions and how one of the purposes of wilderness therapy is to get to the bottom of our *feelings,* and a major goal is to learn to articulate our *feelings* so that we may better communicate the hot-button topics that have driven us to being where we are today.

I'm glazed over by the end of that rule and just say, "I understand."

But Dax tells them he bleepity-bleep-bleep-bleepity-bleep-bleep understands.

I hold my breath, expecting them to go ballistic, but Nash just smiles at him—like he really does think it's kind of funny—and says, "That was your last cigarette, sailor. In the field there will be consequences."

When The Rules are finally done, they make us walk in a sandwich line through the building—John and Michelle ahead of Dax and me, Nash behind us. John's man-bun is right in front of me, and it's pretty impressive. I can do a bun with mine, but not like his. Not even close.

We stop at a room with a carved wooden sign over the door that says GROUND CONTROL, where an old guy with knotty knuckles and a scar across his cheek hands three walkie-talkies to the hippie-dippies. "Fully charged," he says. "You're good to go."

"Thanks, Tom," John says.

"See you on the airwaves, Major," Michelle says, which makes the old guy laugh.

They move along, but I hang back for a second, looking inside the room. The wall clock says it's 5:15. There's some electronic equipment on a table, big maps on the wall, and next to the map a whiteboard with lists of names in different colors—GRIZZLY, BUFFALO, SNAKE, FOX, and BADGER.

Nash pushes me along, and when I've caught up with the others, I ask, "How many campers are out here?" because every heading on the whiteboard had a list of names.

"Too many," John says, and Michelle adds, "We wish there wasn't the need."

Dax turns his head to whisper, "Right. At what it costs to put us here? They're lovin' it."

"What's it cost?" I whisper back.

"Let's just say you could be driving a new car."

"*What?* Are you serious?"

"Yup. But instead you get to sleep in the dirt."

There's a truck waiting for us outside. A really old, beat-up pickup truck. And I am getting royally ticked at my parents all over again for wasting so much money to send me to Desert Jail when a guy steps out from behind the wheel of the truck. He's young. Like he might still be in high school. And he's . . . gorgeous. Wild black hair and dark, red-tinged tan, and silver jewelry.

I can't help staring.

In the middle of Ugly Acres, there's . . . *that?*

"We ready to do this?" he asks, and when the hippie-dippies tell him yes, he says, "Packs in back," and slides into the driver's seat.

"Wren's up front with me," Michelle says. "Dax, you're between John and Nash in back." Then she hands Nash a bandanna and shakes one out herself.

There is a god, I tell myself as I scoot in next to Mr. Gorgeous. *He has a plan.*

Michelle gets in, shoving me closer to him. So close that our legs are touching. I'm suddenly floating on a big hit of happy.

And then Michelle says, "Wren? Hellooooo, Wren?"

"Hmm?"

"I need to blindfold you."

"What!?"

I look in the backseat.

Dax is already blindfolded.

"You've got to be kidding!"

The truck is fired up. Rumbling.

Mr. Gorgeous is looking at me. Waiting. "Campsite locations are secret," he explains. His eyes are jewels, deep, clear, hypnotizing.

"I hate you!" I tell Michelle.

And then she wraps me in darkness.

12

I'm blindfolded for what feels like an hour, jostled around on a dirt road, breathing in dust, feeling like I'm on a sketchy version of Disneyland's Raiders of the Lost Ark ride. Like in another turn we might go crashing down a mountain.

Then I remind myself.

We're in the desert.

The flat, ugly desert.

So why does it feel like we're going uphill? Doing switchbacks? Teetering on the edge of the earth?

"How much longer?" I ask. I sound so pathetic, but I'm hating every bump and turn and not being able to see.

"Remember the rules we went over?" Michelle asks. "We don't discuss the future."

"It's not the *future*. I just have to pee!"

The driver laughs. "Right out of the Rabbit playbook."

I can't see him, so, gorgeous or not, I hate him now, too. "You're a terrible driver!" I tell him.

He laughs again. "You want me to slow down?"

I sink deeper into my seat and shut up, but there's an angry beehive buzzing in my head, and the longer I sit in the dark, the more I poke at it. One thought flies into another, swarming around until I want to attack everyone and everything. My mother, my sister, my father, my so-called friends, my school, these hippie-dippie shrub huggers and their dilapidated truck.

Then we come to a stop.

I go to take my blindfold off, but Michelle grabs my hand. "Not until I tell you."

"We here?" Dax asks from the backseat.

"Wren is," John tells him. "You've got a little ways to go."

"Fabulous," he says like he's spitting nails. Then, as Michelle's leading me out of the truck, he calls, "Bye-bye, birdie. Be a good little chickadee!"

I tell him to shut up in a way that will have consequences in the field.

After the truck drives off, John's voice says, "We've got your pack."

"Michelle?" I ask, feeling weirdly panicked.

"Right here," she says. "Nash is with Snakes. John and I are with Grizzlies." She grabs my arm. "Let's go."

"Why do I still have to wear this blindfold?"

"We do it to minimize runners."

"Runners?"

"If you don't know how to get out of here, you're less likely to run away." She pulls me along. "We don't exactly lock you up, you know."

"Unless you call five hundred square miles of land being locked up," John adds.

Five hundred square miles.

Five hundred square miles of sand and scrub and *wind*. Because what I'm feeling is not a breeze. I can actually hear it howling.

I stumble along, blind, linked to Michelle by the arm, thinking that walking the plank for some cutthroat pirates would be better than walking across Utah for these guys.

I picture the Peter Pan ride. Flying through the air with my brother next to me, shouting, "There he is! There's Captain Hook!" as we sail through the dark.

Mowgli loves the Peter Pan ride.

Suddenly we stop, and Michelle grabs my shoulders and turns me. And turns me again. Like I'm seven and about to pin the tail on the stupid donkey.

Finally she takes off my blindfold. "Okay," she says with a big gust of air. Like *she's* the one relieved. "Welcome to the field. Time to start carrying your own supplies."

John hands over my tarp pack and helps me wrestle into it. I notice right off that the earth around us is different. It's not flat—we're walking between two sandy cliffs, maybe thirty feet tall—and the dirt is a pale orange.

John sees me looking around. "The cliffs are made of sandstone," he says. "And what we're walking in here is called an arroyo. Also known as a wash."

Michelle adds, "Flash floods can tear through here, but we're not in danger at the moment." She eyes the sky, which is the color of steel. "Although we are supposed to get some rain tonight."

The plants are bigger, too. There are even some that might've grown into actual trees if they weren't trapped in the desert. We walk by a small grove of them and they smell like pine, but . . . not. And they're *not* pines because they have berries. Berries that look like hard gray peas.

"Those are junipers," John tells me.

Like I care? I want to tell him to shut up and quit watching me.

I put my head down and keep walking so he won't see me noticing anything else, but he still has plenty to say. "You're in Paiute country," he tells me.

I have no idea what he's talking about, and I don't care. I just keep my head down and hike, feeling the seat belt straps cutting into my shoulders, wondering when this nightmare of a day will finally be over.

But can the shrub hugger take a hint?

No.

He starts spewing random facts about junipers. How the "Paiute" used them for everything. The bark for roofing and weaving, the wood for building and fuel, the berries for food and fighting asthma, the twigs for coughs and colds . . .

Shut up, shut up, shut up.

When he finally takes a breath, I ask, "How much farther?"

At the same time, John and Michelle sing out, "Are we there yet?" and laugh.

"You're hilarious," I tell them. "And what's the deal with not talking about the future? Aren't we supposed to plan for the future? Isn't the future what everyone's all about?"

Neither of them says anything.

"Why can't you just tell me how far I have to hike? I'm dying, you know that? It has been a really long, awful day."

They don't say anything for about twenty steps, and finally

Michelle sighs and says, "I know it has, and you're doing really great."

"I am not. I'm *dying*."

We keep hiking.

Even more than a toke or a drink, I'm jonesing for my phone. Jonesing bad. "Can you at least tell me what time it is? I hate not knowing what time it is."

Michelle looks at the sky and finds the sun, glowing behind the steel sheet of clouds. "Around six. Maybe six-fifteen."

"Sunset's around eight," John says. "But I think we might get that rain before then."

"Yup," Michelle says. She looks at me. "You're going to want to get your tarp up before it starts. We probably should pick up the pace."

"Pick up the pace?" I practically break down crying. "Noooooo."

"No fun sleeping in a wet bag," John says.

I trudge along, exhausted and hungry and hurting, thinking, *My parents got suckered.*

Suckered bad.

13

"Gullible," Meadow had said. "Parents are so gullible."

She meant hers, too.

Actually, she meant every parent she'd ever conned, even the ones who were teachers. Although with teachers it was harder. "You can only use the puppy-dog eyes and beg for understanding so many times before a teacher's onto you," she'd explained once when we were having a quick blaze in a Wing-7 bathroom. I was still in sixth grade, but Meadow insisted on rotating bathrooms from her wing to mine, dodging kids who might narc if they knew where to find us. "What you've got going for you with parents," she said, "is that they *want* to believe."

And she was right.

The proof started one night at dinner when Anabella looked at me across the table and said, "Are you really hanging out with that girl Meadow?"

It was only a few days before winter break, and Meadow

had been on me to spend nights at her house, but I didn't know how I was going to make that happen. There was no way my mom would let me spend the night at someone's house if she hadn't met them.

And I sure didn't want her to meet Meadow.

"Her name's *Meadow*?" my mom asked, perking up.

"She's a seventh grader," I said. "We met in the Commiserating Club."

My mother gave me a confused look, so Anabella explained. "Their names?"

My father studied me. "You're still grousing about your name? So it's a little different. So what? It makes you unique."

"I'm in middle school now, Dad." I looked back and forth between my parents. "Did you two ever think past the nest phase of my life?"

Mom completely glossed over her responsibility in the naming thing and said, "Well, I'll bet Meadow is a unique individual."

Anabella snorted.

In a prim and proper ladylike manner, of course.

"What's wrong with her?" my mother asked, zeroing in on Anabella.

"She looks . . ." My perfect sister gazed at the ceiling, searching for the perfect word, then shot her perfect diction directly at me. "A bit trashy." She took a bite of Panda Express chow mein noodles. "And that's being charitable."

"She is not trashy!"

"Can you say eyeliner, hello?"

"Eyeliner?" my mother gasped.

I leaned in and frowned. "She's a seventh grader, Mom! Kids wear makeup in middle school."

Anabella was quick to cut in. "I don't. And neither do my friends."

I gave her a sneer. "Well, goody for you."

My mother was really looking at me now, studying me. "Do you wear makeup?"

"No!" It was almost the truth. The two times Meadow had pushed her black pencil on me, I'd put on a little but worried the rest of the day that I might run into Anabella in the quad. My sister didn't seem to notice if I was eating alone or looking lost or lonely, but she'd sure notice a little smudge of black around my eyes. After I told the almost-truth, I blurted, "And Meadow is really nice! And makes time to talk to me—" I glared at my sister "—which is more than I can say about *some* people."

"What is going on?" My mother raised her eyebrows at Anabella and me. "Are you two okay?"

"We're fine," we both muttered.

I kept my head down and ate orange chicken until my mother said, "Why don't you invite her over sometime?"

I quit chewing. Yes, she was looking at me. "Meadow?"

"Of course."

I tried to smile. "Sure, if that's okay."

"Of course it's okay," Mom gushed. "Where does she live?"

"I have no idea." That was all truth.

"Well, it can't be too far. How about this weekend? We could pick her up."

I frowned. "You might want to stop making playdates for me, Mom. I'm in middle school."

Mom frowned too. But it was a confused frown. Like she wasn't sure what to do.

Then my father gave me one of his dissecting looks. "Or maybe you *don't* want us to meet her?"

Anabella did a subsonic snort and I just couldn't take it. "Quit judging!" I snapped at her. "You don't even know her!"

She gave me a wicked-queen smile. "So bring her over."

"Is she nice?" my brother asked.

His little first-grader voice was so innocent and sweet, I just wanted to wrap him in a bear hug. "Yes," I said. "She's very nice."

"Will she play *Jungle Book?*"

"Maybe. I could ask."

"I get to be Mowgli," he said.

"You always are," I told him with a smile.

"And you be Baloo!"

I kept smiling. "Of course."

He wiggled in his seat a little. "So bring her over!"

Anabella smirked. "Yeah. Bring her over. She could play Kaa."

I slammed down my fork. "You're the snake, not her!"

"Girls!" Mom cried, looking at us like we were strangers.

My face was flushed hot, but I tried to stay cool, telling my mother, "I'll ask Meadow if she wants to visit."

It was a lie. There was no way I could have Meadow over. One look at her and my parents would freak out. But I did *tell* Meadow about it at school the next day—not asking, just telling—and then she went and said, "Perfect! Once they get to know me, they'll trust you to hang at my house. I've got this. I've totally got this!"

"No! I—"

"Trust me, Wren. I know how to work this!"

The whole thing made me really nervous. But she showed up at our house on Saturday with her hair tied back in a bow, riding a bicycle with a lidded basket in front that had a *cat* latched inside it. She had little pearl earrings in, and there wasn't a trace of makeup.

My brother went nuts for the cat, my mother went nuts for her and actually let her play her precious piano—an heirloom most people don't get to touch.

Even Anabella broke down and admitted she was wrong. "I don't think that's the person I was thinking it was," she whispered to me.

Meadow stayed for three hours, using lots of pleases and thank-yous, and when she left, she told my mom, "Thanks so much for inviting me over to your beautiful home, Mrs. Clemmens. I had a wonderful time!"

Outside, she got on her bike and waved back at the house like she was starring in some fifties movie. Then she gave me a wicked grin and pushed off, whispering, "We are going to have the best winter break ever!"

She wasn't lying.

14

The walk along the bone-dry arroyo goes on forever. I'm hot. Sweating. Little flies buzz around my head. My pack must weigh fifty pounds. I keep stopping to drink from the canteen they gave me, until Michelle warns, "That's your ration of clear water for the week."

"For the *week*?" It's a big canteen, but not enough for a *week*. And there's another empty one wrapped up inside my big blue tarp—why didn't we fill both of them?

I'm about to ask when she says, "You'll be purifying local sources for most of your water needs." She gives me a stern look. "My advice is save that for when you need good-tasting water."

"I need it now!"

She shrugs and keeps moving. "Use as you see fit."

Her attitude makes me mad. Like she doesn't care if I'm dying of thirst or if I run out of water. So I ignore her and take a drink. And another. And another.

Michelle and John both know what I'm doing, but neither

of them says a thing or even raises an eyebrow. They just keep walking.

"Do you remember the achievement levels?" Michelle asks me.

"You mean that I'm a Rabbit?" I ask back.

"Right. So Rabbits are kept separate from the students on other levels."

"We're called *students*?"

She shrugs. "*Campers* seems to misrepresent a bit."

"So does *students*," I grumble. "Just get real and call us inmates."

From behind me, John says, "Guess you've never been to jail."

I look back at him. "Have *you*?"

He just smiles.

"Oh, *great*," I cry.

My parents are definitely idiots. Gullible idiots. Ones who don't think twice about sending their daughter off with *convicts*.

"Back to achievement levels," Michelle says. "Once you're able to do certain tasks, you'll be moved up to Coyote and can work with the other girls. Until then, the Grizzlies won't be interacting with you, and that includes talking."

Sounds like starting middle school all over again. Not that I care. The only thing I want—the *only* thing—is to collapse somewhere and be left alone. My head aches, my feet are killing me, and I feel like I've got a big, sweaty boulder strapped to my back.

"You got that?" John asks.

"Yeah, I got it."

"The other thing," Michelle says, "is counting. If you're

going to use the latrine and don't want someone watching over you, you need to count so we can hear you."

I perk up a little. "There'll be a bathroom?"

John laughs. "Metaphorically speaking."

"It's a hole," Michelle explains. "Dug by the girls."

"And when you use it," John says, "you count until you return to camp."

"You can sing instead," Michelle says.

"Or tell a story," John adds. "Anything loud enough for us to hear."

"But *why?*"

Michelle trudges on. "So we know you're not running off. Once you advance to Coyote, you can stop counting."

"How long does that take?"

"A few days? A week? Depends on you."

"So for the next maybe *week,* I've got to count *out loud* every time I have to go? What if I get . . . you know . . . constipated?"

John chuckles. "It happens. You keep counting."

"This is a nightmare," I mutter.

We keep trudging along, and just when I'm sure I'm going to keel over dead, we cut out of the arroyo and go through a grove of junipers. The path is narrow—barely even there—and leads us up, up, up.

My pack feels like it's doubled in weight since I started hiking, and I'm so exhausted, I can barely walk. Then my nose picks something up. "Smoke!" I whisper. "I smell smoke."

Michelle turns. "That's my girl," she says, and she seems . . . *proud.* "Congratulations. You made it."

"We're at camp?"

She nods as we crest the rise. "Welcome home, Wren."

15

"Home" looks like a homeless camp, with blue tarps strung up between scraggly trees, anchored with rocks, wide open on both ends. There's a fire in the middle of camp with half a dozen girls sitting around it on rocks, scarfing food from tin plates with . . . sticks?

Yes, sticks.

The girls are all sorts of shades and sizes, but the thing that binds them together is a layer of dirt. They all look grubby.

Dusty, dirty, grubby.

"Grizzlies!" Michelle announces. "This is Wren, our new Rabbit."

I stand there dazed by the surrealness of what she's just said.

In what universe does this make sense?

And yet they all act like it's normal. "Hey, Wren!" a few of them call out while the rest of them turn back to their tin plates.

The Grizzly version of school.

Except that they all look older than me—some of them a *lot* older. And even though I feel like the walking dead, caked in dust and sweat from the longest day of my life, *they* look worse. Their pants might once have been sand tan like mine, but they're now two shades darker. And their bandannas, wrapped around their heads or tied at the sides of their pants, are limp and oily.

John breaks away from Michelle and me to sit by the fire while an Asian guy and a white woman sporting what's basically a buzz cut make their way toward us. I can tell they're jailers, not inmates, by the color of their pants—army green instead of tan.

"Welcome aboard," Buzz Cut says. She's got a crooked smile and an eyetooth that sticks out like a fang. "I'm Dvorka, one of the field staff."

"And I'm Jude," the guy says. He's wearing his bandanna around his forehead, his black hair shooting up behind it.

Michelle eyes the sky and nods for me to follow her. "We've got to get you set up before the rains start."

"We're ready for it!" one of the inmates calls as we walk past the fire ring. "Mia and me are roomin' together tonight so my tarp can collect some of the sky's fine wine!"

"Yip-yip-aroooo!" another girl howls.

I figure it out.

They're Coyotes collecting rainwater.

I haven't seen a drop of water the whole time I've been here—no river or lake or even puddle. So despite my miserable state, I already know—if we really have to drink from "local sources," then having a stash of fresh water would be something to yip about.

Michelle stops walking and looks around. "Right here is good," she says. We're standing in a random place, away from the other tarps. "Get your cord. Let's set you up."

I have no idea what she wants me to do.

"Your cord," she says. "The one that's holding your pack together? We need it to put up your tent."

I just stare at her.

"Now?" she says.

I dump my pack and then just stare at *it*. I am *so* tired.

"Before the skies open up?"

I start to undo the parachute cord, but it's not easy. And gets all tangled. And I'm *so* tired.

Michelle just stands there, watching.

"A little help, please?" I ask. I mean, can't she see I'm in pain? Is she that heartless?

Apparently, yes. She just looks at the cord and says, "You can do it."

I hate her. To the moon and back, I hate her. And now I'm mad enough to tear the cord free, and since she doesn't want to help me, I no longer want her help.

I lash the cord so it's strung between a couple of trees, then dump everything out of the tarp and onto the ground and hang the tarp over the cord.

It sags. Badly.

"Let me show you a magic knot," she says. "It'll keep the cord from slipping."

I don't want to know about any stupid magic knot. I don't want anything from her! I snarl at her, untie one end, yank the cord tight, and tie it again.

I don't need any stupid magic rocks, either. I straighten the tarp, find some rocks, and anchor the corners. It's not rocket science. Or even algebra. It's a two-sided tarp tent.

"I know you're mad right now, Wren, but please let me give you some pointers."

I don't look at her. Don't talk to her. I just tug and anchor and straighten. My tent is still saggy in the middle, but who cares?

Looks good enough to me.

"Wren—"

"What!"

"It's about to rain."

"And you've given me this wonderful tarp to protect me. Thank you so much."

I'm pouring sarcasm all over her, but it doesn't seem to sink in. She shakes her head. "The tarp won't—"

"It's *fine*."

She tries to tell me I need to trench around my tarp. She wants me to find a rock and *dig*. I've been up since 3:47 a.m. and she wants me to dig. With a rock!

I yell at her to leave me alone.

She tries to tell me what to do with something called a ground cloth.

I scream at her to LEAVE ME ALONE!

Finally she does.

It's such a relief to be left alone. I unstuff my sleeping bag, which is mummy style and puffs up big and fluffy. I stretch it out on my pad and get comfy on top while I eat a power bar that's in my rations and wash it down with water from my canteen.

My head's splitting and the power bar makes me kind of

nauseous, but at least I can lie down. I crawl into the bag with my boots and pants and everything on, and the world spins as I lay my head down.

I am *so* tired.

I close my eyes. And even though I fight them back, tears squeeze through until I finally just let them loose, sobbing silently until I'm all wrung out.

And just as I'm sinking into sleep, surrendering to the darkness of the worst day ever, I hear a rumbling overhead.

A low growl of warning.

Then the sky opens up and rain comes pouring down.

16

The rain scares me at first because it's so loud—like thousands of little pellets slapping and bouncing off a plastic shield. But then . . . it's okay. I'm safe.

See? I tell myself, thinking about Michelle and her stupid magic knot. *I'm fine.*

But then the middle of my tarp sags and water starts running off it in a stream, pooling on the ground outside, seeping under the edge of the tarp and inside my tent.

It's dark, and there's no flashlight in my supplies. John gave Dax and me some line about the moon becoming our nightlight, but that's not exactly working for me right now.

So I can't *see* the water, but I can feel it. First just a little. Then more. And more. Pretty soon, a lake forms by my ground pad. "No!" I squeal, and wrestle out of my sleeping bag. "No! Stop! Nooooo!"

The water doesn't listen to me. It keeps running in, making its own little route right through my tent.

"Help!" I scream. "Somebody help! I'm drowning in here!"

All I hear is the rain.

Pellets of merciless rain.

I pick up my sleeping bag, scrunch it to my chest. Pick up the jacket. The extra clothes. Anything cloth.

I'm on my knees, on the pad, trying to see in the dark, and what I'm thinking is *I want my phone!* My phone with a built-in flashlight that comes on when I tell it to and doesn't hide behind clouds or go from round to crescent to *gone.*

They didn't even give us matches. Probably because I wouldn't just light one and use it to see what's going on—I'd *torch* something!

I can feel water all around me. I'm furious and panicked and desperate. How do they expect me to sleep in a lake?

"Help!" I cry. "Somebody, please help!"

I wait, holding my breath, clutching my sleeping bag and the clothes. But nobody comes or even invites me into their tent.

Well, forget this. I can't stay in here. The middle of the tarp is completely sagged in. It's going to collapse on me any second!

I remember that somewhere in my stuff there's a poncho. My mind screams *put on your poncho and get out* because the tarp feels like a trap. Like I'm sinking inside a plastic cave.

I scramble around, looking for the poncho.

I'm desperate for the poncho.

Where is the poncho?

And then, suddenly, the rain stops.

All at once, it just stops.

I keep ahold of everything, waiting. I don't know if the clouds are done or just resting. Are they reloading or moving on? I hold my breath, not knowing what to do.

"Tomorrow I'm washing my hair!" a voice calls. "I am so stoked!"

"Yucca shampoo!" another voice calls.

"Do you think it'll really work?"

Michelle's voice weaves through the darkness. "It works great."

"Good night, y'all," comes the first voice.

"Yip-yip-arooooo!"

And that's it. Nobody asks if I'm okay. Nobody checks on me. Nobody even seems to know I'm here.

"I need help!" I call.

Nobody answers.

"Is anyone going to help me?" I scream. "The ground is soaked. I don't know what to do."

There's a stretch of silence, and then Michelle's voice says, "You'll figure it out."

"Are you *serious*?" I cry. "I'm in a puddle of mud! How am I supposed to sleep?"

I wait for an answer, but the only sound is the drip-drip-drip of water from the trees. "I hate you!" I scream out into the dark. "This is *abuse*. You should be *arrested*."

More silence.

I think about going around and ripping down all the other tents. Then maybe they'll know how it feels.

"Who are you really mad at here?" comes Michelle's voice.

"You!" I scream. "You knew this was going to happen!"

But there's a sick feeling in the pit of my stomach. Like a

stone in my gut, heavy and cold. And when she doesn't say anything back, I start to cry. "Please! What am I supposed to do?"

All I get back is silence.

And the drip-drip-drip of water from the trees.

17

For the next two days, I cry and I sleep. I don't let anyone see me crying, and I hate that I do it. But I'm so mad. So, *so* mad, and it sometimes comes out as tears.

I don't say a word—unless I'm squatting over a hole, counting. The counting is humiliating, but it's better than having Michelle or Dvorka stand by with one eye on me in case I make a break for it.

Whatever "it" is. There's nothing but desert for as far as I can see. I'd be buzzard bait in no time. If there are even buzzards out here.

The morning after the sky tries to drown me, I stretch all my wet stuff out on a big bush to dry. It's a needly bush, with a fat trunk and long, sagging branches. It looks angry. Like it's glowering at the world. And since that's something my mother accuses me of doing, I feel at one with this bush.

Man-bun John comes over and gets all chitty-chatty. "Nice way to use the arms of a pinyon," he tells me. "The tree is an amazing resource, on so many levels. The Paiute lived off the pine nuts and heated the resin to waterproof baskets; they used the wood for fuel and building . . . even chewed the pitch like we chew gum."

I don't know who the Paiute are, or care how the tree was used. He's either showing off or trying to get me to talk. Well, I'm not impressed, and I'm sure not falling for the talking thing. Like I haven't spent the last year dealing with therapists and counselors who do the same exact thing? The difference here is, I'm not out the door in forty-five minutes, so I'm not going to play along.

"Have you smelled it?" John asks, then sticks his face in a branch and takes a huge, exaggerated whiff.

I don't say a word to him, since that's exactly what he did to me when I was drowning in my ridiculous tent. When I begged for help and nobody came.

I hate him.

I hate all of them.

Later, Michelle tries talking to me. She explains why nobody could help me when it rained. "We don't force the students to listen, Wren. We can't stop the rain. Or the sun, or the wind. We can only try to help you prepare for it. If you're unwilling to listen or take advice, that's your choice."

I look straight ahead.

I know I can wear her down.

Make her apologize.

Have her say, *Come on—let's start over.*

She's not my mom, so she's holding out longer than Mom ever did, but she knows she's wrong. She knows this is abuse!

"Well," she says, taking a deep breath, "you're going to get

67

pretty tired of eating power bars . . . and you're going to run out. Your other rations require cooking, and in order to cook them, you need to use local water and learn how to build a bow-drill fire. Have you read any of your handbook?"

I stare straight ahead.

"Well . . . if you want help learning how to build a fire, or how to find local water, let any of the field staff know."

Then she walks away.

I'm expecting Jude to come over next and try out his counseling chops on me, but he never does.

Something about that tweaks me.

What game are they playing?

The next day, Dvorka hands me an envelope and tells me I can write a letter home. I scrawl three notebook pages hard and fast, telling my parents what they've done by shipping me off to Desert Prison. How I'm living in the dirt with no food or water, how I had to squat and cough, and now have to squat and *count.* How nobody here cares if I die, and if this keeps up, I'll be dead by the end of the week. I tell them all about the rain and the flood in my stupid tarp tent and how nobody would help me. I tell them that I heard the other girls talking about killing a scorpion, and if I die they can spend the rest of their lives knowing they killed me. I also tell them they'd better not tell my brother anything bad about me. I do a lot of underlining, and scribbling out, and I sign it "Heartbroken and Dying, Wren." Then I seal it in the envelope and hand it over to Dvorka, hoping it's my ticket out of here.

Dvorka takes it and says, "Did you tell them how we're mean and horrible and trying to kill you?"

My face gives me away.

"They'll call, we'll talk, it'll be okay," she says, wagging the envelope. "All students write one of these. Good to get it out of your system."

I want to snatch it back and rip it up, but she's already walking away.

Later, they sic a therapist on me. I'm sitting on a rock by myself in the shade of the glowering pinyon when she walks up. I'm trying to keep out of the sun and the wind, but I'm still miserable because the tree smells like Pine-Sol.

I hate Pine-Sol.

It reminds me of hugging the toilet.

The therapist's name is Tara. She's got an Australian accent, hair the color of dirty carrots, and freckles.

I hate her, but at least she doesn't beat around the bush. "Do you want to talk about it?" she asks.

Her voice sounds like honey. Sweet, warm honey.

I glare at her. It's dirty warfare to send someone to talk to you with a voice like that.

"You're full of rage, I can see that," her uber-cool accent tells me.

I hate that I love her accent.

Why couldn't *I* have a voice like that?

"Do you see any reason—any reason at all—why your parents might have sent you here?"

I just stare straight ahead.

Maybe I should run away to Australia. Find an accent and some freckles.

"We're here to help you, Wren. We need to get to the bottom of your feelings. We want to help you communicate. Not just yell or blame or storm away, *communicate*."

She waits. It feels like an hour, she waits.

I keep staring, straight ahead, breathing in Pine-Sol.

"I understand the rain caused a problem the other night. I understand that you're mad at everyone here." She pauses. "Tell me, are you also a little mad at yourself? Because that would give us two sides to talk about."

I'm not about to cop to that—what they're doing to me is child abuse and they know it!

She just sits there, and so do I. Finally she says, "You hear the other girls laughing?"

I hate the sound.

Don't they know I'm miserable?

Doesn't *anyone* care?

"Each and every one of them was right where you are and hated it too. Look inside your heart, Wren. You don't have to carry all that anger. Not just about the rain. About everything that brought you here. Let's unload it, unpack it, and move forward without it."

Typical therapy mumbo jumbo.

I won't look at her, so she finally stands. Her Aussie accent drops down to almost a whisper. "It'll be a long, miserable eight weeks if you don't start dealing with your feelings, Wren."

She leaves, and I sit under the Pine-Sol branches wondering what my parents will do when they get my letter.

Wondering if Anabella is secretly laughing.

Wondering if Meadow and Nico know what's happened to me.

Wondering if anybody anywhere cares.

18

Nico.

I met him last September while I was walking home from high school. He was in a lowered Mercedes getting high with a friend in the student parking lot.

"Hell-ooooo," he called out the window.

I tried not to do the whole who-me? thing. It had been a long two weeks of being a freshman and trying not to seem like one.

"Yes, you, beautiful," he called.

I tried not to blush, which is always pretty hopeless.

He was wearing Wayfarers. His dark hair had buzzy sides, with ocean waves cut in and a swoop-flip top. The tips were bleached blond. It was amazing.

He flashed me a smile—it was a little cockeyed, with a dimple.

My heart started pounding.

Be cool, I told myself as I walked by. *Be cool.*

"You got a smartphone?" he called.

I gave him a look. A don't-be-a-dork look. Of course I had a smartphone.

"Mine's dumb," he called after me. "Because it doesn't know your number!"

I turned back and smiled, and he grabbed at his heart. "Please tell me you have Band-Aids!"

"What?" I laughed.

"'Cause I just fell, really hard!"

"Shut up!" I laughed.

He started the car, then pulled up and cruised alongside me as I kept walking. "Who *are* you?"

"My name's Wren."

"Like the bird?" He turned to his friend. "Biggy-boy, my heart's all atwitter!"

"Shut up," I told him.

"Get in," he said.

And I did.

Half an hour later, I was drunk on Fireball Whisky, and in love.

"He *kissed* you?" Meadow gasped the next morning. "I couldn't get him to say hello to me last year, and believe me, I tried!"

It was nice to be at the same school as Meadow again.

It was great that we'd patched things up.

I'd really missed her.

She held her head. "So let me get this straight. You hit on him in the parking lot—"

"I wasn't hitting on him! He was hitting on me!"

"Whatever. You flirted. Then he gave you a ride home,

and when he was dropping you off, he kissed you? Like, *kiss-kissed* you?"

I giggled. "Unbelievable, right?"

"No kidding! So . . . what was it like?"

I tried to explain, but that was hopeless too.

"Does he know you're fourteen?"

"No! I told him I'm sixteen!"

"So he thinks you're a *junior*? You do not look like a junior." She frowned. "Wren, you are in way over your head."

It was fun seeing her so thrown off her game. She'd thrived on being a year ahead of me, knowing more, being the boss. But for once I was leader. It felt good. "Well," I said with a laugh, "I'm gonna learn to swim."

"You don't understand." She lowered her voice. "He's a *senior*."

"So?"

"So when he finds out you're a freshman, you are *gone*. Even if you were a sophomore, he wouldn't touch you! Seniors don't go out with the underclass—they just don't."

I gave her a little smile. "Well, I'm a junior, right? So it's cool."

She didn't seem to agree, but what did I care? Nico was worth whatever lies I had to tell to keep him.

But the next day, I saw him with another girl at lunch. And when I made him run into me later, he told me he'd found out I was fourteen and he couldn't afford the "jailbait." None of my promises made it through the Wayfarers. "We need to keep it cool." He flashed that dimple. "Maybe when you're older."

I broke down in the first bathroom I could find. What did

it matter that I was fourteen? Why did I have to be fourteen? What was I going to *do*?

I couldn't get his kisses out of my mind. Not that day, or the next, or the next. I still haven't gotten them out of my mind. I fall asleep some nights reliving them, pretending I'm in his arms, tasting the smoky cinnamon of Nico's lips.

19

My biggest worry about high school was actually my sister.

The narc.

For all her sports, clubs, running for office, and AP classes, she still managed to find time to corner me in the hallway outside my pre-algebra class a couple of weeks after Nico had kissed me. "Nicholas Simms is a wrecking ball, Wren," she whispered, looking around. "Do you know how many girls he's been through?"

With Anabella, it's always wise to play dumb. "What are you talking about?"

"He's hit on every girl at this school, including me! He was relentless! And disgusting! Do not fall for his act, Wren. He is seriously bad news. And a stoner!"

"A stoner? How do you know?"

"He has a reputation! People talk!"

"So you believe the gossip around here—is that what you're saying? Because if I were to believe all the things I hear about *you* . . ."

"Me? What do you hear about me?"

I laughed. "You don't want to know."

"Yes! I do!"

It was fun to see her so shocked. So worried that someone might be saying something negative about her. Which they weren't, but I was having a good time faking her out. "Look," I said, being cagey, "the point is I *don't* believe them. I know it's gossip. So lighten up, would you? Nico's just a friend."

"He's a wannabe gangster! And Sam Biggs? His sidekick? I heard he *knifed* somebody."

I laughed. "Biggy's harmless. Sweet, funny, and harmless."

Like I knew. Like they'd even really talked to me in the two weeks since The Kiss. I'd just been fluttering around the outer circle, hoping to be invited in—something she must've noticed.

Then I added, "And see? There you go judging and believing gossip." The halls were clearing because the tardy bell was about to ring, so I gave her a smile and said, "Just be glad I don't believe the gossip about you," and ducked inside my classroom.

It was the first time I felt like I had power—any power at all—over my sister. It made me happy. Like, giggle-inside happy. Meadow noticed it when we were getting high under the bleachers at lunch. "What's up with you?" she asked, holding in her breath.

"Nothing." But I couldn't help giggling.

"Tell me!" she said.

Two weeks earlier, I would have, but I knew she was the reason Nico had found out so fast that I was fourteen. I'd guessed, and Nico had given her up with a shrug. If it hadn't been for Meadow's weed, I'd have dumped her as a friend that very same day; but I put up with it because getting high with her was the only part of school I liked, the only thing that got me through the day. And since she pinched the weed from her parents, who were big-time users, it was free and easy and I wasn't about to blow that again. I'd learned my lesson the hard way back in eighth grade. I didn't need a refresher.

But in the last two weeks, I'd learned another lesson the hard way. I couldn't trust Meadow. At all. Telling her about Nico had been a huge mistake. I wasn't about to tell her about Anabella. Even though I hated Anabella.

I was stoned, and being at the crossroads of hating Anabella and not trusting Meadow was confusing. So I shook the thought off and passed back the joint. "There's nothing to tell, but . . . is there something in this?" I asked, leading her off track. "It's making me feel all goofy."

After school, I timed things so I was leaning on Nico's Mercedes before he got there.

"Little bird," he said like I was a naughty puppy, "we talked about this."

Biggy was with him, sweating in the afternoon heat. "Hey," I said to him, "is it true you knifed someone?"

He grinned. "Which time?" And they both cracked up.

I pushed off the car. "My sister seems to think you guys are wannabe gangsters and stoners. She says I need to stay away from you."

Nico's dimple appeared. "And yet, here you are."

"Brave, right? Because according to her, you're relentless and disgusting." I looked him right in the Wayfarers. "Which I guess is why you got nowhere with her."

His movements slowed. He pulled down his shades, peering at me over the tops of them. "And who is your sister?"

I felt the creep of a smile—my plan was coming together. "Anabella Clemmens."

He stared at me. Then: "Ana Clemmens is your sister?"

"Didn't I just say that?" I crossed my arms. "You're supporting her assertion that you're not too bright."

"Assertion?" he asked, flexing an eyebrow.

Biggy laughed. "Dude. Ana Clemmens."

"Ana definitely asserts," Nico said, nodding. "And I see it now. Sisters, but like day and night."

I shrugged. "Let's go with processed and organic."

He laughed. "Okay. Let's go with that."

"Dude," Biggy said again. "Ana Clemmens."

Nico pushed his Wayfarers back into place and beeped open his car.

"Get in," he said, showing me his dimple.

He didn't have to tell me twice.

20

It's been five days since I was abducted. I've been keeping track with hash marks on my pants, which are already filthy. Today I did the crosshatch thinking I was almost an eighth done, but according to the jailers, I still have seven weeks and four days to go. How is that fair? My only hope is that my parents read my letter and *do* something about this.

I was nauseous for most of Day 2. Even barfed once. So besides drying my stuff and putting up with hippie-dippie jailers trying to get me to talk, I slept a lot, which helped. The third day was actually the worst because I felt sick, had a crushing headache, and couldn't sleep. I tried to hide it, but I spent a lot of time crying.

Then yesterday I got my appetite back in a big way, and today my headache is finally gone, but my food is, too. At least the stuff I can eat without cooking. Or adding water.

Oh, right, water.

I'm totally out.

Michelle refilled my canteen once and warned me that the next freshwater drop wouldn't happen for a while, and that I'd better learn how to find my own before my refill was gone.

I gave her the silent treatment. I figured it would rain again. Or that she would give me another refill. It would be child abuse not to, right?

But it hasn't rained. Instead, it's been like living in a huge hair dryer during the day and a freezer at night. Michelle and the others don't seem to worry about being accused of child abuse. They tell me to use my sunblock, that my microfiber mummy bag is rated to twenty below, and that, no, they're not going to refill my canteen.

I've been planning to steal water from one of the other inmates while they're busy gathering wood or working on their curriculum or whatever, but I haven't had a chance. Everyone keeps their containers near them like gold.

So I'm dying of thirst and hunger and have been eating raw beans and rice, which is like chewing on gravel. There's been no chance to steal rations, either. They're hidden in secret stashes. Like Nico hides his drugs.

It's afternoon, and I'm still in my tent when Dvorka squats down at the opening and hands in a tin cup.

There's an inch of water in it.

I lock eyes with her for a good long stare. Her buzz cut has already grown out a lot. I can see why she keeps it short. I've got mine back in a braid, but it's feeling oily. Annoying.

Finally I grab the cup from her and down the water.

"Come on," she says softly. "Leave your anger here for a little while. Let's go find you some water."

So that's her plan. The measly gulp she's given me is just

a tease. A taste. I can hear Nico laughing with Biggy. *The first one's always free.*

"Wren?" Dvorka says. Still softly. Like she's waking me from a dream. "You in there?"

I don't like hearing Nico's laugh in my mind. Not when he laughs like that.

I look at Dvorka and nod.

"You'll need both canteens, your billypot, and the clear tubing that's in your supplies. Oh, and bring a bandanna."

It takes me a while to find the tubing. It's rubber-banded into a small bundle and reminds me of biology class, where I sit in the back row, trying to disappear. It makes me wonder if anyone's noticed I haven't been in class. That I've actually disappeared.

A sick feeling in my stomach tells me they have not.

Dvorka is waiting for me outside the tent. She gives me a closed smile but doesn't say a word or try to cheerlead me along, which is a relief. We go in the opposite direction from the latrine, up a ridge to a flat area where we can see for miles.

Miles and miles.

And miles.

And *miles.*

All of it desert.

I'm panting hard, and Dvorka stops and asks, "How are you feeling?"

I give in. "Hungry. Thirsty. A little dizzy."

She nods. "You are one strong young lady, you know that?"

The way she says it is not chummy, or like she's trying to sell me on something. She just says it. So I confess, "Not feeling that at the moment."

"No kidding. But you have definite willpower."

I snort. "My father calls me willful, and he doesn't mean that in a good way."

"Depends on how you direct it," she says, then gives a hint of a fangy smile. "Right now you're going to direct it at finding a water source."

I look around. "So how do I do that?"

The fang stretches. "Let's start with direction. If the sun rises in the east and sets in the west, point to north."

I don't know what the actual time is, but I do know the sun is on its way down, so I point to what I think should be north.

"Willful and smart," she says. There's no judgment in it. Or selling. She just says it like it's a fact.

A good fact.

About *me.*

"We came *up,*" she says, "so we could look *out.*"

I scan the area with my hand to my forehead like a sailor. "I see no water."

She laughs. "Me either. What I do see, though, is a north-facing canyon, a dry riverbed, and a line of cottonwood trees."

I look to where she's pointing. "This is not helping my thirst."

"I could lead you to water, but I want you to be able to find it yourself."

My father muttering about leading a horse to water spooks around in my head. He's made me despise that expression. And what does he know? Show me some water. Watch me drink.

For some reason, thinking this fires me up. "What's a north-facing canyon? Besides one that faces north. What's that matter, anyway?"

"They're cooler because they spend less time being exposed to hot sun from the south. So rainfall stays longer, sometimes for months. And if it's rainfall, it's safe to drink." She watches me and seems to be checking for boredom. "The cottonwoods only grow where there's a steady water source; and the riverbed may be dry now, but the trees let me know that water does flow through there. The night it rained? You can bet there was water in that bed."

"I know all about water in the bed," I grumble.

She laughs. "You are *quick*, too," she says. "So what happened to your water? The stuff that got you wet?"

"It . . . evaporated?"

"Exactly. And what happened to all the water that ran off these highlands and into that canyon and flowed down the riverbed?"

I look out at the riverbed. You'd never know there had been water in it. And it had *poured*. Could the trees have sucked it all up?

Impossible.

Could it have evaporated?

That doesn't seem right, either.

I think back to walking up the wash—the riverbed, the arroyo—to camp that first day. How sandy the ground was. How it shifted under my feet.

Suddenly I know. "It went down! The water seeped in!" I am so excited. So stupidly excited. "It's underground!"

She smiles full fang. "Lead us to water, Wren."

21

When we get to the riverbed, we cross over to the north-facing side and Dvorka shows me how to track down water that's slowly seeping out between rocks. We start near some green plants at the base of a rocky area and work our way up to a small pool of rainwater trapped in the rocks. "Since it's rainwater and pretty fresh, you can just drink it," she tells me. "The water we'll get from under the riverbed we'll have to filter and purify."

I'm dying for a drink. And I can see the water, but the opening's not wide enough to dip a canteen or billypot inside.

She opens one of her cargo pockets and stretches out her length of plastic tubing. "Shall we?"

Oh! A *straw.*

I stick one end of mine down into the water and suck on the other. What comes up is cool and clear. It tastes, *feels,* wonderful.

Dvorka and I look at each other while we drink, and I flash

back to being a kid, sharing a smoothie with my mother at Juice Jive in the City.

All of a sudden, my eyes are stinging and there's a lump in my throat and I can't drink anymore.

Dvorka stops drinking too. "You okay?"

I nod and then shake my head and then nod again.

She waits, then says, "Want to talk about it?"

I shake my head some more and go back to drinking. I concentrate on the end of my tube instead of looking at her. She doesn't pry, doesn't make me lie. It almost makes me want to tell the truth.

"Well," she says, sitting back when we're done, "I brought something you might like." She pulls a can out of her pocket.

"Peaches?" I squeal.

She laughs. "Let's get this party started!"

She produces crackers and a tube of peanut butter. I eat with my fingers and a stick. I shove and slurp and make happy moaning sounds. She laughs and says, "First water is a milestone worth celebrating."

When the food's gone and washed down with what water's left in the rock pool, Dvorka puts all the garbage back in a cargo pocket and says, "Let's go fill those canteens."

What this means is: Let's dig a hole in the dry riverbed. With a rock. The weird thing is I don't mind. Somehow this is exciting. Like I'm digging for buried treasure.

About four inches down the dirt is wet, and by the time I'm down a foot, I've got water seeping in from the sides, pooling at the bottom of my hole.

"Eureka!" I cry.

Dvorka is digging her own hole. "Keep going," she says.

"The deeper you can make it, the easier it'll be to collect. And make the hole wide enough for your billypot."

So I do, and when I've got my own well of water, she has me scoop it up with the billypot and pour the water through my bandanna and into the canteens. The water's kind of murky, and it doesn't take long for my bandanna to have a layer of silt on it.

When the canteens are full, Dvorka hands me two tablets. "Put these in to purify the water. You need one per quart. They take half an hour to work, so no drinking before then unless you want to risk getting the runs." Next, she shows me how to sterilize the threads and cap, then hands me a little metal tube with tablets of my own. "Always carry these with you."

I take the tube and slip it into my pocket. It feels important somehow. Like a secret password. It's *not* a secret *or* a password—it's just pills to keep me from getting the runs— but it feels like I'm being trusted with something. Or being let in on something. Maybe it's the way she gave them to me. I don't know.

I fill up the billypot and lock on the lid, thinking I can filter and purify it later.

"Smart," she says, flashing her fang. "Most Rabbits don't think that far ahead."

On the hike back, I ask how I can stop being a stupid Rabbit and she asks if I've read the handbook.

I have not.

"It's in there," she says. "But basically, you can't get to Coyote without water and fire."

"So maybe tonight we'll do fire?"

"It usually takes a couple of days to master fire. Sometimes longer."

"Seriously? Why?"

"It's easier said than done. Read your handbook. Get the basics down. I'll help you find supplies, but prepare to be frustrated." Another fangy smile. "Who knows? Maybe you'll manage to get it in a day. Maybe you'll put *willful* to good use."

It feels strange to have her turn the word around like that. Being called "willful" has always meant I've been bad. *Angry. Defiant. Hostile. Argumentative. Insolent.* Oh. And let's not forget *bratty.*

But here was a new way of looking at willful.

Of looking at *me.*

When we're nearing camp, Dvorka reaches into one of her magic pockets and hands me three string cheese packets, a power bar, and some dried apricots. "I know you're out of rations," she says. "I think you've earned a night off the raw beans and rice."

I take them and thank her. And I try to hide my glassy eyes.

"Once you have fire," she whispers, "your whole world will change."

I nod and head for my tarp tent, where I stash my dinner and dig up the handbook.

I'm going to figure out how to make fire. And I'm going to be *willful* about it.

Watch me.

I'll do it in a day.

22

I miss my phone. I don't like not knowing what time it is. I hate not being able to look things up. How much longer is it going to be light out? Do I have time to figure out how to make fire today?

"The sun's your timepiece," Michelle told me when I brought it up before.

Yeah, and the moon's my flashlight.

You can see why I hate her.

But I have water and food and daylight, and nobody's bugging me. The other girls are quiet, hanging out in their tarp tents, writing in notebooks, so I start leafing through my Wilderness Handbook—which is just a bunch of hole-punched papers held together with brads. There's an introduction—I skip that. There's a greeting from somebody named Soaring Eagle—I skip that. There's a section titled MOVING FORWARD—I skip that, too, and I'm getting annoyed. I flip to the back, but there's no index. If we're supposedly students and this is our handbook, shouldn't there be an index? I don't want to read a bunch of stuff from some guy named Soaring Eagle. I just want to make fire!

Then I come to calendar pages.

Three of them.

April.

May.

June.

In tiny print inside each day's box is information: Dawn, Sunrise, Sunset, Twilight, Moonrise, Moonset, Day Length. Tonight's sunset is at seven-fifty-four. I am so excited to see this. It's like a gift.

The first thing I do is find my pen and cross off the five days I've been here: April 3, 4, 5, 6, 7. Then I go back to the 3rd and begin to count off eight weeks, but stop as my finger touches down on May 22.

My birthday.

My *birthday*.

I'm going to turn fifteen in the *dirt*?

I get mad all over again. I hate my parents harder than ever. How could they do this to me? HOW COULD THEY DO THIS?

I flash back three months to January. Back to my mother's fortieth birthday. My dad had reminded me that we were celebrating that night and had given me forty dollars to buy her something on my way home from school. "Put some thought into it, Wren," he'd said. "This is not an easy milestone for her. If you get stuck, a nice card and perfume is a safe bet."

Mom had been down on me a lot, mad at me a lot,

disappointed in me a lot since my first-semester grades had come out. I was a freshman and failing. "How is this possible?" Mom had wailed. "You are smart. You are very smart! How can you be *failing*?"

Then some other stuff happened over winter break. Stuff that gave her clues. And then, of course, there was the narc.

So my plan was to be smiley-happy-helpful *reformed* Wren for her birthday. I'd been trying to reset the clock with her, because it was ticking like a time bomb. Even with my "new expensive counselor" reporting that I was making "great strides searching for answers," Mom now acted suspicious of everything, always wanting to know where I'd been and who I'd been with.

So I was planning to get one of those sentimental cards and some perfume at the mall, but after school I was with Meadow, and on the walk over we passed by a place that does body piercing.

It was across the street from the mall in a converted old house with stained-glass decorations and large crystals in the shape of teardrops hanging from the porch awning. We were stoned and the crystals were dazzling. Sparkling and colorful. Like rainbow tears of a lonely giant. I couldn't quit staring at them.

"If you shoplift the perfume," Meadow whispered, "you could get one of these." She pulled up her shirt a little so I could see that her belly button was pierced. There was a crystal jewel right in the middle of it. It was beautiful. A little gemstone cave.

"When did you get that done?"

"Yesterday. Right here." Meadow dropped her shirt and headed up the walkway. "Come on. Tanner's cool."

"Tanner?" I followed her up to the porch, staring at the rainbow tears, then followed her inside the house.

Tanner was head-to-toe tats, with quarter-sized gauges. "Uh . . . ," he said, glancing around like someone might be watching even though we were the only ones there. "I'm lookin' at underage?"

"Remember me?" Meadow asked, showing him her belly button.

He didn't seem to but said, "Oh, right."

Meadow hitched a thumb at me. "She wants one too."

"I don't know, man. I need a parent's signature."

"I got something better than a signature," Meadow said. "Like last time?"

"Oh, right," he said when she handed over a baggie of weed.

"And she's got the forty," she said, looking at me.

I handed over my cash.

"All right," he said, taking it, "but let's make it quick."

It was quick. And pretty painless. I left with a crystal in my belly button, just like Meadow's. It made me happy that we matched. Any problems we'd had in our friendship were stupid. *This* was what it felt like to have a sister.

"See?" Meadow said, laughing, on our way out. "Way better than perfume."

"But I still need to get the perfume."

"So let's go!"

We went into the mall, but by the third store the weed had worn off and I was starting to lose it. "Why do they keep it in cases?" I whispered.

"So people can't steal it?" She thought that was hilarious. "Let's try Ross," she said.

But the perfume was locked up in Ross, too.

"What am I going to do?"

She shrugged. "Get something else?"

"Like what?" I was running out of time and in a panic.

"Does it matter?" She led me to tall shelves near the back of the store. Shelves of junk people use to decorate their houses. "Here," she said, snatching up a glass bird. "It's pretty. She'll think it's sweet and sentimental. Done."

I looked at the price: $8.99.

"She won't know it's cheap! It's art. Come on. Let's get this done."

I didn't pocket the bird right then. I put it on a shelf at waist height, then made a note of the surveillance cameras as we went to find some clothes to use as cover. I picked out three random tops, then went back to Home Décor, where I palmed the bird as I walked by without even slowing down. It was the size of a pear and I slipped it into my hoodie pocket, holding the clothes so no one could see, then went to stand in the dressing room line.

"We're clear," Meadow said after scoping things out.

When it was my turn to get a number for the tops, I asked the attendant what time it was. When she told me, I gasped and said, "Oh, wow! I had no idea! I have to go. Sorry!"

I left the clothes with her and walked toward the entrance, pressing my arm against the glass bird to keep it safe while I had a fake conversation with Meadow about the time. "I can't believe it's so late! I was supposed to be home by now! I'm going to be in such hot water!"

We made it out the door.

We made it down the corridor.

We were home free!

And then out of nowhere a mall cop was bearing down on us.

Meadow said, "We gotta split up," and took off down the escalator, leaving me to get busted.

The rest was a nightmare. My parents didn't believe that I'd lost the money. They didn't believe I was just holding the bird in my pocket and forgot. They didn't believe a single word I said. Not even "I'm sorry!" I was officially the worst, most disappointing daughter ever.

So yeah, staring at the handbook calendar, I get why my mother is making me spend my fifteenth birthday in the dirt.

This is payback.

Bitter, petty payback.

23

I am so mad at my parents for sending me away to live in the dirt as some spiteful revenge. They have the nerve to call *me* petulant and childish? What hypocrites.

I wind up digging through the handbook, looking for how to make fire. If I can't get out of the desert, at least I can get out of being a Rabbit. Seeing what the other girls are allowed to do—just seeing them be together—makes me feel so left out.

So alone.

HOW TO MAKE A BOW-DRILL FIRE is three pages long. There's a list of parts, a diagram, and instructions. The list says I need to find or make a fire board, a spindle, a bow, cordage, a socket rock, a fire pan, and a tinder bundle.

I have no idea what any of those things are, but the descriptions and diagrams help. The fire board—which is just a flat piece of wood—and the spindle—which is a stick in the shape of a big, dull pencil—have to be made from matching kinds of soft wood. I wouldn't have a clue what soft wood is, but in parentheses it says that cottonwood, yucca, or sage heartwood all work.

It feels strange to realize I know what two of those plants are.

The bow—which looks like a crude violin bow—can be made from any kind of wood.

The fire pan is just a dry leaf or a small piece of dry wood—any kind.

And the tinder bundle—also called a nest—can be made out of dry grass or juniper bark.

Juniper.

I feel a little lift inside.

I know what that is, too!

The socket rock is a palm-sized stone with an indent—either natural or nicked in—and in the parentheses next to cordage it says *provided, but can be made from yucca leaves.*

Provided?

I study the diagram. Cordage is just a cord, and if I can find one that's "provided," it's going to be a lot easier than making one out of yucca leaves because I don't know how you can possibly make a cord out of yucca leaves. If you can even call them leaves. Yuccas look like woody desert pineapple plants with extra-long, sharp spears. Cord from that? Impossible.

I start searching through my stuff, which is a mess. There are baggies of dried lentils and beans and macaroni sitting in between stuff like clothes, notebooks, toilet paper, deodorant, bug repellent, and sunblock. It's all a big jumble, and for some reason *that's* making me mad, too. Plus, everything's gotten dirty. Gritty and dirty.

I rummage around for a while but don't find any "cordage," and when I can't stand being in the tent another second, I go out looking for a palm-sized rock with a dent in it.

When I wander past the outskirts of camp, Michelle tags along.

"Just don't talk to me," I tell her, and she doesn't.

Which is awkward after a while.

"What's sage heartwood?" I finally ask, still looking for rocks.

She points out one of the big ugly shrubs that seem to cover the desert.

"Seriously?"

She gives a little shrug and a closed smile.

I frown at her. "Look. You can talk. Just don't get all chatty, okay? I'm not gonna see the beauty in the landscape. I don't need to hear how I'm screwing up or how I should contemplate what's brought me to this place." I snap off a dead-looking branch from a sage bush. "It's payback, by the way. The reason I'm here? It's my parents getting back at me for messing up my mother's fortieth birthday."

She looks at me and gives a nod, but she doesn't say anything.

I point at another sage bush. "How am I supposed to get a fire board out of that?" I kick at it with my boot. "I don't have an ax or a knife or a saw."

She pulls a folding knife out of her pocket and thumbs it open. "You ask for help."

"Why can't I have one of those?"

"Why do you think?" She holds my eyes with hers. "You'll get your own when you're on Elk."

"Not Coyote?"

Michelle frowns. "Not all Coyotes can be trusted."

I drop the subject and let her help me. She points out a sage bush that's split down the middle and half dead, then shows me how to use the knife and a rock to wedge off a board. What we wind up with is crude and splintery and more a shingle than a board—maybe three inches wide, ten inches long, and less than an inch thick—but it looks like the diagram in the handbook and it makes me smile inside.

My first fire board.

"Can I use the knife to whittle down the end of this stick?" I ask, thinking the branch I snapped off will work as a spindle.

"You need one that's straighter," she says, "with no nubs, if possible."

So I find another branch and she lets me whittle the end. "Always cut away from yourself," she says. And after watching me a minute, she asks, "Have you ever done this before?"

I want to lie so she doesn't think I'm lame, but my head shakes out the truth.

"That's okay." She takes it and demonstrates. "It's more a flick than a cut." She makes a few more strokes, then she hands it back and watches me adjust. "That's it."

The knife's sharp. I like the way it feels to shape the wood. *Flick. Flick. Flick.* Even after I'm done, I want to keep working on it. *Flick. Flick. Flick.*

"How about making yourself a spoon while you're at it?" Michelle asks.

So I really get into that, splitting wood, rounding it, flicking out a shallow scoop, and then smoothing it all down on a rock.

"Nice!" she says, admiring it. She hands it back and says, "You'll also need a pilot hole and a notch in your fire board," and shows me where they should go.

By the time we head back to camp, I've got a spoon along with a fire board and a spindle; I've found a good socket rock and a branch for the bow, which is now notched and ready for cordage; and Michelle's helped me gather dry grass and juniper bark for the tinder bundle.

The sun is just dipping out of sight on the horizon as the blue tarps come into view. "It's seven-fifty-four," I announce. "Twenty-five minutes 'til dark."

Something about knowing this makes me feel anchored. Like I have a toehold on what's going on. Plus, I'm holding everything I need to make fire.

Well, except for the cordage.

But that's somewhere in my tent!

Michelle gives me a small grin. "Someone's been reading her handbook."

I try to hate her for saying that, but right now I just don't.

24

I'm inside my stupid tent, eating my last string cheese in the dark, watching the campfire burn, while the other girls are sitting around it laughing, when one of them squeals, "Mokov!"

It sounds like she's seen some exotic bird, but out of the darkness comes this man with two long silver braids dangling over a leather vest. Under the vest, he's wearing a dark green thermal shirt, and his pants and hiking boots are just like the jailers', only something about him seems really different.

All the girls get to their feet. "Mokov!"

"Hello, Grizzlies," he says with a smile.

Dvorka is suddenly at my tent. "Come with me," she whispers. "You don't want to miss this."

I scramble out of the tent. "Who is that?"

"Mokov. It's story time."

I stop. *"Story time?"*

She waves me to follow. "Legend time. He's Paiute."

"What *is* that?"

"It's a Native American nation," she whispers. "Just come!"

Since I'm still on Rabbit, I'm not allowed to sit by the fire on a rock or log. I've got a second-row seat with Dvorka, in the dirt.

"Do you want anything to eat?" one of the Grizzlies asks the Mokov guy. "Or drink?"

"The land has nourished me," he says with a nod.

I pull a face at Dvorka.

"Don't judge," Dvorka whispers. "Just listen."

The Mokov guy spreads his arms. "Sit, girls. Tell me how you've been."

All the Grizzlies sit and look at him like he's a god. "We gathered rain and washed our hair," one of them says.

"It was awesome!"

"We used yucca root!"

He nods his approval, then asks, "But tell me—have you been able to move forward in your quest?"

They all look away. Mostly down.

"It's not easy," one of them says.

"I'm still so angry," another one adds.

He nods. Like he's thinking. Considering. "Anger is a dry riverbed. You should follow it only if it leads you to the springs of forgiveness."

The Grizzlies stay silent, their gazes down, but I'm staring right at him, thinking he can't see me in the second row.

"Hello, young one," he says, looking right at me. "Welcome."

Dvorka elbows me, so I give a little wave.

I feel like such a dweeb.

One of the Grizzlies peeks up at him. "Will you tell us a story?"

The rest of them look up and start begging like little kids. "Please???"

I squint at Dvorka. "Are they *serious*?"

She shrugs. "There's nothing like a story told by Mokov." Then she adds, "Traditionally, the full legends were only told in the winter or fall, but he thinks there's value in sharing shortened versions with us." She lowers her voice even further as we watch the others. "Most Native American tribes have nature-centered spiritual traditions where everything has life and the power to direct its energies. The humans and spirits in their stories often take on the forms of animals." She zeroes in on me. "Storytellers were the ones who passed along the tribe's history and beliefs. These are sacred legends, told in a traditional way. They are not to be ridiculed."

She's so serious.

So concerned.

Stories where animals talk seem like baby-book stuff to me, but I nod at Dvorka and whisper, "Got it."

The Grizzlies are holding their breath, waiting for this Mokov guy to speak. Even the fire is quiet, not popping or crackling, and the flames seem to be dancing in place, waiting, while the smoke rises straight up.

Finally he begins.

"In the Long Ago, there was no fire in our lands. Lizard was lying in the sun to keep warm when he saw something falling slowly from the skies. 'What is this?' he asked as it descended to earth.

"All the people gathered to look. 'This is ash!' Coyote exclaimed. 'There is fire in another country!'

"'We must have fire!' Rat said. 'It will keep us warm on winter nights!'

"'But how?' Rabbit asked. 'How will we get it?'

"So Coyote made a plan. He and the others followed the winds west, toward the fire. Along the way, Coyote positioned people at stations. 'Wait here,' he told Rat at the first station. 'Wait here,' he told Rabbit at the next station. He did likewise with the others until at last Coyote arrived at the fire. Many people were dancing around it. He watched patiently, devising a plan to steal the fire. Cleverly, he made a false tail from shredded bark and grasses and entered the dance. The other dancers did not notice anything strange about him until he dipped his false tail in the flames, stole the fire, and fled.

"The dancers, not wanting to share fire, began to chase him. Coyote ran to the first man he had posted and passed the fire to him. This man ran to the next and passed the fire again. And so it went until the fire was passed to Rabbit and then to Rat.

"Still the people chased, demanding fire be returned to them. Rat ran to the top of a tall rock with a sheer face and put fire in a large pile of brush. The people could not reach him and pleaded with him to give their fire back.

"Rat, realizing fire should belong to them all, threw the brush in all directions, where it scattered far and wide and set a spark in all the brush across the lands." Mokov spreads his arms wide. "And this is why, to this day, you can still make fire from the brush."

No one says a word when he's done. They just sit staring into the fire.

"Wow," one of the Grizzlies finally says. "I'm going to think of that every time I start a fire."

"Another story?" someone asks.

"Yes, please! Another!" the Grizzlies beg.

So he tells a story about a deadly warrior with a stone shirt who was killing members of a tribe and how Snake found the warrior's weakness and saved them. As punishment, the stone-shirt warrior's offspring were turned into terrapin, which Dvorka explains to me is turtles.

And then comes another story about how Packrat got his patches. It's obviously a story about being deceptive, but I find myself listening to every word. I see myself in Packrat—which is probably the point for all of us here—but, weirdly, I don't mind. Watching Mokov tell the story by firelight, watching him move his hands or hold them up toward the sky, watching his braids sway like silver snakes on his chest as he speaks, seeing his wrinkles deep with shadows . . . it's like he's something right out of his Long Ago.

There's also his voice. It flows, soft and warm and deep, and seems to cast a spell around us. About the time he's done I realize that his stories feel like lullabies. Lullabies from a different world.

Mom used to sing soft, quiet lullabies to Mo.

She used to sing them to me.

A rock forms in my throat when I realize that this feels like that.

Like something from *my* Long Ago.

Mokov rises to his feet and wishes us peace. We all stand, too, and watch as he turns and walks away, disappearing into the darkness.

25

I'm up before sunrise, counting out loud at the latrine. John's sitting by the fire, his man-bun frizzed and frayed, stirring something in his billypot. Everyone else is still in bed.

John keeps an eye on me as I gather twigs and wood from the outskirts of camp and pile them in a clearing away from the other tarp tents. I make a circle out of rocks, and inside it I set up a little tepee of twigs and wood, just like I read about in the handbook. All I need now is to find that cordage. Something I have yet to do because my "room" is a mess.

How many times have I heard *that* in my life?

But this really is a mess. A dirty, gritty mess. At home, Mom would have threatened and begged and finally broken down and cleaned it, but that's not happening here. And it's so bad that even *I* can't stand it.

I drag everything from inside the tent, shake it out, dust it off, organize it, and put it back, finally getting the plastic ground cloth laid out flat under everything else.

Nowhere in any of my stuff do I find the "provided"

cordage. When I tell John, he says they issued me some and he can't give me any more. "Are you saying you guys never make a mistake?" I ask. "I'd steal a piece from my tarp cord, but it's barely long enough as it is."

"Sorry, Wren" is all I get out of him.

The other Grizzlies and Jude are up now, hanging out with their billypots around the fire, making oatmeal. Jude hasn't looked too happy lately. And even from across camp I can see the bags under his eyes. Wonder what *his* deal is.

Whatever.

Like I care?

I turn my focus back to the cooking oatmeal. It smells so good.

It smells so *unfair*.

I have oatmeal. I have water. I have a billypot and a spoon. I could be making some too, if I could have a little corner of their stupid fire.

Which I can't, since I'm still on Rabbit.

Which I'll be on until I can start my own fire.

Which I can't do without the stupid cordage, and I sure don't want to waste time making some out of yucca leaves.

I go back to my tarp tent totally tweaked and hungry. But when I kneel down to retie my boot because the lace has come undone, my mood suddenly changes.

Cordage.

Not the stuff they supposedly issued me.

My bootlace!

It's not flat and cottony like a regular shoelace. It's round and tough and plenty long enough to string across my bow stick.

I whip it out of my boot grommets, hold it up, and face the

oatmeal eaters. "CORDAGE!" I shout. "I'm gonna make me some FIRE!"

Some of them laugh and wave their stick spoons. Jude gives me a halfhearted thumbs-up while John calls, "Inventive!"

I don't see Dvorka, and Michelle's just dragging herself out of her tent, looking totally hungover.

"Lazybones!" I call at her. "I've been up for hours!"

I hear my mother in my voice, which is weird in a very bad way.

Who says "lazybones"?

Dorky moms, that's who.

From reading the handbook, what I get is that if I turn the stick in the fire board fast enough, I'll make a little coal that I can transfer into my "nest" and fan into flames.

So I gather all my fire-kit parts in my extra bandanna and take the handbook with me to my fire ring. Then I sit in the dirt and tie the bootlace onto both ends of the curved stick to make it into a bow, and I twist the middle of the spindle stick into the middle of the lace like the diagram shows. So basically I have something that looks like a crude violin bow with a stick tangled up in it.

Following the directions, I rest the whittled end of the spindle stick in the fire board pilot hole, slip a scrap of wood partly under the notch in the fire board, put the socket rock on top of the spindle with my left hand, put my right foot on top of the fire board to anchor it, take a deep breath, and pull the bow.

In that single pull, the whole thing collapses.

I don't know why.

I review the diagram in the handbook, assemble the parts again, take a deep breath, and pull.

The whole thing collapses again.

I let out a curse, not knowing Michelle is standing right behind me, ready to assign consequences for my language. All she says, though, is "Your cord isn't tight enough. It has to be way tighter than you think."

So I sit back down in the dirt and retie the cord.

"Even tighter," she says. "It should be hard to twist the spindle in."

So I pull as hard as I can, wrap the cord in the bow notch, and tie it off.

She nods. "That should do it."

I have a real hard time twisting the spindle in, but this time everything stays together when I start moving the bow back and forth. The spindle wood squeaks against the fire board. *Rrreeerh, rrreeerh, rrreeerh, rrreeerh, rrreeerh, rrreeerh, rrreeerh.*

That's all.

It just squeaks.

"You have to go faster," Michelle says. "And push down harder with your socket rock. You need friction. Lots of friction."

So I lean into it, pulling and pushing, pulling and pushing as fast as I can. The cord snakes back and forth around the spindle as the spindle squeaks in the fire board. *Rrreeerh, rrreeerh, rrreeerh, rrreeerh, rrreeerh, rrreeerh, rrreeerh.*

And then, like a genie rising out of the wood, there's smoke.

"Smoke!" I cry, thinking that any second the fire board is going to burst into flames.

"Keep going!" Michelle says. "You have to keep at it."

And then I remember that the fire board's not supposed to burst into flames. This sawing back and forth is supposed to make a glowing ember that I have to transfer into the tinder-bundle-nest-thing, and *that's* what's supposed to burst into flames.

But . . . where's the ember? All I see is smoke. And my arm is getting really tired!

"Don't stop!" Michelle cries.

"But it's not working! Where's the ember?"

"In the fire pan!"

I stop to look.

"No!" she cries, and hits a palm to her forehead.

I pick up the fire board and see a little sooty pile on the piece of wood underneath. *"That?"*

She sighs. "You were just getting started."

"Just getting started? My arm is about to fall off!"

"Give it another try."

So I do.

And I get an ember—a little spot of glowing red in the middle of a small pile of sooty black. I transfer it into the tinder bundle, but the ember goes out.

So I try it *again.*

And I get another ember.

And the ember goes out in the tinder bundle.

I try once more and the same thing happens. "Why do we have to do this?" I yell at her. "My arm is dead! And what's wrong with *matches?* We can have pills to purify water—why can't we have matches to start a fire? This is stupid!"

She studies me. "Have you had breakfast?"

"I've got no food!" I yell at her. "Everything I have has to be cooked! Your rules are stupid!" I point at the campfire, burning away. "Why can't I just use that?"

She stands up, dusts off, and says, "You'll get it." Her voice is calm. Neutral. Like she doesn't care one way or the other. "And when you do, things will change." She starts walking off. "If you can start a fire out here, you can start one inside yourself."

"What's *that* supposed to mean?"

She keeps walking. And instead of explaining, she calls, "Soak some oatmeal. Eat it cold. It's not great, but it's edible."

I kick my fire board; I kick the bow.

I hate this place.

I hate it so much.

26

I eat cold oatmeal. It's lumpy and gross. It's not the instant kind, either, so there's no sugar or flavor. It's just paste.

I'm wishing I'd saved a few of the dried apricots that Dvorka gave me, but they're long gone. And adding powdered milk just makes it worse. I flash back to spoon-feeding Mo when he was a baby. His little tongue pushed out more oatmeal than it took in. Now I get why.

Although his oatmeal wasn't all lumpy-bumpy.

And he didn't have to eat with a rough wooden spoon.

Gross as it is, I'm still hungry, so I make more. I stick the billypot in the sun and hope some of the building heat from the sky will soften my oatmeal. Then I sit in the dirt in the shade of a juniper tree and watch the rest of the Grizzlies doing some dumb trust-building game. There are blindfolds involved. And zombie walking.

I'd rather eat pasty oatmeal.

After a while, I go to check the billypot oatmeal to see if

it's gone from crispy to pasty. Not yet, but maybe I'll eat it anyway.

Then I hear footsteps behind me. On the other side of the juniper tree. They sound like running footsteps. *Human* footsteps. But who would run in this dusty heat? I tell myself it must be some sort of animal, but then I hear panting.

Human panting.

Then there's rustling and more panting, and the branches of the juniper are bouncing around.

"Hey!" I call out, because now I can see boots.

Boots that are just like mine.

I move closer, and I really don't get what's going on until I hear a curse. And another curse. And then a voice says, "Don't give me up, Wrenegade."

My breath catches. Only one person's ever called me that before.

Michelle's voice comes from behind me, "What's that?" And then she sees him.

Dax cusses again, dives out of the juniper, snatches up one of my canteens, and takes off running straight through camp and into the open desert.

"Hey! That's *mine*!" I shout, and try to go after him, but my one boot is still missing the lace, so I can barely hobble.

"We've got a runner!" Michelle shouts, then whips her walkie-talkie off her belt as John grabs his water and goes after Dax.

"It's a boy!" one of the Grizzlies squeals like a little girl. Trust-building blindfolds go flying, and all the Grizzlies run to the edge of camp to try to get a glimpse of Dax. "A boy," they say like they're dreaming.

To them he may be some mythical being, but to me he's a thief. I had *just* filtered that water! It's all I had left!

"I wonder what group he's with," one of the Grizzlies says, her voice floating through her own Dreamland.

"Snake," I tell her.

She gasps and her eyes go wide. "Oooh. Adjudicated."

"A bad boy," another one says.

A third one snickers. "Aren't they all?"

The whole group laughs. And then one of them asks me, "How do you know he's from Snake?"

"I rode in with him from the airport. His name's Dax."

"Daaaax," they murmur, watching him grow smaller and smaller as John chases after him, his man-bun busting loose, his long hair flying.

Dvorka's coming to break up our little party, so one of the girls leans toward me and says, "Would you bust out that fire already? Get off Rabbit. We need a little sister."

"Rules!" Dvorka says, charging in.

"How far's Snake camp?" one of the Grizzlies asks her. "I think maybe we want to go exploring." But I can tell she's just baiting Dvorka away from the rule breaking they did in talking to me, because while Dvorka's going off about not-even-thinking-about-it, the girl who asked her is giving me a secret grin and jerking her head over to my little bow-drill fire stuff. "Get going," she mouths.

The truth is I've been feeling left out and ignored. Like everyone else belongs and I'm not fit to be in their group. But now I've got an excited flutter in my stomach. The other

Grizzlies *want* me to move up to Coyote, to join them around their campfire.

They're *rooting* for me.

I eat my soaked oatmeal fast and get back to my fire setup. I twist in the spindle and get a comfortable stance with my foot anchoring the fire board. Then I start sawing back and forth. Faster. Harder. Faster. Wisps of smoke come up, teasing my nose, my senses. Pretty soon, I'm breathing hard and my arm is getting tired.

Faster, the smoke teases. *Make me burn.*

Behind me I hear *Clang, clang, clang.*

A spoon beating on a billypot.

Another spoon and pot join in. *Clang, clang, clang. Clang, clang, clang.*

They're beating in time with my sawing.

Clang, clang, clang. Clang, clang, clang.

A third pot starts up, then a fourth, urging me to keep going, to try harder, to go faster.

Clang, clang, clang. Clang, clang, clang.

My arm's in pain, my heart's pounding, I'm panting like I've run the mile, but I can't stop now.

Clang, clang, clang. Clang, clang, clang.

Dvorka's voice beside me says, "You've got a cherry. You must. Transfer it into the nest."

My hands are shaking from fatigue. Shaking as I transfer the glowing ember into the tinder bundle. Shaking as I blow, gently blow, into the nest. The little fibers of grass and bark crawl red and curl. I blow again, and smoke billows through the nest. I blow again, begging it to come to life, begging for a flame.

And then *Whoosh.*

"FIRE!" I yell at the top of my lungs.

I put the tinder bundle inside my tepee woodpile, where the flame spreads and crackles and pops to life.

"FIRE!" I yell again, and do a little dance while the billypot drums go wild.

27

There's a ceremony involved in moving from Rabbit to Coyote. It includes a blindfold—of course—and hiking to a secret place with the other Coyotes.

I'm a little nervous. I've heard that coyotes move in stealthy packs. That they lure smaller, unsuspecting animals to remote locations by acting friendly, then circle them, kill them, and tear them to bits.

The dog-world version of school.

It's slow going, getting to the secret spot. There's uphill and blindness. There's whispering.

I hate whispering. At school, at home, in the store ... it always feels like it's about me. Even when it's probably not, it feels like it probably is.

The Coyotes finally sit me in the dirt, and when someone removes my blindfold, I find myself in a small circle with three girls and Michelle. In the center of the circle, there's a branch of sage, a leather cord with a white bead strung on it, a canteen, and a ziplock bag of M&Ms.

M&Ms!

"Welcome," one of the girls says. She's African American, with hair fluffed out above her headband bandanna. She's the same one who broke rules to tell me to get going on starting a fire, but now she sounds so official. Like she's conducting a tribunal, where my crimes will be exposed. Where I might be executed.

Or get some M&Ms.

I'm so confused!

"I'm Mia," she says. "I'm on my third week. I'm seventeen. My aunt took me in when my mom left. My uncle abused me. I got way into drugs. Got violent at home. Tried to kill my uncle. My pastor started a collection at church to save my soul. I wound up here."

She says all this like a list.

It's not some wild story, it's facts.

Just facts.

"I'm Shalayne," the next girl says. She's fake blond, with a dark root line. "I'm also in week three, also seventeen. My parents are divorced. I'm a pawn in their war. Started drinking and smoking weed at thirteen. Didn't even try to hide it. They sent me to counselors, rehab, AA, nothing stuck. My dad remarried. I tried to burn down his house. Got sent here."

Again, it's like a list.

Just the facts.

"I'm Hannah," the third girl says. She's got a pixie cut and blue eyes so big they're like oceans in her face. "I'm sixteen. This is my second week. I started drinking when I was eight. Just doing what my mom did every night. Got into drugs, did the street-hustle thing. My dad came back into my life, and after a few months of trying to fix me, he took me on a 'road trip' and left me at base camp."

A silence falls over the circle as they all turn to look at me. I point to myself and pass a questioning look around the circle.

The answer comes in their stares.

Yes, it's my turn.

I sit there, petrified because I've never admitted any of it. Meadow knows, Nico and Biggy know, but none of us actually *talk* about it. And I've sure never confessed any of it to people I don't know. And sure not to an *adult*. All the school counselors I've been called in to speak to? All the therapy sessions I've been to? I've lied and denied and detoured. I've talked about little things like they're big things. Cried, just to make sure they knew I was serious. I've learned the dance and can do it in my sleep. Or completely wasted.

I look around the group.

They're still staring at me.

Calmly.

Kindly.

Waiting.

"I'm Wren," I say.

My chin starts to quiver.

Why is my stupid chin quivering?

"I'm fourteen."

A lump lands in my throat.

What's the *matter* with me?

"We moved. I started middle school. I had no friends."

I sound so pathetic.

So whiny and pathetic.

Especially compared to them! I haven't been abused, my

parents aren't divorced, my mom's not an alcoholic. . . . I've got nothing tragic to flash.

Still, they look at me.

Calmly.

Kindly.

Waiting.

"Middle school sucks," Shalayne offers.

Mia nods, her fluffy hair waving a little. "But that's not what got you here."

I look down.

"No one's judging," Hannah whispers. "We've all been where you are."

I sneak a look at Michelle. I hate that there's an adult here.

"Yes, even me," Michelle says. "Why do you think I'm willing to do this? I've been right where you are, Wren. It's frightening and painful, but if you walk through this fire, it'll make you stronger."

I want to yell, *What's with you and fire?* I want to fight back. Lie! Escape!

Instead, it's the truth that escapes. "I smoked my first joint in sixth grade." My throat is suddenly dry and raw, my heart is pounding, and I can barely breathe. "I started drinking after that. Started stealing, lying . . . hating. Got in with some older guys. My sister narc'd on me. Things spiraled. I went ballistic. Here I am."

I've said it to the dirt, but I've said it. And I feel sick about it.

Weak.

Disgusted with myself.

They've finally broken me. After all the counselors and

therapists, after all the framed therapy certificates I've seen hanging on office walls, after all the chairs and couches and action-figure playacting, after all the lying and denying, all the diverting and skirting, I've finally given up the truth.

In the desert.

In the dirt.

I turn to the side and puke.

28

Moving from Rabbit to Coyote is a ritual. There are steps. Solemn stares. The burning of sage. The eating of candy.

It reminds me of the things I had to do to hang with Nico and his friends.

As we sit in our solemn circle in the dirt, Mia asks, "What do you bring to the group?" When I sat in Nico's car, Biggy asked, "What's in it for us?"

I don't know how to answer Mia any more than I knew how to answer Biggy. My mind went blank then, and it's blank now. I can think of absolutely nothing I bring to the group.

I am worthless.

Totally worthless.

Michelle coaxes. "You can build a fire. You can find water."

"All of them can do that," I whisper.

"You are tenacious, determined, and strong," Michelle says in a firm voice.

Nico had said, "She's a minor, smart, and fast."

What Nico meant was that I could carry and deliver drugs and not go to jail if I got caught. And if the heat was on, I had a good chance of ditching the cops on foot. I didn't understand that when Nico said it. His words were wrapped around me, silky smooth and soft, and he was looking at me like he was finally going to kiss me again. He pulled back at the last second, but I knew he wanted to, and that meant so much.

And now . . . what do Michelle's words really mean? *Tenacious, determined, and strong* sound good, but they seem desperate. Like she's trying to cover up that I have nothing.

Mia nods as the words float away, but it's a contradictory nod where yes means not-good-enough. "Can you cook?" she asks.

I look at her straight on. "Is there a microwave?"

The other Coyotes snicker.

"How about gather firewood?" Shalayne asks.

"Or dig? Like, with a shovel?" Hannah asks.

I shrug. "I guess. . . ."

"So . . . you got anything you can teach us?" Mia asks.

"*Teach* you?"

Hannah nods her pixie head. "I've been teaching them to draw."

"And I make killer scrambled eggs," Shalayne says. "Which, believe me, is a skill you want on your team when you're dealing with freeze-dried."

Mia doesn't volunteer anything. She asks, "How about talents?"

"Yeah," Hannah says. "Like if you were going to be in a talent show, what would you do?"

I give her a little squint. "Hide in the bathroom?"

The Coyotes look uncomfortable. I feel completely stupid. Maybe I'll be stuck on Rabbit forever.

Michelle tries again. "I understand you have a close relationship with your little brother."

I want to glare at her, but there's a sudden ache in my heart.

And my eyes are stinging.

"How do you entertain him?" she asks.

I shrug. "I don't think you have computer games out here." But the truth is those games were never as much fun as playing *Jungle Book*. Or even reading him Disney stories. There's a collection of Disney kid books in his room, and when he was younger, he'd make me get in his bottom-bunk fort and read those stories.

That was before we moved.

Before we each got our own room.

Before everything changed.

"Wren?" It's Michelle's voice, prompting. "You were thinking about . . . ?"

I just shake my head.

But they're all quiet.

Waiting.

The silence is not something I'm used to. At home it gets filled in with advice. Instructions. Reprimands.

Here, they just wait.

"I used to read to my brother," I finally say. My voice is small. Unsure. "He loves Disney stories."

"*Nemo!*" Hannah cries. "My all-time favorite story—*Nemo!*"

The Coyotes shoot their favorite titles around—*Aladdin,*

Toy Story, 101 Dalmatians, Zootopia—until they get to *Frozen* and I cry, "No! Not *Frozen*. Anything but *Frozen*."

Mia nods. "I hated *Frozen*."

The other two frown at us. "How can you hate *Frozen*?"

Michelle intervenes. "I think what we can derive from this is that Wren can serve as storyteller."

"Storyteller? No! I could never be like that Mokov guy. I just read to my brother."

"But I'm guessing you've read the same stories over and over and over?" Michelle says.

I nod. "So true."

"Which means you probably pretty much know them by heart?"

I think for a minute. "Yeah. I kind of do."

Michelle smiles, very pleased. "Hmm," she says. "Disney stories as oral tradition? Interesting! They do contain metaphor. And moral consequence."

"Hey, don't ruin them with analysis," Hannah says with a frown. "Leave our childhoods alone."

Michelle laughs. "Point taken."

"Do you know how long it's been since I've seen *101 Dalmatians*?" Shalayne asks with a faraway look. She turns to me. "Can you tell that story . . . do you know it?"

"I do."

"Do you do voices?" Hannah asks, ocean eyes wide.

I am feeling weirdly exposed. "I do."

She claps her hands. "Awesome!"

Shalayne laughs. "We could do the Twilight Bark!" And she and Hannah throw back their heads and yip and howl and bark like idiots.

Michelle gives Mia a nod, and Mia hands me the sprig of sagebrush. "Walk with us, Wren. We invite you to be our storyteller."

Hannah and Shalayne jump in, tag-teaming me. "That doesn't mean you don't have to bust out a fire." "Or gather wood." "Or bring home water." "Or dig the latrine!"

Mia ties the cord with the white bead around my neck, and the others pull theirs out of their shirts—all white beads on cords.

"You get a new bead at each level," Michelle explains. "A yellow one when you advance to Elk, an orange one at Falcon."

Then they open the M&Ms and we glut on chocolate, and the whole time I'm thinking how different things are out here. First *willful* became a compliment instead of a complaint, and now I'm a *storyteller,* and that's considered a good thing. At home that word is on my parents' rotation of synonyms that included *liar* and *prevaricator, fibber* and *fabricator, con artist* and *dissembler.*

I pop in a fistful of M&Ms, wondering how being called the exact same word can make a person feel so completely different.

29

The first time my mother accused me of telling stories, I was actually telling the truth. It was back in seventh grade, and there were a hundred questions she could have asked where I *would* have lied, but for this specific question—had I borrowed her diamond necklace—I didn't have to. "No" was technically the truth.

What I'd done was steal it.

Steal it and sell it.

It was definitely not a "borrow" situation—there was no chance she'd be getting it back.

"Have you asked Anabella?" I asked my mother when she didn't seem to believe me.

"She told me to ask you."

"Why? She's the one who wants it. For winter formal, right?" I swept an arm across my jeans and Minnie Mouse T-shirt. "Not seeing much need for diamonds with the clothes I wear. Now, Anabella . . ."

Mom pressed. "She thinks maybe you didn't want her to wear it?"

It was true. And truth, Meadow had taught me, is best avoided through redirection. "Why would I care if Anabella wore it? *I* sure don't want to wear it!" I gave her a hard look. "And why do you always believe her and not me?"

"I don't. I treat you equally. And fairly." She squirmed. "I just want to make sure you're not . . . telling stories."

"Thanks, Mom. The vote of confidence is so comforting." I looked her right in the eye. "I did not borrow your necklace. Go cross-examine Anabella."

"But she's the one who noticed it was missing!"

"When?"

"This afternoon!"

"While you were at work? Why was she even in your jewelry box?" I crossed my arms. "Or maybe her discovering it missing is just a clever ploy to seem innocent? She's very good at that, if you haven't noticed."

She paused. Blinked. Shook her head. Left the room.

And from down the hall came Anabella's whine: "Why would I take a necklace you told me I could borrow?"

Soothing words came out of Mom, but from my eavesdropping spot outside Anabella's room I couldn't quite make out what they were.

"I planned my whole outfit around that necklace!" Anabella cried. "She has it, Mom. She has to!"

"I do not!" I said, walking into her room. Then I ripped into her about being the worst sister on the planet for accusing me.

Things got louder from there.

What I learned from the necklace incident was to not steal your parents' *stuff*. Stuff is risky. I didn't even get much for the stupid necklace. Pawn shops are a rip-off. The only really good part was messing up Anabella's perfect princess plans.

The other reason I stole the necklace is that no one can live off twenty bucks a week allowance. Even Anabella griped about it. Being in seventh grade, I was on the middle school's prepaid meal plan, but Anabella was now in high school, where there were options. So her whining got *her* somewhere, where mine did not. Which was, as usual, unfair.

Meadow was totally sympathetic when I complained about it. "No one can live off that," she said. "Go to the movies once and it's gone."

"Exactly!"

We were getting high in a faculty hallway bathroom during nutrition break. Every wing at the middle school had a faculty bathroom. They were basically locking closets with a toilet, a sink, a vent fan, and air freshener. But since teachers hardly ever used them, Meadow had devised a system to make them into our own private stall. It included an Out of Order sign, a locked door, and heavy doses of air freshener.

It was genius.

"You should pinch cash from your parents," Meadow was saying.

"Are you serious?" I handed the joint back to her. "I'd be petrified of getting caught!"

"Pinching is an art," she told me. "The trick is to *pinch*, not grab. Like, if you're going to pinch from your dad's wallet, take one bill. Don't get greedy." She held in her breath and handed the joint back. She exhaled slowly. "How do you think I've kept us in weed for over a year? I *pinch* from their stash. If I took too much, they'd notice."

I tried it at home that night. Dad's wallet was always on him, but Mom kept her purse and keys on a little desk in an alcove near the kitchen. Mo was asleep, Anabella was holed up in her room, and Mom and Dad were watching TV. I sneaked to the alcove, opened the purse, opened the wallet, slipped out a twenty, then returned everything to the way I'd found it.

I went back to bed with my heart pounding. Twenty bucks! Just like that! No asking, no begging, no thank-you notes to write . . . it was the best, easiest twenty bucks ever!

And I was sure Meadow was right.

My mother would never notice.

30

It took until spring break, but my mother did notice.

First she came up short at the farmers' market.

"Why do you even buy stuff here?" I asked, trying to re-direct. "We just throw it away."

"We do not." She was practically pouting. Like I had hurt her feelings. My mother has great intentions to go organic and "reduce our carbon footprint," but nobody in the family likes what she does with kale or Asian eggplant or bean sprouts, and you won't catch that woman on a bike. She doesn't even own a bike. And since we moved from a small, tri-level apart-ment in San Francisco to a sprawling single-story house in Orange County, our footprint went from lizard to T. rex.

She also went from working part-time to working full-time. Dad is an "imaging professional," which means he does MRIs and CT scans, and Mom works billing medical claims. When they both got offered jobs at Kaiser in Southern Cali-fornia, Mom told us again and again how much sense it made to accept them. Mo was starting first grade and she didn't need to be home so much anymore; taking the new jobs and getting out of San Francisco meant they could afford to buy a house instead of rent an apartment. We'd have space. Maybe get a dog. It was all rosy. A dream.

Except nobody was ever home. Mo went to after-school day care, Anabella found an instant circle of friends, I found Meadow, and the dog was a rabbit that died after three weeks.

When we lived in San Francisco, Tuesday was taco night and Thursday was spaghetti night. The other nights were wild cards, but I always looked forward to Mom's cooking on those two nights. Everyone did.

After we moved, Domino's and Panda and Taco Bell became our dinner choices.

We even stopped transferring it to plates, because, I mean, why?

Mom and Dad were also too busy or tired to notice that Anabella and I were fighting, or that Mo would wake up alone in his big new room and start to cry. They didn't notice that I'd go into his room and tell him a story—just make up a story—until he fell back to sleep.

All the extra space did was give us room to drift apart.

Mom was still rifling through her purse to pay the kale man. The total was almost thirty dollars—way too much for what we were getting, if you asked me. I'd pinched two twenties the night before, thinking there was a lot of money in her wallet. I didn't know the rest of the bills were all ones.

"Just leave the beets and kale and . . . whatever that root thing is," I suggested. "No one's going to eat them anyway."

"Yeah," Mo said. "I hate kale."

The veggie peddler turned to help someone else. Mom ignored us and tried to unearth her missing money. "I don't understand this," she muttered. "Am I losing my mind?"

I cooled it for a few weeks after that. But when she was flush again, I resumed pinching. I was more careful, and took less, too.

Then one morning in the commotion to get out the door to work and school, Anabella spun me around as I was going by her in the kitchen. "That's a Jack Wills hoodie?" she gasped. "How did you get that?"

"It's Meadow's." I'd prepped that lie for other clothes I'd worn, and it was a good thing, because I really wasn't expecting to have to use it now. "She lets me borrow stuff all the time." I couldn't help throwing in a dig. "Like sisters are supposed to."

"It's nice that you think of Meadow that way," Mom said. She was wetting down Mo's hair. "Too bad you and Anabella don't like the same clothes. I always loved trading outfits with my sister."

Anabella was giving me a suspicious look. "That's a hundred-dollar hoodie," she said. "And brand-new."

I wanted to kill her. Why couldn't she just mind her own business? It *was* brand-new but made to not look it. Everyone else in my family would have thought it was a five-dollar thrift-store find. But no, not Anabella.

The narc.

Mom was distracted, but not completely. "Wow. Better not spill your grape juice on it!"

On her way out the door, Anabella cornered me and said, "I'm not stupid, you know."

"About what?"

She pointed a finger at me as she left to catch her ride. "You know exactly what," she said. "I suspected before, but now I know."

I grabbed the door. "Suspected *what?*"

"You know what!" she yelled up the walkway. "And I'm going to prove it!"

I closed the door thinking, *I hate you. I hate you so much.*

31

I didn't know exactly what Anabella was going to try to prove, so I had to be careful about everything. And it came at a really bad time.

"My parents know," Meadow informed me as we were lighting up in the Wing-8 faculty bathroom that same day. "They moved their stash."

I stopped midpuff. "What happened? Are you grounded?"

"I'm alive." Meadow took the joint back. "At least they're not *your* parents, right?"

That was an understatement. Meadow's parents were living off a trust fund and basically just hung out watching Netflix in their condo all day. Meadow said they never smoked in front of her, but you didn't have to look or smell too hard to figure out that the downstairs TV room was a stoner temple.

"I know how to score some," Meadow was saying, "but you're gonna have to chip in."

"Can't you just find where they put their stash? It's gotta be somewhere, right?"

She laughed. "So you *want* me to get killed—is that what you're saying?"

"No! But—" I explained about Anabella. "So I have to be really careful for a while."

She puffed down the joint until there was nothing left to smoke. I felt like she was hogging it. Making a point. Though I wasn't sure what the point was.

She flicked the nub into the toilet and flushed. "You can just quit if you want. . . ."

The thought of quitting felt like spiders crawling under my skin. Getting high with Meadow was the only thing that made school tolerable. "Well, what's it cost?"

"What have you got? I'll see what I can score."

I turned over fifteen dollars, and the next day she handed me a skimpy baggie of weed and a package of rolling papers.

"You're kidding, right?" I asked.

"Don't I wish."

So I had to find a way to get some cash, but Anabella was now watching me like a hawk. She thought she was being sly, but I was watching her like a hawk now, too, so I noticed things.

Her door left open a crack at night.

The money left as bait in our bathroom.

Her spying through my bedroom window.

What a stalker!

I had to go past her bedroom door to get down to the alcove where Mom's purse was. I'd seen Anabella sneak down there a couple of times, so I was pretty sure she was setting up something to trap me. I didn't think it was anything sophisticated like a video camera, but I wasn't a hundred percent sure.

This was Anabella, after all.

But I suspected it was something more like sticking a twenty up from the rest of Mom's cash so I'd be tempted to take it. Like when we were little and we played Old Maid—she'd stick the bad cards up a little so I'd reach for them without thinking.

Well, I wasn't her gullible little sister anymore. I wasn't going to take whatever bait she'd set up, and I also wasn't going to call her on any of the stuff she was doing. If I sprang her traps, she'd just set others up.

Instead, I stayed away from Mom's purse, called out, "Hey, Anabella—is this your money in the bathroom?" and made like I was doing my homework when she was spying through my window.

And I smiled.

Smiled a lot.

Which drove Anabella nuts.

Then one night I had an idea for how I could turn the tables. I could almost not believe how brilliant the idea was. A lightbulb hadn't just come on, it had exploded in my mind.

I waited for Anabella to do her ridiculous evening routine—brushing her teeth, flossing her teeth, brushing her teeth again, rinsing with mouthwash. Gargling with mouthwash. Cleansing her face, moisturizing her face. Lotion everywhere—hands, toes, elbows, arms, calves. Brushing her hair—*brush, brush, brush,* to one hundred. Tying up her hair to give it volume the next day. Rubbing beeswax into her fingernails.

Sharing a bathroom with Anabella is a nightmare.

When she was finally done, I waited a good fifteen minutes, then walked down to the alcove, making just enough noise to alert Anabella. I stood in the alcove for thirty seconds, killing time, then hurried back to my bedroom.

Anabella scurried out of her room and down the hall like the rat she is. I slipped out of my bedroom and crept after her like a cat. And just as she was checking inside Mom's purse, I took a picture with my phone and screamed, "Mom! Dad! Come quick!"

Mom and Dad came flying into the alcove like the house was on fire and ran right into Anabella, who was so shocked that her hand was still in the cookie jar.

"Anabella!" they gasped. *"You?"*

It was one of the best nights of my life.

32

I'm a Coyote for one night—just one night—when reality comes knocking. The sun isn't even up yet when it starts. "Rise and shine, Grizzlies! We're striking camp."

I don't really know what this means.

It sounds like picket signs will be involved.

At the moment I don't feel like picketing or protesting. At the moment I'm warm and cozy in my mummy bag, looking out my tarp tent at the soft glow of a new day. There's the crackle of fire, the smell of sagebrush shriveling to ash. I am lying in a cloud of smoky content.

With me, I've got the memory of last night. Being accepted into the circle around the campfire. Meeting the other girls—Brooke and Kelsey, who are in their fourth week and a level ahead on Elk, and Felicia, the only Falcon, who is in her sixth week. I'm not great with names, so I was glad at least the *F* was a Falcon. It helped.

We ate a warm meal of rice and lentils, and nothing had

ever tasted so good. And being the storyteller was fun. I did part of *101 Dalmatians,* and the Coyotes especially loved me!

"Rise and shine, Grizzlies! We're striking camp!"

It's Michelle, busy at the fire, hyped up like she's been pinching from an illegal stash of caffeine.

"*Now,* ladies! Unless you want to hike on empty stomachs!"

Grizzlies groan, but none of us get up.

Michelle's tent is already down and bundled into a pack. Dvorka's is too, and I can see her working on dismantling John's tarp. The sun crests the horizon and glares across camp, and Jude staggers around his stuff like he's not really sure what he's doing.

"What happened to John?" I call out. "Did he catch Dax?"

Across camp, Mia sticks her fluffy head out of her tent. "That's right—what happened?"

Shalayne's ratty bleached mop appears. "Yeah, what happened?"

Hannah moans from inside her tent, which is right next to Michelle's spot. "How can you not know? The stupid walkie-talkie was going all night!"

"So?" Shalayne asks. "What's happened?"

"John will meet up with us later today. Dax is in custody and going back to court," Michelle says, sounding totally testy. "Now let's move. It's going to be a hot one."

"What about my canteen?" I ask. "Dax stole it."

"We'll deal with that later."

"But—"

"Let's *go.*"

I stay put. "Maybe we would if you weren't being such a bossy grouch!"

Camp goes quiet. Even the fire quits crackling.

"Not cool," Felicia says.

Without a word, the other girls all get up and get busy.

"You're kidding, right?" I ask, but no one answers. They just go about their business, stuffing away their bags, tearing down their tarps. I can't believe it, but I know the signs. I've been here before.

Shut out.

Shunned.

Blacklisted.

But why?

I tear down my tent and work at packing up my stuff like everyone else is doing. I'm terrible at it. I only really did the tarp-pack thing that first day, and I don't remember how to do it. I feel like kicking my stuff. Yelling at it. At everyone. Why am I being treated like rotten fish? Is there a secret Fish level they didn't mention? A place to which you get exiled if you say something wrong? I didn't even say anything wrong! I just stated facts. Michelle's tired and grouchy! They're all tired and grouchy! Why else would I be exiled to Fish?

"Need some help?"

It's Mia. I'm suddenly jealous of her hair. It's like a crown, puffed and proud behind her headband bandanna. My hair's dirty and gross, and even braided back, I want to cut it off.

"Why did everyone shut me out?" I whisper.

Mia unfolds my tarp, bringing me back to square one. "You don't get it now, but you will."

"Get *what*?"

"How much Michelle cares. Her and Dvorka both." She drops her voice. "You're on Coyote now. You don't dis them. Ever."

"But I didn't—"

"Yes"—she holds me with a hard look—"you did."

I'm dying to argue. Dying to say, *What Utopia are you from where you think that was disrespectful?* But her list from yesterday plays through my mind—abused by her uncle, hooked on drugs, tried to *kill*—and I feel more lost than ever.

So I'm just quiet as she shows me how to fold the pack, how to keep my fire kit, a canteen, the billypot, and some food strapped outside the pack so it's easy to get to.

"Thank you," I tell her when I'm packed.

"We need breakfast," she says. "Believe me, you want to eat."

The other Grizzlies are already cooking oatmeal, whispering. I'm sure it's about me, because they go mute when I arrive. Mia offers to cook my oatmeal with hers, and when it's done, she scoops some across to my cup and shares her brown sugar.

No one says a word.

I watch Michelle, who's across camp having a powwow with Dvorka and Jude. It seems pretty serious. Maybe they'll get rid of me, too. That would be good, right? Anything's better than sleeping in the dirt, right?

They finally come over to the fire ring, and Dvorka asks, "How we doing?"

Everyone nods. No one speaks.

There's a battle raging inside me. I want to shout, "Really? *Really?*" I mean, how stupid is this silent treatment? And at home that's exactly what I would have done. I would have stormed out of the room cursing and slamming doors and hate-hate-hating until the house was bursting with it.

But there are no doors here.

There is no place to hide.

And as hard as I might try, I could never fill the desert with hate. The wind would just blow it away.

And, weirdly, I don't want to hate on them.

Even more weirdly, I want to say something I haven't said in a long, long time.

Have not said honestly, anyway.

Even thinking of saying it is putting a rock in my throat. I don't understand why I want to, don't even *agree* with it, but it's like I need to stand up and say it.

I have no idea why I need to *stand,* but I do.

So I do.

And then I freeze in place.

Everyone looks at me.

Waits.

I can barely breathe as I look right at Michelle and remember how she helped me build my bow and spindle and board, how she trusted me with her knife, how she cheered when I lit my first fire, how she made me believe I *could.*

"I'm sorry," I choke out. "I'm sorry I was disrespectful."

And then my eyes burn with tears and I sit down trying my hardest to hate this place for making me want to say that.

For confusing me so much.

33

My apology works like an unmuting. Grizzlies are talking to me again. *Smiling* at me.

I should be happy, but instead I'm suspicious. Are they all just minions? Is this actually some desert cult? Is Michelle the supreme leader? Do they put behavior-mod drugs in the oatmeal? Is that why I got emotional? Should I try to barf up my breakfast?

We finish packing, put out the fire, scatter the ashes, cover the latrine, "remove all traces" until there's no "impact on the environment."

"Excellent," Dvorka says, looking around. Then she assigns duties. "Coyotes, work out the tarp; the rest of you are on resupply." She looks at the sun and frowns. "Let's do this!"

I look at the sun too and try to calculate the time. If sunrise was around seven and sunset is around eight, then, horizon to horizon, that's thirteen hours, which puts us at about nine o'clock. Maybe nine-thirty.

"Wren!" Mia calls. She's with Shalayne and Hannah by the stretcher—a tarp lashed between two wooden poles. All week, the stretcher has been propped against a pinyon tree, off to the side of camp, and I figured it was for in case someone got hurt. But this morning we've been putting supplies on it. Stuff like a griddle, some big pots, a couple of large, empty plastic containers with spigots, the collapsible shovel, rope, and two metal snow discs.

I didn't ask about the snow discs. I just did what I was told and figured there might have been snow. Somewhere. Before.

But now suddenly it matters. Every ounce on this tarp matters, because Mia is telling me and the other Coyotes to pick up the ends of the stretcher poles.

"You're serious?" I ask. I'm already carrying a gazillion pounds on my back. "And why do we have to haul around snow discs?"

"High or low?" Mia calls to the other Coyotes, ignoring my questions.

"I'm for low," Shalayne says. "Until we get to flatlands."

"I'm good with that," Hannah says.

"Low it is," Mia says. "On three."

"Would somebody please tell me what we're doing?"

"It's not rocket science," Mia says. "One . . . two . . ." She frowns at me. "Grab your end, Wren!"

There's no pretending I don't know what she's talking about. I reach down and grab my end of a pole, and on three, the four of us lift the tarp stretcher.

The stuff on the tarp bangs and clangs and settles into the middle. I feel like one of those porters we learned about in fifth grade—slaves who had to carry rich people this way. Only the rich people sat in chairs. Or in little enclosed carriages.

The whole group starts moving, walking in kind of a line—a dust-covered chain gang with Dvorka in the lead, Michelle at the rear, and Jude up between us porters and the other Grizzlies.

As we hike along, my hand starts sweating and hurting. Pretty soon, my arm is stretched out, aching, and I'm mad. I get now why everyone was happy that I advanced to Coyote. It wasn't that they cared about *me*. They knew a move was coming up and wanted me to help carry stuff!

I'm back to hating on them. Hating hard. I feel tricked and stupid. Like I did when I finally figured out what Meadow was doing.

This is just like that.

Meadow had made me believe that she was my friend.

She'd made me believe that she liked me.

It was all just a lie.

A cold, heartless lie.

34

When I had to start paying for weed, my allowance bought me maybe four joints a week, which was not even enough to get me through school and left zero money for anything else.

Mom's purse was no longer an option, Dad kept his wallet on him at all times, Anabella's cash was hidden behind about eight layers of security, and Grandma's birthday money stopped when I turned thirteen.

"Should have thanked her last year," Mom said when I opened my Happy 13 birthday card and there was no money in it.

Her voice was frosted with I-told-you-so, and it tweaked me. Even on my birthday, she couldn't take my side. Why not frown at the *card* and mutter, "What kind of grandmother cuts you off after one year of forgetting to send a thank-you note?" Her own mother had died, and I could tell she didn't really like Dad's mom, so why not sigh and say, "You know she's vindictive and miserly," and then make up for it by giving me some birthday money?

But no. She just couldn't help giving me that disapproving look.

Even on my birthday!

We were in the living room by her grandmother's piano, so I went for a backdoor approach. "I sure miss *your* mom. Remember how she used to sit on the bench with Anabella and me and tell us the *Tale of the Piano?*" The *Tale of the Piano* was a long story about the piano's life, which included time in great-grandmother's Nazi-occupied apartment during World War II. I thought bringing it up might make her realize I wasn't getting any birthday money from *her* mother either, but all it did was make her break down in a puddle of tears.

It was Meadow who came to my rescue. First she offered to sell my stuff on Craigslist, and when I'd sold off everything she thought I could get anything for—including my Jack Wills hoodie—she said, "I think it's time for a little S'n'R."

"S'n'R?"

She lowered her voice. "The fine art of Steal-and-Return."

"Steal-and-Return? What's that?"

She laughed. "You steal, I return."

She explained that it was complicated because without a receipt you usually get store credit when you return something, which you then have to use to buy something else, which you then return with the receipt, and, depending on the store, you can wind up with another store credit because your receipt said you used store credit to buy what you're returning, but at some stores you can cash out.

Like I said, complicated. And it involved shoplifting, which

I was new to at this point and made me crazy nervous. But I was nearing the end of seventh grade and Meadow was finishing eighth, which meant she'd be at the high school in a few months while I'd be stuck in middle school for a whole year alone. I knew I had to do something.

I took a deep breath. "Okay . . . how do we do this?"

She started me off with a tour through Walmart. We acted like we were browsing shelves, while she filled me in on surveillance cameras and how to shield what I was doing from them. I'd had no idea they were even up there, because they didn't look like cameras. They looked like big smoky Pokéballs hanging from the ceiling, but they were actually dangling eyeballs, watching our every move.

"Don't look at them!" Meadow said through her teeth.

It was hard not to, now that I knew they were there. And now that I did know, I was totally creeped out. Who was watching? Was it a whole bank of cops looking at monitors in some back room? Or was it just one creeper with a Big Gulp and a mountain of junk food? Were people watching us *right now*? Could they tell we were up to something? Was everything being recorded?

"Never look right at them," Meadow whispered, guiding me along. "Just scan the area where you're going from a distance, then remember where they are and stay cool. Cool is the key. Lose it and you're locked up."

"But we're minors, right? They can't lock us up!"

She gave me a sharp look. "You don't ever want to have to play that card, and you do *not* want to wind up in juvie." She pulled me along. "So focus. What you're after is small, high-value items."

I could figure out what that meant, but it sounded so strange coming out of her. Like she had a PhD in shoplifting. So I squinted at her and said, "What?"

"You know, like makeup? High-end earbuds? Anything that costs a lot but is small enough to slip into a pocket. Obviously, the bigger the price tag, the better."

Obviously.

She steered me around a little more, giving me tips and ideas on what to say if I got caught. "Oh, I'm so sorry! My hands were full and I forgot I put that there!" Stuff like that. "And be contrite!" she told me.

"Contrite?"

"You know, apologize. Be sorry. Act innocent!" She grabbed my arm and led me to the door. "Come on—let's get out of here."

"We're not taking anything?" I whispered.

"Are you kidding? The way you've been acting? It's waaaaaay too hot in here right now."

The next day, she took me to a drugstore near school. "Why here?" I asked. I was whispering even though we were clear across the street from the store.

"Less cameras, and I've had good luck returning stuff here."

We stayed across the street for a few minutes while she gave me more instructions. Then she sent me off by myself. "You'll be way less conspicuous by yourself," she said. "Don't be nervous. Just do what I said. You'll be fine."

So I went inside, got a handbasket, and hung it on my arm, just like she'd instructed.

I felt like a dorky Red Riding Hood.

I walked the aisles casually, adding stuff to the basket—a loaf of bread, a L'Oréal lipstick, a box of caramel popcorn, a can of iced tea. When I put the iced tea in the basket, I palmed the lipstick back out of the basket, rounded the aisle corner, and slipped the tube into my pocket. I shopped around a little more, then went to wait in the register line.

When it was my turn, I smiled at the clerk and said hello as I put the basket on the counter.

The clerk was older than my mom, with tight curly hair. She welcomed me in a bored voice and didn't even look at me, just started ringing things up.

"Oh, no," I said, digging through my jeans pockets.

She'd already scanned the bread, but she stopped when she saw that I had one measly dollar in my hand.

I gave her a desperate look. "I left my money at home!"

She canceled the sale and put the basket aside. "Next!"

I left the store, sweat popping, heart pounding. I started across the street, hearing Meadow's voice loop in my brain: *Do not look back, stay cool. Do not look back, stay cool. Do not look back, stay cool.*

I made it halfway across the street.

Nobody was shouting at me to stop.

Do not look back, stay cool. Do not look back, stay cool.

I was almost across the street.

Nobody was clamping a hand on my shoulder.

Do not look back, stay cool. Do not look back, stay cool.

I reached the other side and finally risked looking back.

Nobody.

Suddenly there was this *rush.* This really strong electric *high.* Every cell in my body tingled. I was flying!

"Look at you." Meadow laughed as she ushered me down the street. "I have never seen you smile this big."

I slipped her the lipstick.

"Nice," she said with an approving grin.

I was on top of the world, totally hooked.

35

That summer, I got to be a pro at lifting. Not just stuff Meadow could return to keep me in weed, either. I got stuff for me, too. Candy bars, nail polish, makeup, clothes . . . By the time I was in eighth grade, it didn't even faze me anymore. Lots of times I did it just because I could.

And then the day before my eighth-grade spring break, Anabella came to my room and said, "I owe you an apology."

She was a sophomore now and hardly even acknowledged my existence, let alone spoke to me when Mom didn't make her. So an *apology*? My brain could almost not translate.

"Huh?" I said, looking up from my phone.

She came in a step farther, stared at the floor, and frowned. "Remember last year how you told me that that Jack Wills hoodie was Meadow's and I basically called you a liar?"

"Uh, yea-ah."

"I was wrong. I'm sorry."

My head was spinning. This made no sense. "Why are you bringing this up now?" I asked. "It's been over a year."

She shrugged. Still looking down. "I see her in it all the time at school."

Before I could think, I was saying, "You *do*?" Then I tried to cover up by laughing out, "It's gotta be pretty thrashed by now."

"No, it still looks good." Suddenly her phone was in my face, with a picture of Meadow wearing my Jack Wills hoodie.

What went screaming through my brain was *She said she sold it on Craigslist for twenty bucks! She gave me three measly joints for it!* But I managed to nod and stay cool. "Yup. That's it."

She was studying me now. "So, you know, I'm sorry I treated you like that."

"No big," I said, hoping she couldn't see the steam coming off me.

She started to go, then turned back. "I'd like to start over with you someday. I don't like that we hate each other."

"Oh, so you hate me? Is that what you're saying?" I went back to browsing my phone. "So nice to know."

"Wren, look. I'm not—"

"Just leave."

She did.

I sat on my bed thinking about Meadow. I tried to come up with ways she could have my hoodie without having lied to me. Like: she sold it, then saw it at Goodwill and bought it. But I was grabbing at shadows. She knew I loved that hoodie. She would have told me!

And then the paint I'd brushed over other things started cracking.

I was always the one who lifted, she was always the one who returned. "It's complicated," she'd explained again when

I'd offered to do the whole thing myself. "You don't want them to get suspicious."

But it never really made sense. Suspicious of what? It's not like we always used the same store. We had a rotation system going! And wasn't it more suspicious if the *same* person returned things? And why was she always telling me what to steal? Like, down to the brand name!

Everything was fine as long as I didn't ask questions. But the times I did, it felt like I was in gym trying to shoot a hoop with someone's arms out, blocking. Out! Up! Out! Every time I asked something, I got swatted down.

So I quit trying to make the shot. What did I care, anyway? What I passed off to Meadow somehow got turned into weed, and that was what mattered. I kept doing my part, she kept doing hers. It had gotten me through the torture of middle school, right?

But seeing Meadow in my hoodie, knowing she had lied . . . it tweaked me.

Really tweaked me.

And she'd been wearing it all year? It was almost spring break and I'd never seen her in it, which told me she didn't want me to know she had it.

So the paint was cracked.

Cracked and peeling.

But something else was starting to bother me.

Why had Anabella taken the picture? She'd used it like proof. But why did her apology need proof? She could just have said she was sorry and that would have been enough.

But she'd come in with the picture ready.

She'd really wanted me to *see*.

I sat in my room and thought.

And sat.

And thought.

And finally I just knew.

Anabella wasn't apologizing.

This was classic two-faced, phony Anabella—she'd come in to narc on Meadow. I actually growled at the doorway where she'd been. I *hated* her.

But as much as I wanted to chalk the whole scene up to Anabella being the most despicable sister on earth, I couldn't ignore the awful, gut-burning feeling that Meadow had spent almost a year taking me for a ride.

36

The first day of spring break, I just showed up at her house.

"Meadow!" her dad bellowed from the door. "Your friend's here!" He smiled as he stepped aside, letting me in. "How's it goin'? It's been a while."

He'd put on weight since the last time I'd seen him. There was a full-on roll coming over the waistband of his shorts, and his face looked puffy beneath the stubble.

"Good," I said. "You?"

"Hangin' in there." He looked around. "Excuse the mess. It's been a little . . ." His voice drifted off, then came back full force. "Meadow!"

"I know the way," I said with a laugh, and pointed to the stairs with a question mark on my face.

"Sure, sure, of course. She's probably got the earbuds in again."

At the top of the stairs, I turned left to Meadow's wing. Her parents had a bedroom around the stairwell and down the other hall, but Meadow said that they slept in the down-stairs TV room, so she was pretty fearless about smoking weed in her bedroom. "They're on their own cloud," she told me the first time I spent the night. And it was true. They never, ever checked on her. It was like she had the whole up-stairs to herself.

I listened outside Meadow's door for a minute and could hear the tinny buzz of headphone music. I tapped just so I could say I'd knocked, turned the knob, and peeked inside.

She was on her back on her bed, earbuds in, eyes shut. The room was a disaster. I hardly recognized it. No way I could sleep on a pad on the floor like I used to.

I slipped inside and closed the door. There was evidence everywhere: nail polish, sunglasses, jewelry, clothes . . . I crept around the room collecting all of it in a cloth-lined wicker basket that was supposed to be used for organizing. Then I spotted my Jack Wills hoodie lying in a heap by her bed and quit tiptoeing. I was *mad*.

"Hey!" Meadow cried, sitting up. "What are you doing?"

I shoved the basket at her. "Here! Label that Wren's Stuff!" I picked up my hoodie and put it on. "You *liar*."

"Aw, maaaan," she said, looking down.

"This is why you never invite me over anymore! This is why you never want to Facetime. This is why you want to be the one to cash in. You don't actually do it! You *liar*."

"It's not like that. It's . . . complicated."

"I'm done falling for that, Meadow. It's really simple—you're a *liar*."

"Look. I had trouble returning stuff. They're tight about it now. I didn't tell you because I didn't want you to feel bad."

"You really think I'm stupid, don't you? Well, I'm not! The only thing I was stupid about was trusting you! But I totally get it now. You never had to buy on the street! Your parents never moved their stash! You've been pinching from them this whole time!"

She switched into battle mode. "Yeah, well, you know what?" she said, standing up. "You never even offered to pay! You—"

"You were getting it for free!"

"I taught you how to pinch from your parents, and you never even thought to offer me any of it!"

"You get twice what I do for allowance!"

"You went out and bought hundred-dollar hoodies! Like I could afford to do that?"

"If it bugged you, why didn't you say something?"

She was glaring at me now. "You never even said thank you!"

That stunned me. "*Thank* you?" It had never crossed my mind to thank her. Maybe because I thought hanging out in the bathroom getting high was doing her a favor? But that hadn't been the case since early in sixth grade.

"I thought you seeing how much the stuff actually costs might give you some appreciation! But no. Never once did you thank me. For anything!"

I went at her a different way. "I thought you liked hanging out with me!"

"What do I get out of it? I do all the work and you get all the pleasure!"

"Pleasure? *What?*"

She snorted and sat back down on her bed. "In case you

haven't noticed, I'm the brains, you're the leech." She waved at the door. "Go. And good luck scoring on your own."

She was dismissing *me*?

"I am not going to let you turn this around! You're the worm here. You've been lying to me for a year!"

She lay down and started to put her earbuds in. "Yeah. And you've been leeching for about three."

I stormed out of there. Meadow was a complete *liar* and the worst friend ever! I didn't need her! Who needed her? Our friendship was a habit, was all. A bad, empty habit. I was done. D-o-n-e, done!

Which was easy that first week.

And harder the next.

I tried making new friends, tried living clean.

By summer she was back in my life.

37

It feels like we've been hiking with the tarp stretcher for at least four hours, but when I look at the sun and divide up the sky again, I calculate that it's only been about two.

Two sweaty, miserable, dusty hours across the desert.

We've traded sides and high-low positions a couple of times to relieve aching hands and arms. My bandanna's now wrapped around my stretcher handle to keep the hot spots that were raging at me from turning into actual blisters. I've been quiet and mad while the other Coyotes have been talking. They chitchat about school, complain about haters, joke about guys. And Mia and Shalayne bust out hip-hop lyrics like their tongues are tap-dancing.

I march on, head down. What is *wrong* with them? Don't they know we're prisoners? That we're just a chain gang, being forced to lug a ridiculous pile of junk through the desert?

"Terrain" seems to be Dvorka's favorite word today. She's called back stuff about rocky terrain, mountain terrain, rugged terrain, and desert terrain. . . . I'm sick to death of it. So now when she pipes up about the *floral* terrain, I grumble, "The only *trr-ain* I want to hear about is one that'll give me a ride out of here."

Mia—who's working the back end of the tarp stretcher with me—hears and tosses me a grin. "Choo-choo."

And then suddenly we're logjammed, with Hannah and Shalayne stopping dead in their tracks. I snap, "What the—" but then I see the carpet of yellow flowers ahead. It's the size of a football field. I blink, sure it's a mirage.

"Springtime in the desert," Michelle says behind us. "There's nothing like it."

I look at her. "But . . . ?"

She laughs. "A little rain goes a long way when the land is parched." She nudges her head up, telling us to keep moving. "Sometimes it doesn't take much for what's dormant to bloom."

She says this carefully. Like she's putting words on one of those justice scales, balancing them. And in the back of my mind, I get that I'm supposed to feel the weight of what she's saying, but I ignore it. What I need is the *lift* I'm getting from seeing this field of bright, beautiful flowers.

Next to me, Mia seems to be feeling it too. "Wow," she says under her breath.

"You haven't seen this before?" I ask.

She shakes her head. "This is a first."

As we move closer, I ask, "We're walking *through* it?"

"We're heading for that canyon over there," Dvorka calls from up front.

And that's when I actually look around. I've been so busy

looking down, being lost in my own head, hating on Dvorka for being so chirpy about *terrain,* that I haven't noticed much but the ache in my arms and the sweat, sticking dirty shirt to hot skin, beneath my pack. But now I see that, even without the flowers, things are different. There's a rise of smooth sandstone on the left, another on the right, and the walls have wavy stripes of oranges and whites that remind me of saltwater taffy.

The taffy-candy walls also make me feel disoriented. How can we be in a canyon—or heading for a canyon—when we've been walking either level or uphill all morning?

I make the mistake of asking Michelle, "Aren't canyons supposed to be *down?*" It sounds stupid the minute it's out of my mouth, so I say, "Never mind."

"No, you're right," she says. "We think of canyons as being down. Most people go to the rim of, say, the Grand Canyon and look in. But if you were to follow the Colorado River instead of driving to the rim, you would enter the Grand Canyon from the bottom. That's just like out here, but on a bigger scale. The Colorado River cut the Grand Canyon into the earth like floodwaters cut into these sandstone canyons."

Mia glances at Michelle, then grins at me. "I'm gonna picture us rafting down a river of daisies."

I try to go with that image, but there's noise in my head.

Noise telling me that we're walking *upstream,* not down.

Noise telling me there's no such thing as a river of daisies.

Besides, even I know these aren't daisies. They're low to the ground. And the petals look rough, not smooth. The plants crunch underfoot but seem to spring back, undefeated.

Like it's going to take more than being walked on to bring them down.

From up front, someone starts whistling "Follow the Yellow Brick Road" from *The Wizard of Oz*. It's the Falcon, Felicia. Then the two Elks join in. Behind us, Michelle laughs, then whistles along.

I feel like a dorky dwarf from *Snow White,* caught in a Wicked Witch nightmare.

"Hey!" Shalayne calls. "It was fields of poppies in *The Wizard of Oz*." She shifts her hold on the tarp pole. It's an angry move that throws the rest of us off balance. "They were red," she shouts. "And they put Dorothy to sleep!"

"But the Yellow Brick Road was yellow!" Brooke-the-Elk singsongs back.

"But the *road* wasn't *flowers!*" Shalayne shouts. "And we're not headed for Oz! We're in the freakin' desert heading for more freakin' desert, and we haven't stopped walking in fifty hours! I need to rest!"

"It's the flowers," Brooke calls. "They're making you sleeeeeepy."

"No," Shalayne shouts, "*you're* making me *mad*. If you had to haul a stretcher like we do, you'd be hungry and tired too!"

"Hey, I paid my dues," Brooke calls.

I am so stunned and happy that someone else is miserable and up for a fight that I keep my mouth shut. The Yellow Brick Road spat has ground us all to a halt again, and from the front end of the stretcher, Hannah looks back at us. She seems exhausted, but more than that, she seems . . . panicked?

Michelle must see it too, because she breaks protocol by talking about the future and calls, "On the other side of that canyon is our resupply. We're almost there. You can make it, girls."

I've heard the Grizzlies talking enough to know that "re-supply" happens about once a week and means fresh water, food, and letters from home. I know exactly how I feel about fresh water and food, but letters from home?

A knot forms in my stomach just thinking about it.

"Let's giddyup!" Mia calls, and we start to move, but three steps forward Jude—who hasn't said a single word the whole day—goes down with a thump and a clang and a groan, right in front of us.

Ahead of us porters, Dvorka and the others keep hiking.

"Hey!" Shalayne screams at them. "Are you totally *oblivious*?"

Michelle's already up at Jude, taking his pulse, while the four of us Coyotes put the stretcher down and crowd in.

"Get me some water," Michelle says, and Mia's handing hers over before the words are even out. Michelle tries to sit Jude up a little, but he's not taking water. "Get his pack off," she commands, and Hannah and I dump our own packs and jump in to help.

Dvorka has rushed back and is squatting beside Michelle, asking, "Heatstroke?"

"He just went *down*," Michelle says, her voice low, guarded.

"His vitals okay?"

Michelle nods as Hannah and I peel off Jude's pack; then she tries again to get him to drink water.

Everyone's circled around now, watching. "Maybe it *is* the flowers," Hannah whispers to me.

I start to give her a look like *You nuts?* but stop when I see her ocean eyes are swimming.

"He'll be fine," I whisper.

But her eyes aren't drying up, they're flooding.

"What's wrong?" I ask. "Why are you freaking out?"

"Poppies," she whispers.

"Poppies?"

She flings tears away. "I thought I was better."

I'm not following. "Better?"

"Just the connection sends me back."

I'm still not following. "What connection?"

"Poppies." She slides a desperate look my way. "You never did H?"

My eyes go wide and my heart catches. *The Wizard of Oz* . . . the Deadly Poppy Field . . . I'd never even thought about why the poppy fields were deadly, but now I get it. Opium. Heroin. It comes from poppies.

When I first heard Nico talk about "H," I was clueless. He and Biggy were talking in code. It took me about two weeks to break that code, and by then I was in too deep to have second thoughts.

"Did you?" Hannah whispers, demanding an answer.

I shake my head, and the truth is I *haven't* done heroin.

What I *have* done, though, is deliver it.

"Then forget it," she says. "You wouldn't understand."

"But these flowers are not poppies!" I whisper. "They're gnarly desert daisies. And they're not even why Jude passed out. He's got heatstroke."

"I know," she whispers, but her chin's quivering and her ocean eyes are filling up again. "I think about it every day. I *fight* it every day. I thought I was winning, but this . . ." Her voice fades into sobs.

I still don't really understand why a field of yellow flowers is making her lose it. What I *do* get, though, is that she's hurting. Hurting bad. "Hey," I whisper, and before I can even think about what I'm doing, I scoop her into a hug and hold on tight as a tidal wave floods my shoulder.

38

The hike out of the flower field and through the taffy canyon is a solemn march. Jude's awake, but shaky and nauseous. Michelle's managed to get water and Gatorade into him and sponged him down to cool him off. We've been moving through shade wherever we can, but the sun's almost straight overhead, so there hasn't been much of it.

The two Elks are toting Jude's pack on one of the snow discs, while Dvorka and Felicia-the-Falcon try to keep Jude on his feet and moving forward. Michelle's put a buffer of distance behind us, but I can still hear bits of what she's saying on the walkie-talkie. Basically, Jude's going home.

"Wish I'd thought of that," Mia says in my direction. A few steps later, she mutters, "But maybe I'm glad I didn't."

"You serious?" I ask.

She shrugs with her free arm. "It's weird. This is starting to feel normal."

"And that's a *good* thing?"

She's quiet for a long stretch, but I can see her thinking. Finally she says, "I like how I feel strong now. All I ever felt before was angry." She gives me a smirk. "I used to think it was the same thing, but it's not."

I'm quiet for a long stretch after that, doing my own thinking. I start out with my sights on the truth in what she's said, but as I move toward it, I spin out remembering all the ways I hate Anabella for being such a selfish narc, and Mom for always taking her side, and Dad for ignoring everything, and Meadow for betraying me.

I arrive, instead, at angry, and yes, I feel strong.

Vengeful.

Unstoppable.

"Quit pushing!" Hannah calls from in front of me.

I snap out of my thoughts and ease up. Who says anger isn't strength?

Then Dvorka cries, "There it is!" like we've arrived in Oz. She's pointing to the same truck that dropped me off . . . how many days ago? According to the hash marks on my pants, it's been only seven, but it feels like a month.

Two men are hurrying toward us. One's John, the other's Mr. Gorgeous.

Both Elks race ahead, the snow disc bouncing up and down between them. "Silver Hawk!" Brooke squeals.

"He's mine!" Kelsey cries.

I look at Mia. "Silver Hawk?"

"You didn't meet him on the drive in?"

"Nobody told me his name."

"Well, now you know it."

"It's Silver Hawk? Seriously?"

"That's how he introduced himself. He's Mokov's grandson." A helpless sigh escapes her. "His eyes give me chills."

I decide we're all idiots, and while the counselors deal with Jude and have a hush-hush confab, I work at ignoring Mr. Gorgeous Silver Hawk instead of fawning over him like the rest of the girls.

It doesn't help that he's dispensing cups of cool water from a big plastic drum in the bed of the truck. Or that he's handing out deli sandwiches. Or that he says, "Looking good," when he hands me mine.

"Liar," I say back, but I can't help smiling.

―――――

Resupply means we each get our own personal stash of food, issued in ziplock bags. Dry stuff like granola, powdered milk, rice and beans, lentils, trail mix . . . stuff that we're supposed to self-ration over the coming week. They also issue group food that the Elks are in charge of and will have to carry on a snow disc.

The Elks try to keep me from nosing in, but I manage to identify a sack of corn masa, powdered eggs, peanut butter, honest-to-God apples, cheese sticks, brown sugar, and *potatoes*.

Huge, whole potatoes.

But . . . how are we going to cook those? And why lug them anywhere when there's the lightweight just-add-water freeze-dried kind out there? As much sense as it *doesn't* make, I am excited to see real food.

Resupply also means refilling our personal canteens and, for me, getting one to replace the canteen Dax stole. I'm careful not to drink a single drop out of my new supply and instead ask Silver Hawk for cup refills out of the big drum until I can't swallow another drop.

Silver Hawk also fills the group water dispensers. They're clear and collapsible, and we've been carrying them empty on the tarp stretcher, but once they're full, they get strapped onto a snow disc for Felicia-the-Falcon to tote along. Water's heavy. Eight pounds a gallon, if I remember right. About time Coyotes weren't doing all the work.

Through the resupply and lunch, Jude sits in the front seat of the truck looking miserable while the counselors rotate huddles. With each other, with their walkie-talkies, with Silver Hawk. There's a lot of nodding and wrinkling of brows, but they're all smiles when it's time to head out. "Jude's leaving the team," Dvorka announces. "Let's give him a fond Grizzlies farewell and get back at it. We have miles to go before we sleep."

When a fond Grizzlies farewell turns out to be a lukewarm "See ya," and "Take care," I mutter, "I guess you guys didn't like him much?"

I'm standing in a little pack with the other Coyotes. "He joined us the day before you did," Mia says. "We barely know him."

Hannah seems to be over her poppy meltdown. She smiles at me and says, "Yeah. We know you better than him, and you've been off limits for most of it." She looks toward the truck. "I think he was dealing with his own stuff."

Shalayne is in a way better mood now, too. Amazing what some food and rest will do. She says, "I guess some of us are just tougher than others."

Mia gives her a playful shove. "Girl, you spent your first three days crying."

"You *cried* your first three days?" I ask, pretending I didn't.

Shalayne groans. "Am I *ever* gonna live that down?"

Mia zaps me with a wicked look. "Maybe we should bring up your first days?"

Mia and Shalayne tease, "Help meeeee!" and we all laugh, even me.

Then Shalayne sees Silver Hawk getting behind the wheel of the truck and cries, "Take me with you!"

"Or stay!" Hannah shouts. "Pleeeease?"

Silver Hawk flashes a smile and waves out the window. Then he's off in a cloud of dust.

And, with a "Heave ho," so are we.

39

According to my sky-dividing calculations, it's somewhere between four and five o'clock when we finally stumble into camp. I've got blisters on my feet and my hands, and my back and shoulders are caked in salty sweat under my pack. I'm dying for shade. Everyone's miserable, even our jailers.

"What a team," John tries as we set down the tarp stretcher. His voice comes out flat. Exhausted. His man-bun is frayed and frizzed.

"You only hiked half," Brooke-the-Elk grumbles.

"But I did about twenty miles yesterday, bringing in Dax," he points out. "He didn't exactly give up easily."

I want to ask about Dax, but I notice the other Grizzlies scoping out the camp. I'm not sure how it works, but I don't want to get stuck with the worst spot, so I do a quick gauge of the sun's path. The campsite has scattered pinyons and junipers, with one area that would work as a little harbor of afternoon shade. I hurry over to it and dump my pack, claiming it.

"Hey!" Felicia says, looking at me like I'm sitting at a seniors-only table in the school cafeteria. Which seems to be how things play out here, with the Falcon and Elks acting like upper class to the Coyotes' lower class.

Since Felicia's like the senior in the group, she's probably used to getting her way, but before she can actually complain, I call, "Over here!" to Hannah, who comes shuffling toward me, followed by Shalayne and Mia.

"Wait, what?" Felicia calls, looking to our jailers for help. "Aren't we going in order?"

"You are really brave," Hannah whispers.

"Are there rules?" I whisper back.

"Unspoken ones, yeah."

John and the other counselors are watching, but they don't interfere.

"Seriously?" Felicia asks them, and when they don't make a move, she huddles with the Elks, looking over at us from time to time.

The Coyotes are acting nervous, twitching. I don't want to give up the shade, but I also don't want trouble. And even though there's no way we can all string up tents in Shady Harbor, I call over, "We can all squeeze in!"

But the Falcon and Elks don't want to hang out with a pack of Coyotes. They turn in a huff and pick spots on the other side of the camp area.

Everyone gets busy setting up their stuff. I really just want to roll out my pad, unstuff my sleeping bag, and collapse, but no one else is doing that. Plus, I know it'll turn cold quick once the sun goes down, so I make myself get to work too. I'm still slow at putting up the tarp, but better than before. And this time I let Michelle teach me her "magic knot" to help tighten my tarp-tent cord. It makes things so much easier.

I've just started arranging stuff inside my tent when John begins barking out words like a roll call.

"Fire ring!"

Brooke shoots off, "Mine!"

"Firewood!"

"Mine!" Felicia shouts.

"Latrine!"

"Wren's!" the Elks and Falcon cry together.

"What?" I ask, not knowing what's going on.

John laughs and keeps going. "Ignition!"

"Mine!" Mia shouts.

"What are we doing?" I ask.

"Community chores," Hannah explains, then calls out, "Latrine assist!"

John studies her and nods. "Fair enough. And very nice."

"Terrain's pretty rocky," Dvorka agrees.

"Pantry!" John calls.

"Mine!" Shalayne and the other Elk, Kelsey, call at the same time.

John considers, then declares, "You'll work together."

This creates instant silence, broken by Michelle, who calls out, "And the field staff volunteers to make family dinner."

A cheer goes up: "Yay!"

A few minutes later, Hannah pops her head inside my tent, collapsible shovel in hand. "Ready?"

I say yes, but it turns out that no, I'm not. It takes us over an hour to dig the latrine. By the time we're done, I've got three new blisters and an attitude to match—I'm hot and hurting and ready to pop.

On our walk back to camp, I turn to Hannah and manage to scrape a thanks from deep inside the way I'm feeling. "I don't know how I could have done that by myself."

"It's the *pits,* no kidding," she says, and grins.

I groan, then go with the stupid pun thing. "You better *wipe* that look off your face."

"*Urine* for it now!"

I stop walking. "Okay, that was just bad."

Her nose twitches in the air, and at first I think she's going to make another stupid joke, but then I smell it, too.

"Wow!" I gasp, and the pit-digging torture instantly vanishes from my mind. "Is that . . . onions?"

"And . . . hamburger?"

Our noses pull us along to camp, where we find a fire ring that already looks like it's been there a week. The jailers' tents are up, the fire is blazing, and John is just putting the lid on the big black kettle the Elks lugged into camp on a snow disc. "That smells so good!" Hannah cries.

"What is it?" I ask, my mouth watering.

Dvorka arranges ashy-looking sticks from the fire around the kettle. "Peacekeeper pie," she says, putting more chunks of smoldering wood on top of the lid.

"When will it be done?" Hannah asks, her words strung together by a thread of hope.

Dvorka looks around at all of us. Every single Grizzly Girl is standing nearby, drooling. "It'll be about half an hour," she says. "Enough time for you to wash up."

"Wash up?" I look at Hannah. "With what?"

"It's more a wipe down," she says, leading me over to our tents. "Get your washcloth."

"I have a washcloth?"

She laughs. "An eight-inch square of blue cloth?"

"That's a washcloth?"

"Yup. Or you can use a bandanna."

"They're filthy!"

She ducks inside her tent. "Well, find something or you'll miss out on your weekly bathing opportunity."

Hannah waits for me while I find my washcloth. Then we line up with the others to get water from Michelle. "It feels like we're the Seven Dwarfs, getting inspected by Snow White," I whisper to Hannah. She gives me a puzzled look, so I add, "Remember that scene before dinner when Snow White checks the dwarfs' hands and she asks Grumpy when the last time he washed was, and Grumpy says, 'Recently. Yeah, recently!'?"

Hannah laughs. "It's been a long time." Then she asks, "So . . . what dwarf are you?"

I don't need to think twice. "I'm Grumpy. Definitely Grumpy. You?"

"Hmm," she says, then decides. "Hungry!"

"There is no Hungry!"

"There is now!" Hannah laughs.

Ahead of us, Shalayne says, "And I'm Sore!"

Ahead of *her,* Mia calls, "And I'm Tired!"

"We're Grumpy, Hungry, Sore, and Tired," Shalayne calls forward, trying to include Felicia and the Elks. "What are *you* guys?"

They won't play along, though, so we secretly decide for

them—they're Angry, Moody, and Snotty. By the time I get to Snow White—the water-rationing Michelle—and put out my washcloth like the others have done, I'm in a weirdly good mood.

Michelle pours on just enough water to wet the cloth, but that small amount I spread as far as I can. I rub down my face, my neck, my arms, and my hands. It feels cool and smooth and fresh, and I'm amazed by how one small handful of water feels better than any shower I've ever taken.

All of us are quiet, reveling in it, and in the silence, Michelle's words from earlier trickle through my mind. The ones about springtime in the desert. About a little water going a long way when the land is parched.

My eyes are suddenly stinging and I turn away, hiding it from the other Coyotes.

Hannah, though, notices. "What's wrong?" she whispers.

I shake my head. It was just a glimpse, one I don't know how to put into words. But I saw it. *Felt* it.

How parched I really am.

40

Peacekeeper pie. Wow. We're like dogs scarfing down dinner, licking the dish, begging for more. "How?" I ask, taking a second to breathe. "I want to know how."

"To make this?" John asks.

I nod and stick out my plate for seconds.

"You need a Dutch oven. We share this one with some of the other camps," he says, clanging the side of the kettle with the serving spoon. "First you sauté chopped onion and ground beef until they're cooked through. Add a couple cans of beans—kidney or black—some salt and pepper and whatever spices you want, and stir it all together. While that's cooking, mix up some corn bread, then spread it over the concoction like thick frosting. Cover the whole mess with the lid, surround it with hot fire coals, and let 'er rip."

Felicia sighs, "It is so good!"

"I'm definitely feelin' the peace," Mia says, stretching forward for seconds. "Thank you."

"Yeah," we all murmur. "Thank you."

So peacekeeper pie has done its job. But as we finish eating and turn to watch the fire send sparks up into the darkening sky, I notice an uneasiness. An anxiety. It feels alive. Like a dark presence moving around the campfire.

I don't know what it is or if I'm just imagining it, and then Brooke says, "So? When do we get our letters?"

Letters! I'd completely forgotten. I feel a quick jolt of excitement, doused right away by reality. And now I understand the anxiety. None of us came here because we wanted to. We were sent here. Forced here. Abducted and brought here kicking and screaming. And the people who sent us here? They're back home. Reading letters from home is probably the same for all of us—like walking through a minefield in your heart.

Suddenly I don't want any letters. I don't want to hear attacks and excuses and expectations and disappointments. I just want to be left alone with the fire and the stars and the peacekeeper pie humming in my stomach.

I flash back to the letter I wrote my second day in the desert. The things I said about being abused and tortured. The way I tried so hard to guilt my parents into bringing me home. And now, even after the washcloth wipe-down, I'm filthy and I'm full of blisters from walking five thousand miles through the desert and digging a hole for a toilet. My clothes, my *everything,* smell like smoke, my hair is matted to my scalp, and I have never been so sore or tired in my life. So I'm even worse off than I was a week ago, but now . . . I don't want to go home.

It's a shocking realization.

I really don't want to go home.

Dvorka delivers the letters, reading the names by firelight, bringing them to us while we sit waiting, our dinner dishes put aside.

Everyone gets at least one letter and accepts it like a death sentence. Nobody tears open their envelope like they can't wait, but nobody chucks their mail into the fire, either. They just stare at it, turn it over and over, sigh, or hold their breath.

"Tara will be here tomorrow," Dvorka says. It takes me a minute to remember she's the therapist. The Aussie with the carrot hair. "But know the three of us are here if you want to talk things through tonight."

"I'm going to bed," Felicia announces.

"Me too," the Elks say.

They stand up, dust off, collect their things, and dissolve into the darkness without another word.

The rest of us stay and read by firelight. Inside my envelope are two letters. One from my mother, and one from my brother. My mother's is a page and a half, typed in the usual Lucida Handwriting font. My brother's is on notebook paper, written in pencil, decorated with doodles and drawings. He doesn't have much to say. It rained on Tuesday and he has to be a bunny in a school play. There's a No Bunny picture, but what's inside the circle and line looks like a rat with oversize ears. "I hope you're having fun camping" is followed by drawings of a campfire, trees, and a stream. He signs off "Your brother, Morris."

Morris? When did he start going by Morris?

It about breaks my heart.

Then I read Mom's letter.

I don't know what I'm expecting, what I'm hoping for.

Something different than what I get, that's for sure. She's arm's length. Clinical. Telling me how they won't be "fetching" me from "therapy camp," how she's spoken with the director and knows that I've "greatly exaggerated" the situation and "need to stop overdramatizing every little thing."

Easy for her to say from the comfort of her ergonomic chair, typing at her high-speed computer inside the weathertight walls of her climate-controlled house. Wonder just how clinical she'd be acting if *she* was the one getting flooded out of a tarp tent, if *she* was the one squatting over a hole, if *she* was the one digging for water.

She goes on to say how she, Dad, and Anabella are attending therapy sessions twice a week to "better understand our family dynamic and our evolution forward."

She doesn't even sign the letter by hand. She lets Lucida do it for her, writing, *Never doubt we love you, Mom.*

"What a crock," I say to the letter, and head for my tent.

Next door, Hannah is crying. It's sobby but soft, the sound of pain buried in cotton. I'd barely noticed her leaving the fire ring while I was still reading. Obviously her mail wasn't all hearts and flowers either.

At first I think I should leave her alone, but after hearing her cry for a while, I scoot halfway out of my tent and peek into Hannah's. "Hey, whatever they said, forget about it."

She sniffles and wipes her face. "My mom finally wrote me. And guess what? Her being an alcoholic is all *my* fault. She can't be around me anymore. She wants me to go live with my dad. In *Kansas.*"

Oz and poppy fields and yellow brick roads spring to mind. "*Kansas?*"

"Exactly!"

"Maybe it won't be so bad?"

"You don't understand."

I don't, and I know I don't. So, after a little silence between us, I mumble, "Sorry," and start to scoot back into my tent.

She lunges forward, grabbing my arm. "Wren? I'm sorry. Was your letter good?"

I shrug. "Not exactly."

I want to go, but even in the dark I can see that she's tortured by something. Like she's dying to say something.

"What?" I ask.

She shakes her head super fast but then comes out with it. "Thanks for your help in the poppy field today."

"They were *daisies*," I remind her, even though they weren't daisies either. "And there is no Oz. Not in Kansas or anywhere else."

She says something, but it's so quiet I can't make it out.

"What did you say?"

"I can't remember the last time someone's hugged me, is all. Yours really got me through my freak-out. I'm glad you're my friend."

Her friend.

The last time I made a friend, it was Meadow. I'm not even sure what the word means anymore.

"Me too," I tell her, and pull back into my tent.

41

Meadow is not my friend. I know that. I don't really know what she is, and that confuses me. I *want* her to be my friend. She's fun and smart and daring, but she hides her heart.

Or maybe she has no heart.

I forget that sometimes. I slip up. Let her in on something. Give away too much. In the moment she's sympathetic and understanding and totally on my side. But later she cuts me open with the things I've told her and leaves me alone to bleed.

I tell myself not to trust her.

I swear I'll never tell her anything personal again.

And then I slip up, get cut up, and bleed.

After we had the big blow-up in her room during spring break last year, I really tried to make new friends. My problem is I don't seem to know how. I tried when I started middle school and couldn't break in anywhere. Which is how I wound up with Meadow. Almost three school years later, when I tried again, things were even worse.

I didn't just try. I *really* tried. I was so mad at Meadow and wanted to show her I didn't need her, didn't *want* her in my life. I started smiling at people at school. I said hi to everyone around me in class. I tried sitting with different groups at lunch.

But it was awkward. For them, for me, for everyone. All through middle school, I'd been sitting in the back of the class, phone in my lap, texting Meadow. All through middle school, I'd either been holed up with Meadow or hiding out at lunch, texting Meadow. All through middle school, I'd been running off after school to meet up with Meadow. And now I wanted to talk?

Plus, I had no weed, and I didn't know how to get it. I was testy and antsy and thought about it a lot. A *lot*. Once I'd made it through, "Hi! Mind if I sit here?" I'd zone out. Or fidget. I took up biting my nails. Biting them until they bled.

I tried scoring some weed from an eighth grader who had the reputation of being a stoner, but he shut me down. "Dude, seriously? You need to stop judging people. This," he said, doing the game-show prize display thing all up and down his grunge look, "is the result of self-sustaining lifestyle choices. I stress the word *choices*." He sneered at me. "Smoke that."

He sure sounded stoned to me, but I was now freaking out thinking he might tell someone I'd asked, so I said, "Just testing," and took off.

"Narc!" he called after me.

So yeah, I didn't try that again.

I was so desperate to break free from Meadow that I even worked at getting my grades up. And they did come up. A little. But the whole time I was miserable. Miserable and invisible.

I passed the one-month mark. A month that felt like ten years. I made it six weeks. Seven. And then one day, there she was, waiting for me after school. "You made your point," she said, falling into step beside me.

I was shocked to see her. And unbelievably happy. I didn't let on though, snarling, "Why are you here?"

She smiled. "Goofy girl, I miss you!"

I kept walking, not saying a thing, not looking at her, not letting on that my heart was pounding.

"Look," she said, "I'm sorry. I got greedy. It wasn't cool. I should've just been straight with you."

I had worked so hard at building a fort around me, protecting myself from all things Meadow. I'd put every trace of her in a box in my closet. I'd been clean for almost two months. By now I should have been bulletproof, but instead I felt lost. Empty. And so incredibly alone. My fort turned out to be a wobbly house of cards, and the soft breeze of Meadow's voice knocked it over. "Really?" I whispered.

She laughed. "I was an idiot, okay? Can we please be friends again?"

I told myself that this is what friends do—forgive and forget. I told myself I'd done things wrong too. I told myself things would be different.

We got stoned in the park that afternoon, and in no time she was back to slicing and dicing me with things I'd tell her.

She wasn't a friend.

I knew that.

But I pretended she was, because without her, I had nothing.

42

I fall asleep thinking how strange it is that at home I was desperate to make friends and couldn't, and out here in the desert I made one without even trying.

I sleep like a rock. No dreams. No tossing and turning. Just deep, heavy sleep.

I wake up in mummy position—on my back with my ankles crossed and my arms folded over my chest, the sleeping bag like a sarcophagus around me.

It's barely light out and there's a bird twittering. I stay in mummy position, listening. It's a friendly call, followed by silence. Another call, more silence. It makes me wonder—what's it saying? Is it lost? Lonely? Why doesn't another bird answer?

After a few more calls, the bird goes quiet. I wait, wondering if it's flown away or just given up. It makes me remember eighth grade, when our psychology teacher, Mr. Wexler, asked, "If a tree falls in the forest and no one is there to hear it, does it make a sound?"

Hollister Keegan, the class brainiac, said it didn't, so most of the class went along with him. He lined out some complicated reason that made Mr. Wexler exclaim, "Excellent!" Then Mr. Wexler buzzed around the front of the classroom asking, "Who agrees? Okay! Okay! Who else?" while one hand after another popped up.

I kept quiet, thinking they were all idiots, glad Mr. Wexler didn't notice me slumped in my chair at the back of the room.

But now I wonder if maybe I was wrong. What if a bird sings in the desert, and there's no one there to hear it? Does it make a sound? And if it does, and no one answers, is it really just the same as silence?

I start to think that maybe I've imagined hearing a bird. Maybe I *was* dreaming. I go to roll over. To get up. To shuffle out to the latrine and maybe see my phantom bird. But the minute I move, I discover I'm stiff as a board, sore beyond anything I've ever felt from gym class. Every little move causes pain. "Ohhhh," I groan, falling back into mummy pose.

I give it a minute and try again, but another groan comes out, even louder.

I hear Hannah moan, "Me too," from next door.

It takes a while, but we stagger out of our tents at about the same time. She looks wild, her pixie hair sticking out randomly, her bootlaces dragging, but she's the one who points at me and laughs, "Help! Zombie!"

I laugh, too, and we shuffle, moaning and groaning, toward the latrine.

On our way back, I ask, "Did you hear a bird this morning?"

"Yeah," she says. "That was a warbler."

"A warbler? How do you know?"

"John took us birding last week."

"Seriously? While I was dying in my tent?"

"Yeah, sorry." She shrugs. "Everyone's first week is awful." We shuffle along, quiet, until she says, "Anyway, we saw a yellow warbler, a nutcracker, and a creeper."

"A *creeper?*"

"It's my favorite, actually. Nothing like its name." She grins. "Or guys at school. Creepers out here are cute, with a long beak and a high, tweedly song."

The thought of all these birds in the desert is messing with my head. Crows and vultures, sure. Eagles, maybe. But songbirds? And enough of them to go out birding?

"Hey," Hannah says, nodding over to the fire ring, where John is adding wood and stirring last night's coals back to life. "You want to surprise everyone and make pancakes?"

"Out of what?"

"Community supplies. John'll be all for it."

"Sounds good, but really, you don't want my help. They'll come out terrible."

"Sure I do!" She's wide-awake now, all excited. "I'll teach you! Come on!"

John *is* all for it, and Hannah . . . I don't know. She's nice. Patient. *Happy.* She walks me through every little step— mixing the batter, making a bed of coals, prepping the griddle, testing the temperature, pouring the batter, gauging when to flip by the bubbles forming in the batter, and then, finally, flipping.

I'm really nervous about the flipping. I'm suddenly eight again, back in the kitchen with Anabella, making pancakes on Mother's Day.

I didn't know how to do anything in the kitchen. I was always invited to go do something else when Mom was busy cooking. And since Anabella was bossing me like crazy and told me we didn't have much batter, so I wasn't allowed to flip, I grabbed the spatula when she was taking down plates and tried turning over the pancakes she'd just poured on. By the time she saw what I was doing, the pancakes were pretty much scrambled.

When we served breakfast to Mom in bed, Anabella, of course, explained that the pancakes were ruined because of me. Mom smiled through it all and said that it didn't matter and that they were delicious, but after that I never wanted to cook anything ever again.

"Why are you shaking?" Hannah asks.

I'm staring at the griddle, spatula in hand, terrified.

"Are you okay?"

So I tell her about Mother's Day. I don't mean to. It just comes out.

"Well, let's get you over that," she says, then guides my hand through flipping a pancake. "See?" she says. "Easy." She guides me through a second one, then cuts me loose. By the fifth one, I'm a pro.

John comes over to check on us. "You two ready to open a diner?" I noticed him across camp with Dvorka and Michelle, talking. From the way they kept glancing over, it seemed to be about us.

Hannah laughs. "Just about!" Then she asks, "Can I make peach topping?"

He gestures at the community food stash. "Go for it."

So while I do the next batch of pancakes, Hannah works

at a kettle next to me, talking me through how to make a topping out of canned peaches, cinnamon, cornstarch, and sugar. By the time we're done, the inmates and the jailers are standing in a line, plates in hand, drooling. Felicia and the Elks even say thanks as we serve them.

"So," Hannah says as we finally sit down to eat, "want to open a diner?"

"The Grizzly Girl Café?"

"Perfect!" she says, and the other Coyotes swear they'll come eat there if we do.

Then, at the side of camp, a bird calls.

"The warbler!" Hannah cries through a mouthful of food.

John smiles over at her. "Very good!"

From farther away another warbler twitters. I hold up my finger, hold in my breath, and listen as the birds sing back and forth.

It makes me happier than I can explain.

43

Tara-the-Therapist appears as we're finishing up breakfast. She saunters into camp wearing a light daypack and carrying a walking stick. "Good morning, all," she greets us, her carrot hair bouncy clean, a smile on her freckled face.

I'm instantly suspicious. Something about her looking like she's just returned from a leisurely walkabout doesn't make sense. We arrived exhausted, blistered and dirty, and here she is all Aussie-licious?

I look at the sun, divide up the sky. If sunrise was at about seven, it's still before nine. Maybe only eight-thirty. What this adds up to is there must be a drop-off point not too far from here. Like, a *road*, not too far from here. And unless she started driving when it was still dark, she came from somewhere not too far from here.

It makes me wonder—where *are* we? How much stupid extra walking did we do yesterday? Are they running us in circles?

I'm a little tweaked about it, but I'm still feeling good about the pancakes, so I'm actually more just jealous of her clean hair. I would give a lot right now to be able to wash my hair.

After some small talk about it being a gorgeous day, Tara joins us around the campfire and says, "So? How are you?"

There's general shrugging and looking away, so she says, "Felicia? Let's start with you. How do you feel about going home? It'll be time before you know it."

I lean closer to Hannah and whisper, "She expects us to do this in front of everyone?"

"You'll get used to it," she whispers back. "This is group. She does the one-on-one after."

Felicia tells Tara that she's worried about going home. Worried about losing the control she's found out here in the desert. Worried that old triggers will defeat her. Worried that everything she's learned out here where it's quiet will be drowned out by the noise of what she's known for so long.

She sounds so smart. And serious. And more than just a little afraid to go home.

We move around the circle to the Elks and then the Coyotes. Everyone shares something, which I swear is because of Tara's voice. Low and sweet and musical, it floats through the air, luring the truth to sing along.

A lot of what the Grizzlies say has to do with their letters from home. For most of them, home is a place they miss . . . and also dread going back to. They have hope that things will be different . . . and worry that they just won't be. Tara encourages them to consider a transitional program, which sounds like a halfway house for people not ready to go home.

And then it's my turn.

"Wren?" Tara says. "How are you?"

"Dirty and sore and full of blisters," I hear myself say. And then out of my mouth comes, "But weirdly happy."

Everyone laughs, even Felicia.

I hurry to add, "I made pancakes this morning." As if that explains everything.

Tara gives me a smile that says she gets me, even though she's clueless. "It's easy to see you've come a long way since I saw you last," she says.

I don't like her words. They're *therapy* words. They're adult-who-thinks-she's-smarter-than-me words. But they're wrapped in a swirl of Aussie gauze and it softens them somehow.

"And letters?" she asks. "How were they?"

"I'm not allowed to say."

"Why's that?"

"Because there'll be consequences in the field if I do."

The jailers all chuckle, and it ripples through the Grizzlies as they get what I mean.

"Well," Tara says, "I think everyone agrees that it's not so much surviving out here that's the challenge—it's surviving back home."

I snort. "Easy for you to say, with your washed hair and clean clothes."

"She really has come to life, hasn't she?" Tara asks the jailers.

John looks at me and says, "Tara's right, though. Conquering the wild is nothing compared to fixing the cracks in your heart." He turns to the group. "All of you have been hurt.

All of you need to learn how to *cope*. Once you figure out the basics for survival in the wild, you have to figure out how to survive your issues."

Tara picks up the talk, saying, "And that's what today's about. It'll be a quiet day, writing letters home. Everyone needs to convey their thoughts to at least one person back home. Find a way to express your feelings without resorting to name-calling or"—she sends a smile my way—"language that would have consequences in the field. I'll cycle through and we can talk one on one. You may not feel like writing a letter, but it's the only way your family will understand who you are and what you're dealing with."

Everyone stands like there was some magic signal that meant go to your tents. So I go to my tent. I take out my notebook. I find a pen. I sit cross-legged and stare at a page, trying to figure out how to talk to my parents. The blue lines on the page start to blur together. I don't know what to write. What am I supposed to say? They don't care, not really. They just want me to behave, to be their little bird again.

I fling the notebook aside.

I'm not writing them.

I'm just not.

44

Therapy sessions have always felt like a sick game of cat and bird to me, where the therapist is the cat and I'm the one trapped in a cage. They sit looking at me, the tip of their tail twitching. "What do you want to talk about today?" they purr.

I usually look down and shrug, but what's always screaming in my head is *Nothing, you moron!*

Twitch, twitch. "How was your week?"

Awesome, and you're the cherry on top.

Twitch, twitch. "I care, you know, Wren. I'm here to help you."

How stupid do you think I am?

Twitch, twitch. Twitch, twitch. "How about those exercises we went over last time? Were you able to employ any of them?"

I'm not doing your freak exercises!

Twitch. "Did you bring them with you? Why don't we role-play?"

Because they're lame, you dork! And in the trash!

A claw reaches through the cage bars, straining in my direction. "We can't make progress if you don't open up."

Again, how stupid do you think I am?

"Look, Wren," the cat says, giving up. "I'm here to help you."

That's a crock, and we both know it.

"So why don't you tell me about your day? Let's start with that."

At this point I might chirp out a little sob story. I make it up—the people, what they said, what they did . . . everything. I do this because I'm playing with the cat. I'm perched on their head and they don't even know it.

I also have a little bet going on what their first question will be when I finally shut up. My story ends, and then . . . "How does that make you feel?" mews from the cat's mouth.

Ding-ding-ding-ding-ding! Like I just outplayed you, you stupid machine.

My parents didn't send me to an official therapist until eighth grade, when I was trying to kick my Meadow habit. It took until I was fighting to turn things around for Mom to notice me, and what she decided was that I was depressed. "I really think it would help you to talk to somebody," she said, sitting on the edge of my bed. "I would love it if you would talk to me—I miss you, Wren. But if you're not comfortable with that . . . ?"

In that moment I was tempted, so tempted, to tell her about Meadow. Not the details. Not about the weed. Just that Meadow had lied to me and . . . and that I was really trying to make new friends. But my mom doesn't do quiet. She doesn't know how to wait. So before I could float a balloon to see where it went, she popped it and filled the airspace. "I'm at a loss, Wren, I really am. You're like a stranger to all of us, and I don't know how to break through."

I was instantly glad I hadn't told her anything. She was looking so intense now, crowding me. I wanted to kick her off the bed, make her leave. And the fastest way I knew to do that was to say I'd go to therapy.

I started that week, and after the first session Mom didn't waste her precious time off from work in the waiting room. Instead, she "ran errands." It didn't take me long to figure out that what she was really doing was spending the time with Anabella, getting frozen yogurt or doing some power shopping. It really tweaked me, and all I could think about during my sessions was how Anabella and Mom were out together laughing and shopping and eating yogurt. With sprinkles. And Reese's bits.

Therapy became a nightmare.

"Don't you like Dr. Ramirez?" Mom asked after about a dozen sessions. "She seems so . . . centered."

"I'm supposed to call her Libby," I said. At this point I was back with Meadow and needed to get out of going to therapy. "She has me play with dolls."

"Dolls?"

The hook was in. I just had to tug. "Are you sure she has a license?" I asked. "She spends a lot of time talking about creepy stuff."

"Creepy stuff? Like, what sort of creepy stuff?"

I opened my mouth like I was going to tell her, then stopped short.

"Wren?"

"She stressed confidentiality?" I said, giving her a concerned look. "Some law?"

"That's to protect you, not her!"

I shrugged, she fumed, and that was the end of my sessions with Libby.

It was easy to stay off Mom's radar over summer, especially since she needed me to take care of my brother after his sports camp while she was at work. Anabella, of course, was too focused on her meet-ups and camps and friends to help much, but Meadow and I had no problem "watching" him.

Then high school started, my grades were a disaster, and Mom was at it again. First it was just going to my school counselor, Mr. Miki. I actually kinda liked him. He'd ask me questions like "What are your academic goals?" and "Have you thought about what sort of career you might like?" and "Where do you see yourself after high school?" They were easy to BS, and he didn't once ask me to explore my feelings.

But my grades didn't change, and parent-teacher conferences at school ended with my mom yelling at me on the way home, which made me quit pretending and start flame-throwing, which got me put back into therapy.

First there was Dr. Yalsen—an old lady with a weird accent who, of course, wanted me to talk about my *feelings.*

Then there was Pia Boyd—a skinny woman who must've spent three hours every morning flat-ironing her waterfall of shiny black hair. She had a nose like a crow's and liked to wear black, so the overall package made me want to caw.

Then came Dr. Goth. When I heard his name, I pictured dark clothes and maybe some eyeliner and black nail polish, but instead he looked like a bar of soap in a crooked brown wig. He even foamed at the mouth when he couldn't get me to talk.

I hated all of them, and they hated me. But where I was honest about it, they pretended to be interested, or concerned, or sympathetic.

There is nothing grosser than fake sympathy.

And from a foaming bar of soap?

Please, hate me instead.

My parents started getting into full-blown fights about me. I could hear them through doors and walls, across the house. Anabella would come out and scream at me about them screaming at each other. I screamed right back and threw whatever I could grab. My brother hid in his closet.

All therapy did was make me dig in deeper. All therapy did was make me hate everyone, every*thing,* even harder.

So being at a wilderness camp would be one thing. But this is a wilderness *therapy* camp, and that's a problem. I'll do the endless hiking, I'll sleep in the dirt, I'll squat over a hole, but I'm not talking about, not writing about, my feelings.

I'm just not.

45

I'm curled up on my sleeping bag, half asleep, when Hannah's head pops in. "Hey," she whispers. "You awake?"

"Yeah," I manage. "Kind of."

"You're not writing?" She scoots in a little farther. "You've got to have something to show Tara when she comes around."

"I'm not doing a letter." It comes out a growl. Like I'm mad at her. So I prop up on an elbow and say, "Sorry. I just can't. I was going blind, staring at the page."

"You want to take your notebook and go for a walk?"

"We're allowed to do that?"

"Sure. As long as we're visible from camp." She points off to the right. "There's some trees up on that crest. I'm thinking there might be better than here. My tent's kinda stuffy."

Now that she's mentioned it, I realize that mine is, too. Even with it being open on both ends, it's steamy inside. And smells like hot tarp. "Sure," I tell her, and gather my things.

We tell Michelle what we're doing, then go up to the crest

and settle in the shade with our notebooks. There *is* a slight breeze, but it's not enough to clear the sticky web of anger from my mind. I stare at the page, but I don't put a single sentence on paper. One angry thought leads me to another until my brain is tacky and tangled and I'm ready to scream.

Even if I wanted to write, why bother? Anything I say won't be heard. My parents will just shore up their argument, their point of view, their wall of disappointment. Writing them a letter won't change anything, so why bother?

Next to me, ink is flowing out of Hannah's pen like a flash flood across the desert. I have never seen a person write so much so fast. "Who are you writing to?" I finally ask.

"My mother," she says, looking up briefly before diving back in. "I'm letting her have it."

I want to ask her what good she thinks that'll do. Does she really think her alcoholic mom is going to read it with an open mind? Feel bad for the way she's messed up her daughter's life? Is it going to change *anything*?

"I don't care if she reads it," Hannah says, being telepathic. "I need to get this out." She glances my way. "You should try this. It feels good."

But the thought of doing what she's doing *doesn't* feel good. It feels . . . futile. Like shouting underwater. Or doing CPR on a mannequin. Or drinking cough syrup to cure cancer.

After another minute, Hannah comes to the bottom of her page. She sees me sitting like petrified wood. "You have to write *something*. She reads them, you know."

"Who does?"

"Tara! And then you discuss. It's the process." She flips to a new page to pick up where she left off. "Why don't you write a note to your brother? Just to get you started?"

I like her idea. Technically I'll be writing a letter home, but I won't have to deal with my parents. And by the time Tara rotates around to me, she'll be needing to get back to her magic ride out of here and it'll be too late to write anything else.

"You are brilliant," I tell Hannah, which earns me a big smile from her. And for as mentally blocked as I am about writing to my parents, I suddenly know exactly what I want to write to my brother.

Dear Mowgli, I begin. *Boy, do I have a story to tell you!*

I think a minute, then make a title in the middle of the page:

DESERT BONES

I'm not sure exactly why I make this the title, other than it sounds good and I know my brother will like it.

Next, I add a subtitle:

A Cross-My-Heart, Hope-to-NOT-Die True Story

And after a minute of thinking about the *Jungle Book* stories I've read to him in his old bunk-bed fort, I start scribbling.

> *In the setting sun of the Utah desert, Wren Clemmens*
> *crouches over a piece of sagewood, determined to make*
> *fire. Not with a match, but with simple scraps of wood,*
> *a bootlace, and the unbending will to turn friction into fire.*

Then it just flows out. From starting my first fire to finding water to hiking through the desert with the tarp stretcher to digging the latrine to making peach pancakes over a fire, I turn it all into an exciting adventure where bones dry to chalk in the desert heat and danger lurks around every pinyon.

My brother loves when there are pictures in a book, so I draw what I can—a bow-drill setup, a tarp tent, a fire, a shovel with a roll of waving toilet paper on the handle jammed into a mound of dirt beside a big hole, and a stretcher on the shoulders of four hikers. The pictures take a while because I'm not very good at drawing, but I do my best.

Everyone else breaks for lunch, but I eat trail mix and keep writing. I don't notice the sun shifting in the sky, or that Hannah is gone with Tara for as long as she is. Then Hannah's back, with swollen eyes and a quivering voice telling me she'll see me at dinner.

"What happened?" I ask.

She just shakes her head and stumbles off in a stream of tears, and before I can get up to go after her, Tara approaches. "Ready?" she asks.

"Uh . . . not if you're going to do *that* to me!"

"She's letting go of pain, Wren. She had a tough breakthrough, and it's left her feeling exposed and exhausted." Her accent is still magic, but I notice the smile she gives me doesn't shimmer like the one she had at the beginning of the day.

"If she's letting go of pain, why's it look like she's drowning in it?"

"She'll be fine, Wren, I promise." She nods at my notebook. "So . . . can I have a look?"

I want to say *No*, but I remind myself that there's nothing in what I've written that she can use to "help" me. So I say, "One sec," and scribble *To Be Continued!* and sign off *Wren (aka Baloo of the Desert)*. Then I grab the group of pages and pull them out of my notebook, making a thick tassel of torn holes at the edge. "You guys should really tell the new prisoners how this works," I say, giving her the pages. "If Hannah hadn't explained it, I might have nothing to hand over."

"You wouldn't have written a letter home?"

I shrug. "I'm not great at letters."

"And yet," she says, taking my pages and counting through them, "we have seventeen of them?"

I shrug again, like no-big-deal. "There's illustrations."

She begins to read my letter, and she actually laughs out loud a couple of times, but after she's made it through about three pages she fast-forwards through the rest, then looks at me and says, "This is very entertaining, Wren, but this is not the idea of letters home. The purpose is to explore issues, to get to the root of what's brought you here."

Right. And leave you in a big puddle of pain.

"Oh, I know what's brought me here," I assure her. "A big dude named Joel, a black SUV, a seven-thirty-seven out of LAX, and those guys," I say, pointing to the jailers. "Why write home about stuff my parents set up?"

She's quiet for a very long time, and I catch her eyeballing the sun, estimating how much time she has to hike out before dark.

Adults are so transparent.

I'm pretty sure that if I stonewall a little longer, I can cut the whole "therapy session" short. So I just wait her out. And finally she asks, "How'd you find your mother's letter?"

"I didn't find it—Dvorka handed it to me."

She gives me a little smirk. "You know what I mean, Wren."

"Did you bring shampoo?" I ask. "Because, really, you should share."

Her smirk turns to a frown. "Is this how you handle conflict at home?"

"Are you saying we're having conflict? Because I didn't know that. I thought you and I got along okay. I like your hair, did I mention that?"

Her eyes pinch closed and she lets out a little sigh.

Even that seems to have an accent to it. A little Aussie sweetness.

"I found her letter to be a bit detached," she says. "Guarded. Did you?"

"Do you guys read *everything*?"

She nods. "It's part of the program."

"Do my parents know?"

"Certainly." She takes a deep breath and tries again. "So . . . would you describe the letter as guarded?"

"Sure. That's a fine word to describe it."

"Why do you suppose that was the tone of it?"

For some strange reason, playing with her isn't doing anything for me. So I go back to being petrified wood. Maybe I have the name of a bird, but there's no way I'm interested in this can of worms.

She sits, waiting. And waiting. And waiting.

I see her check the sun again.

"Do you have an envelope?" I ask, hoping to wrap things up. "Because I'd really like my brother to get my letter."

She does have one folded in half inside her pocket, and she hands it over with another sigh. I make it out to Mo-Bro Clemmens at our address and then draw big sunrays all around it. For the return address, I write Desert Bear and draw a snake coiled around it, then give the snake x's for eyes and a funny tongue. I take my letter back from Tara, fold it in thirds, and stuff it inside.

When I hand the envelope to Tara, she gives me a solemn look and says, "I'll give you a pass for now, but next time this will not fly. You're learning how to survive out here, but what really matters is you learning to survive at home."

"No worries, mate," I tell her in an Aussie accent. It comes out sounding chirpy, even borderline manic. I don't care, though. For now, I'm off the hook.

46

I wasn't kidding about not talking about my feelings. I've been here four weeks now and still haven't done it. I also haven't written to my parents.

They *cannot* make me.

Felicia is long gone, and Brooke and Kelsey are on their last week—or at least close to it. We've got two new Rabbits, but there's a big gap between them and the rest of us.

The other inmates seem to really like Tara-the-Therapist, but I still find my whole body gnashing every time she shows up. It's a cold grind in my head, in my gut, in my heart. I want her gone. I want her warm-honey voice to shut up. I know who she is, what she does. She's not fooling me.

She doesn't seem to be on any regular schedule, which tweaks me. I like to know what I'm up against, and this whole camp is like moment-to-moment, which drives me nuts. Some days we do "curriculum" and just hang out in camp doing what's basically hippie-dippie schoolwork about botany or astronomy or geology or math that's "tied to the wild." Some days the jailers take us on day hikes to nowhere. We just hike all day through the stupid desert, have lunch on some bluff, where we're supposed to appreciate the "wonders of nature" and the "magnificent views," then hike back to camp.

And then there's the predawn "Strike camp!" wake-up call that seems to be totally random, too. Could be two days, could be a week. And then we could be lugging the tarp stretcher all day or just a couple of hours. "Embrace the journey," Dvorka keeps reminding us. "The destination is just a mirage."

Whatever the bleep that's supposed to mean.

We've had two washdays where we got rations of "locally sourced water" to do a full sponge bath and wash out our clothes. It wasn't enough water to wash all the clothes—mostly the small stuff like undies, socks, bandannas, and T-shirts—but it was better than nothing. And funny to see underwear dangling all over the place, drying out.

One of the things I hate most about being out here is the stupid gnats and flies. They're little and black and buzz around your head. They've gotten worse lately, and the only thing that makes them disappear is sunset. Bug repellent helps, and smoke from the fire does too. I've gotten used to the smoke but don't like to use the repellent unless the bugs are really bad. When you add up sunblock, bug repellent, smoke, and dust, you wind up with a layer of gross that a sponge bath can't cut through.

I really, really, really want a bath. One I can sink into. One with bubbles up to my neck.

Almost as annoying as the flies are the stupid trust-building exercises the jailers force us to do. Give me a break. All a blindfold does is make me feel trapped. It also covers up the fact that what we're doing is really lame. There's a lot of climbing and spinning around and being led to cliff edges that turn out to be six-inch rocks that couldn't twist an ankle. There's also way too much touching by your "trust partner" involved. They physically move you, which I hate. Let me crawl, blindfolded, through the dirt all by myself. I don't care if I go over a cliff. Just quit muscling me around.

Hannah noticed how uptight I was when we got paired up for trust building today. I was blindfolded and being a real mule, digging in as she tried to maneuver me. But she didn't grumble like Brooke did, or sigh over and over like Kelsey did. She leaned in from behind me and whispered, "Don't worry. I won't let anything happen to you."

Her words seemed to float into my ear. They felt so kind. Sincere. *Truthful.*

I could feel myself let loose a little, and once that started, tears bled into my blindfold. I don't know why. Maybe because, as always, Hannah was being nice to me. Maybe because I knew *she* trusted *me.* Over the last couple of weeks, she's told me so much stuff about her mom and her life. I've held back, but hearing her confide things through our tarps late at night makes me feel trusted, and more than once I've wished I wasn't so scared to trust her back.

Trust between people is a convoluted thing, because which comes first—trusting or being trusted? It's a paradox, as Mr. Wexler used to say. The chicken-or-the-egg thing. He and Hollister Keegan debated it for a whole class period, which was stupid. Of course the egg came first. Not that that stops trees from falling in the forest without anyone hearing them.

Whatever. I was glad the blindfold was there to hide my tears. And I let Hannah guide me for what felt like miles through ups and downs and turns. When we finally stopped and she pulled off my blindfold, we were back to the exact place we'd started. Lame, as always, but I didn't feel completely annoyed like I'd been with Brooke and Kelsey. Instead, I felt weirdly . . . exposed.

"I think it's safe to say," Michelle said to the group when we'd all come back together, "that each of us has felt betrayed at some point."

All the inmates looked down, which told me that I wasn't the only one thinking *No kidding.*

"Learning to trust again can be as hard as learning to love again after we've had our heart broken. It's the other edge of the same sword."

"Amen to that," Mia muttered.

"Likewise," Michelle continued, "holding another's trust is a profound responsibility. And breaking someone's trust is, in some ways, worse than breaking their heart, because it accomplishes both at once." Michelle was quiet, letting that soak in before saying, "This afternoon I want you to reflect on the people who have broken your trust and why you let those people stay in your life, if you did. But you should also reflect on trusts *you've* broken and how those actions have affected you."

"So we're journaling?" Shalayne asked.

"That's one option," Michelle said. "Group share is another, or you can partner."

I didn't want to journal. Between curriculum, journaling, and letters to my brother, I've done more handwriting out here than I have in my entire life, and I'm sick of it. Plus, our journals are supposedly private, but they're hard evidence and not something I want falling into the hands of the enemy, since everything around here seems to get relayed to my parents.

I also didn't want to group-share. Hearing everyone else's stories can be interesting, but even after four weeks, talking about my own stuff still makes me puke. And there's no getting away with fiction out here. I don't know how, but the jailers can totally tell.

So when Hannah caught my eye and said, "Do you want to partner?" I nodded and we went off to a private spot of dirt.

I wasn't planning to spill my guts, but after some back and forth and nudging from Hannah, I heard myself talking about Meadow. About our friendship. About the way she'd betrayed me, cut me open, left me to bleed. It was like I wasn't even me. I was off to the side, watching me talk about Meadow. Hearing me talk about Meadow.

And then I wasn't off to the side, watching, anymore. I was me again, sitting right in front of Hannah, crying about Meadow.

Hannah reached out and held my hands. "That girl is not your friend."

"I know," I said, and completely lost it.

47

I'm barely over my meltdown about Meadow when letters arrive. I hate letters more every week. It's like getting sucker-punched. One minute you're innocently standing there, the next you're doubled over, gasping for air, fighting not to show how much it hurts.

I got sucker-punched for real in third grade when Tex Cauldwell said I cheated in four square. He was right, but my friends wanted him out of the game, too, so his fist became the sledgehammer of justice.

Last week there was a letter from my dad. It was all about him growing up poor and walking seven hundred miles uphill both ways in the snow to get to school so he could get an education and "provide me with a better life." Like he was thinking about things like that in elementary school? Not a chance. As Mr. Wexler would say, my dad's looking back through the distorting prism of self-awareness.

I hated when Mr. Wexler would throw out phrases like

that. Nobody in eighth grade wants to hear about distorting prisms of self-awareness. Nobody except Hollister Keegan.

For some reason, though, Mr. Wexler's sayings keep popping into my brain at random times. Maybe because I'm surrounded by boring nothingness so big that even my dad suffering from distorting prisms of self-awareness seems worth thinking about.

So last time, I got a letter from my dad but nothing from my mom—something that both relieved me and tweaked me. Anabella wrote some phony stuff about how it's just not the same there without me, which, of course, was code for things being a whole lot better with me gone.

Except for Mo, I haven't written any of them back. And I've written him a *lot*. I'm sure my parents read all my True Stories, because why else would Dad say he grew up camping and wished he could be out here with me, starting fires, sleeping under the stars, feeling the cold morning air against his cheeks.

Talk about looking back through distorting prisms. Guess he's forgotten the whole get-up-in-the-freezing-cold-to-use-the-latrine thing. And I bet he's never had to dig for water. Or go matchless.

Tara-the-Therapist says I have to write them back. Every time, that's what she says. "You won't advance to Elk this way," she tells me.

Like I care?

Even though Mia and Shalayne have both advanced.

And Hannah's talking about wanting to.

One of the new Rabbits is named Jolene, and I want nothing to do with her. She's whiny and dying over everything.

She hasn't stopped crying since she got here, and she's not trying to hide it, either. She does these loud, wailing sobs. It's like a fire alarm and fire sprinklers going off at the same time, and the fire department's not showing up to shut things down.

Anyone who's okay with being that loud and obnoxious is going to be awful, even if they do shut up. And if Hannah advances to Elk and I don't, I'll be stuck with the crybaby when she finally moves up to Coyote.

Not liking that scenario.

Not one bit.

So when Tara hands me my envelope of letters and says, "You know what you have to do, right?" I nod.

She studies me, and I can tell she thinks I'm blowing her off.

Which I may be.

I'm not quite sure.

"It doesn't matter how angry or even brutal what you write sounds," she says, pouring warm honey into my ears. "Show them your wounds. Show them your scars. They're willing to listen, but they need something to work with. Someplace to start."

She leaves me with my letters from home, and the first thing I notice is that there's nothing from my brother. It feels like a sucker punch, too. Not a Tex Cauldwell sucker punch, but it still hurts. Didn't he like my True Stories? Doesn't he miss me? Or . . . has Anabella turned him against me? What has she told him?

A panic button goes off inside me as I imagine the ways Anabella could sabotage me. And what's now clanging loud and clear in my mind is: that must be why he hasn't written me back. Especially after last time's really funny True Stories.

The thought makes me feel so helpless.

Helpless and *mad*.

My dad hasn't written either, which feels about right. It's not like he talks much, ever. If his last letter hadn't been handwritten, I would have suspected Mom wrote it for him. Two pages is more words than I've ever seen him string together on paper or out loud. Mom, on the other hand, could fill a book just asking you to get the mayo out of the fridge.

But there is a letter from Anabella. If you can call it that. It's a printout of a screen capture of one of those cheesy ecards about sisters. The big sister has her arm around the little sister, and the caption reads, *Friends may come and go, but sisters are forever.* Under it, written in Anabella's loopy handwriting, is *I want to get back to this,* and off to the side in smaller, tighter loops she's written, *P.S. Meadow is the girl in the article.*

The article?

What article?

All that's left is the dreaded Mom pack—a fat envelope, sealed, with my first name across it, typed in Lucida Handwriting. Like running an envelope through the printer is easier than writing out four measly letters?

Oh, wait. Right. That capital W can be a bear to get as pretty as Lucida does.

I rip the envelope open, right through my name, and the fat pack of pages I unfold is not another typed letter. It's a news article from the Internet. The article is not actually that long, but it's got all the ad graphics along the right margin, so it takes up five sheets of paper. The headline reads: "Senior

Assault Leads to Drug Bust," and beneath it, in full ink-jet color, is a picture of Nico in handcuffs.

My face goes hot as my heart hammers. Nico's been busted? How? Did someone narc on him?

Did *Meadow*? Is that what Anabella's note meant?

I start to read, but I'm distracted by the picture of Nico. Even seeing him in handcuffs, even knowing—and having known all along—that he's dangerous with a big, bold D, his adorable dimple and his warm cinnamon breath flash through my mind, and suddenly I'm aching for Fireball Whisky and weed and the smoky interior of his Mercedes-Benz.

48

By the time I get to the end of the article, I feel like throwing up. Not because of what's in the story—that there'd been a rash of homes in a ritzy neighborhood broken into, only this time the "suspects" had gone from burglary to battery to busted.

It's also not because it's Nico and Meadow in the story—although that *is* pretty incredible. What happened? Nico was always so careful, so cagey. It feels like things have really spun out of control in the time I've been away, and I can't help wondering . . . if I hadn't been abducted to this place, would I be in police custody, too?

So all that is shocking and upsetting, but the reason I'm sick and shaking is because of the note that's gouged in ink across the bottom of the article.

A note that says, *We have accessed your text history.*

I don't know whose handwriting it is. That's how angry the writing looks. And I don't know why it feels like I've come stomach to fist with Tex Cauldwell again, but it does. I was totally stressed about my parents getting into my phone on kidnap day, but as the days went by and none of their letters said a word about it, I figured they'd just put my phone aside and forgotten about it. But no. Anabella was probably up all night every night trying to guess my password. It must have been her. It's always her. The narc.

Hannah swoops in with a smooth, scissors-twist move that puts her cross-legged beside me. "I know that look," she says. She pulls the pages out of my hands. "May I?"

I don't have the strength to tell her no.

I don't even *want* to tell her no.

She speed-reads through the first three pages, then stops to say, "Who's this 'minor female' they keep talking about?"

"It's Meadow."

"Seriously?" She turns back to the paper, and after reading for another bit comes up for air. "Possession of heroin? Does she use?"

The pages are quivering and I remember too late about Hannah's addiction. "She dabbled," I mumble.

Hannah dives back into the article. "You don't 'dabble' in H."

I feel weirdly guilty. It's not like I lived anywhere near Hannah, and it's not like I ever looked at what I was delivering for Nico or knew the people I was giving it to. I didn't even know what it was at first! But I still feel bad.

I try to take back the pages. "Maybe you shouldn't—"

She yanks away, still reading. "This was your *friend*? She sounds psycho! Who attacks an old man? Even strung out, I would never do that."

I want to say that the report must be wrong. I want to say that Nico would never in a million years let Meadow into his group. The night before I got kidnapped, he told Biggy that she was a carnival ride. They'd both laughed that way I hate. Like they knew something I didn't. I wanted to ask what they were talking about, but I kept quiet, kept cool, while I imagined the worst and swigged down Fireball.

I also want to tell Hannah that Meadow would never attack an old man. But I don't say any of those things to her, because the last few months I saw Meadow turn from manipulative to mean, and Nico . . . well, he does like the carnival.

Instead, what stumbles out of my mouth is something I haven't told anyone, ever. "She tried to suffocate me."

"What?" Hannah's focus whips my way. "Meadow did? When?"

"On Groundhog Day. She tried to make a joke about it afterward. Said it was going to be a short winter because I kept popping up."

"So, like, with a pillow, or what?"

I nod. "I was spending the night. She came at me in my sleep."

"For real, or . . . maybe she was just playing around?"

"For real. We'd both been drinking. She was drunk and angry."

"Why angry?"

"She wanted in with Nico."

"This guy?" Hannah says, flipping back to the front page, and when I nod, she does too. "Well, he *is* hot. But . . . 'in' how?"

My mind flashes back to February. To the night at Meadow's house when she spewed hatred about me being a gatekeeper. The night she said I was a pathetic pull toy and a loser who had no idea what to do with a guy. The night I realized she was jealous.

Jealous of me.

Seeing that—really seeing it—gave me a power surge. I tore out of Meadow's house barefoot, and by the time I got home, I was fully charged and ready to fire back. The very next day, I started yanking Meadow's chain like she'd been yanking mine for years. I acted like nothing had happened. I acted like she was my best friend. Someone I could totally trust. And then I started telling her stories that were mostly lies. Stories about Nico and me, about getting high, about using heroin, about sneaking out at night to break into houses and steal stuff. I made it all sound exciting and risky and cool.

And I did it mostly by text.

Texts my parents had now read.

Texts my parents would totally believe after the things I'd actually done.

Hannah's voice pulls me out of my thoughts. "Wren?"

My reply escapes on a gust of air. "I'm in so much trouble."

"What?"

I hold my head remembering things I did in the weeks before I was kidnapped. "I took scissors to my sister's clothes."

"You what?"

"I slashed my Dad's tires."

"Why are you—?"

"I carved a swastika into my mother's piano."

"A *swastika*? Why a swastika?"

I can barely breathe, thinking about it. There's no way I can explain about the *Tale of the Piano*. About how Nazis had lived in my great-grandmother's house and played it, laughing and drinking, while my great-grandmother's family fumed upstairs.

I can hear my grandmother's voice telling the story. *But the piano stood strong and defiant, and in the end, it survived to play a happy tune.*

"Wren?" Hannah's studying me. "Why?"

There's a lump closing off my throat. "Because . . . because I was drunk and mad and I knew it would hurt her more than anything else."

"Who? Your mom?"

"Yes! She loves that piano way more than she's ever loved me."

My eyes fill up. I try to hold back the tears, but they're swelling, teetering, ready to spill over. Even to me my excuses sound lame. Even to me I seem horrible. But where before, I felt like my mother totally deserved it, what lets the flood loose is the sudden, terrifying reality of what I did.

49

I hole up in my tent, my nerves fried, twitching, shaking. If there was Fireball or weed out here, I'd be all over it, but there's not, and I don't know how to deal with this panic, this dread, this *confusion*.

Why do I care what my parents think?

Don't I hate them?

I try to block out what happened when they found the swastika, but the scene is like a wrecking ball, swinging through my mind:

My mother screams. It cuts through the house like a siren. My dad comes running. My mother breaks down, sobbing, wailing.

Banned to my room for "attitude" during dinner, I'm deep into my secret bottle of Dr Pepper Fireball, feeling no pain. What are they going to do? Have me arrested?

"Wren!" my dad bellows. He's a thundercloud rolling my way. I hide the Dr Pepper bottle. Not that they've ever questioned what I'm drinking, but why take chances?

"What's up?" I ask when he blasts into my room. "Why's Mom crying?" It comes out a little slurred, with a giggle I try to mask.

He yanks me up by my arm and hauls me over to the piano, where Mom is draped across the lid like it's a coffin with her firstborn inside.

She sees me and wails, "Why?"

"Why what?" I pretend not to see the swastika. "What's wrong?"

My mom sobs, "How *could* you?

"How could I what?"

My dad shoves me forward, shoves my face at the gouged wood. His grip on my arm is a tourniquet. "ANSWER HER!" he yells, loud enough to blow tiles off the roof.

"Let go!" I shout at him. "Why are you blaming me?"

My sister's at my mother's side, comforting her. "Because you're the only person in this family who would have done it!" Anabella cries.

I sneer at her. "Oh, really?" Dad's still holding my arm, so I wrench free. "Did you ever think," I snarl at my mom, "that maybe *she* did it because she knows you hate me and would automatically assume it was me?"

"That's ridiculous," Anabella huffs.

"Well, then why *did* you do it?" I ask her.

"NO AMOUNT OF DENYING OR REDIRECTING IS GOING TO GET YOU OUT OF THIS," my dad roars, sending more roof tiles into orbit.

"So that's it?" I ask, backing away. "Anabella couldn't *possibly* have done it? One of Mo's friend's couldn't *possibly* have done it? I'm the only one?"

"Anabella would never do such a thing!" my mom wails. "And neither would your brother *or* his friends!"

"But *I* would? I'm automatically guilty?" I stumble into my brother's stuff, which is where he dumped it before racing off to spend the night with some friends. His baseball bat jumps into my hand like it's magnetized. "Okay, well, since you hate me so much, let me give you an actual reason to!" Then I go on a rampage, smashing stuff. Framed pictures, the coffee table, vases . . . anything I can hit. Dad comes at me like a linebacker, but I manage to ditch him and head for the kitchen as mom shrieks and Anabella calls 911.

In the kitchen I smash whatever I can—the counter, the canisters, the faucet—and I'm just swinging for the blender when my dad tackles me.

My face skids along the tile floor, my arms get wrestled behind me. My dad's breathing is heavy, his knee sharp in the middle of my back. I can hear my mother freaking out, but the cool tile against my cheek overrides it. It feels so good. Ice against fever. I wish all of me could feel that way.

And then the world goes black.

———

Later, I saw that night as a victory. My parents were afraid of me. So was my sister. Their solution seemed to be to lay down even stricter rules and cage me. In the days that followed, I played along until they went to bed, then escaped through the window. I didn't know they were plotting a kidnapping.

But now, thinking back to the night of the rampage, what keeps playing in my mind is the real wrecking ball. I woke up from my blackout, on my side on my bedroom floor with my head pounding and my hands tied behind my back. Everything hurt. Outside, lights were flashing blue and red. I staggered over to the window and saw my parents talking to two cops on our porch. When the cops finally left, my parents sat down on the steps, wrapped their arms around each other, and cried.

At the time, what I saw was them crying over the piano and the things I'd smashed.

At the time it was easy to turn away.

And now?

Now I can't seem to block out the way they were sobbing, heaving, collapsing into each other. Over and over the scene smashes through my mind, and what I see now is them *grieving*.

Like someone had died.

50

I can't write the letter. I just can't.

Tara sits with me, tries to get me to open up, tells me it takes courage to face our darkest selves. I know Hannah's spilled what I told her. I'm not mad. I know she's worried. I know she cares.

But I can't write the letter. I just can't.

Tara holds my hands, pleads with me to let it go, let it out. I cry and shake my head, terrified by the panic, the confusion, the memories ravaging my mind.

"You can do this," she tells me. "You can face this and get through it. Let the burden go."

But I can't write the letter. I just can't.

Maybe if I had some weed. Or whiskey.

"Is there something you can give me?" I finally ask. "Something to calm me down?" I break down and beg. "I've seen them give meds to the other girls. Please?"

"Those are prescribed by their doctors back home." She squeezes my hands. "Wren, you're clean. This is the time to figure things out. Numbing the pain won't help you do that." She looks at me intently and whispers, "Let it out. Let it go. Stop poisoning yourself with hatred."

I look down and hold still for the longest time. And when I finally look up, I beg her, "Please? I think I could do it if I wasn't so . . . raw."

She studies me a moment, then leaves without a word. I see her gather the jailers—John, Dvorka, Michelle—and they all stand in a circle talking quietly, heads bowed, hands shoved in pockets.

When they're done, Michelle's the one to come to my tent. She squats in front of it and says, "We need you to pack your things."

Panic swallows me whole. "You're sending me home? Why? What did I do?"

"No!" she says quickly, because now I'm hyperventilating. "We're sending you on a quest."

"A quest?" I'm panting, not understanding.

"Remember how Mia was gone for three days? And then Shalayne?"

I nod. It was against the rules to talk about where they'd gone, but they'd both come back . . . different.

"They were on a quest."

"What does that *mean*? What am I looking for?"

She smiles and stands. "You're looking for you."

"What?"

"Pack. We need you ready to go in twenty minutes."

The second she's gone, Hannah pokes her head in the back side of my tent. "Did I hear right?" she whispers. "You're doing a quest?"

I still can't breathe right. "What does that *mean*?"

"It means you disappear for three days." She looks past me, through the tent to Dvorka, who's heading our way. "You better still be my friend when you're done!"

"Why wouldn't I be?" I ask, but she's already gone.

Dvorka squats in front of my tarp opening. "Pack no food. We'll provide rations and water. But you need to bring everything else for two nights. And just a heads-up—rain is expected."

"Is anyone going with me?"

"No."

Her answer feels like a lock snapping closed. "But . . . where am I going? What am I supposed to *do*?"

"You're supposed to do what you *need* to do, and Tara says you know what that is."

I look down.

"You'll be guided to your quest site," she says. "The rest is up to you."

"Are you *serious*?"

She gives me a little smile. "Have I ever given you reason to think I'm not?" She pats my knee. "Come on. And pack wisely."

I've struck camp enough times now to be quick at it, and by the time Michelle approaches again, I've got my pack bundled tight. Anything I'm not bringing—mostly just my curriculum binder and random clothes—gets put in a Hefty sack.

Michelle is wearing a worn leather knapsack. It's decorated with juniper berries and is full up to the drawstrings. "Ready?" she asks.

"Is that even possible?" I answer, but the packing did help—at least I can breathe again.

She chuckles. "Well, ready or not . . ." She produces a bandanna, snaps it out, then turns it into a blindfold.

I groan, "Seriously?" but I don't put up a fight as she wraps it around my head, turns me a couple of times, and leads me in who-knows-what direction.

We've walked less than ten minutes when Michelle stops and holds me by the shoulders. "You'll be fine," she says softly in my ear. "Let the sun rise inside you."

I'm thinking, *We're here? They're exiling me this close to camp? Well, cool. I can find my way back, no problem. I'll just follow campfire smoke and—*

And then the blindfold is off, Michelle has disappeared, the knapsack is at my feet, and I'm looking into the ancient eyes of Mokov.

Mokov's silver-snake braids sweep against his leather vest as he straps on the knapsack. "Wild Bird," he says, giving me a soft smile. "Come."

Then he turns and heads into the sagebrush without even glancing back.

51

I watch him go, and in my head I'm sputtering, *Wild Bird? What makes you think you can call me that?* But he's already disappearing behind a grove of pinyons, so I hurry to catch up.

He's swift. Silent. Like smoke on a breeze. Me, I'm crunching on twigs and breathing hard, struggling to keep him in sight.

There is no path. No destination I can see. He leads us past pinyons and junipers, down a section of huge boulders, and through a stretch of hard red dirt that funnels into a narrow canyon.

The walls of the canyon have black streaks running down their faces like streams of inky tears. "Where are we going?" I call after him, but it echoes off the canyon walls unanswered.

I follow him through the canyon, over endless brick-red dirt. Finally I shout, "How far are we going?"

He stops. Turns. Waits. "On this journey? Or in life?" He gives me a small smile and begins walking again, this time a little slower. "We travel only as far and as high as our hearts will take us."

"Well, my heart has had enough," I tell him, panting.

He glances back at me. "I like to reflect on things as I walk."

"Reflect on *what*?"

"Hmm," he says, checking the sky as he hikes. "Today I've been considering how life's journey is not about the distance we move our feet, but how we are moved in our heart."

Stupid me for asking. "Look," I beg, "all I really want to know is where I'm going, and how long it's going to take to get there." Then I add, "And also, how it's legal to stick me out in the middle of the desert by myself."

He stops again and studies me with those ancient eyes. But instead of giving me information or even a glimmer of hope that I won't die in the middle of nowhere on this "quest," he says, "There's a wisdom passed through the ages that says that if we walk far but are angry as we journey, we travel nowhere. If we hold grudges as we scale mountains, our view remains the same." He starts off again, saying, "So what I can tell you is that your journey will be long and difficult if you refuse to choose a new direction for your heart."

A new direction for my heart? I follow but let him gain ground on me and play around with the idea of ditching him. He was cool back when he just told stories, but telling me about the direction of my heart?

Who needs that?

But since I have no idea where I am, or how to get back to camp, I follow him up, up, up a mostly nonexistent trail to a mesa, where I find him waiting, looking out across an enormous canyon.

The view catches me off guard, makes me a little dizzy. It's like we've shifted dimensions, entered an alternate universe. There's a river below us—a *river*. It's muddy, tinged red, and lazy, but it snakes along for as far as I can see.

Mokov gives no explanation, no instructions. Instead, he begins a story as I stand beside him, looking across the canyon. "In the Long Ago, Owl gathered the birds for a contest to settle a dispute. Eagle had been leader for many years, and other birds felt it was time to challenge him.

"'It is known far and wide that I can soar highest,' Eagle said, and indeed, in challenges past he had won easily.

"But Crow and Hawk had been preparing for this challenge. Secretly, they had risen earlier than usual each morning for two moons, flying higher and higher to strengthen their powers. 'We shall see,' Crow cawed to Eagle. 'Yes,' agreed Hawk, 'we shall see!'

"Lark, like many other birds, had traveled a great distance to see the contest. And, like many other birds, Lark was resentful of Eagle's place. Emboldened by Crow and Hawk, Lark now stepped forward singing, 'Yes, we shall see!' Excitement ruffled through the other birds. How brave Lark was to challenge Eagle!

"The competing birds aligned side by side, and at Owl's command the contest began. Lark, Hawk, Crow, and Eagle lifted from earth, rising into the air. Lark's wings beat mightily, but before long the little bird returned to earth.

"'You were brave to try!' the other birds chirped. Their eyes returned to Hawk, who was now also returning to earth.

"'Crow is strong,' Hawk said to the consoling flock. 'He might do it!' But Crow, too, could not match the strength of

Eagle's wings. He returned, greatly disappointed. It seemed that, once again, Eagle would win the contest and remain leader.

"To make his victory one beyond question, Eagle did not immediately return to earth but pumped his mighty wings and spiraled toward the heavens, higher and higher. The other birds watched in wonder at Eagle's power and strength. 'Eagle is indeed a great leader,' Crow conceded. 'Yes,' Hawk agreed. 'Eagle is powerful and fearless.'

"But then, just as Eagle had exhausted himself and could fly no higher, Hawk saw something shoot upward from between Eagle's mighty shoulders. 'Look!' Hawk exclaimed. 'It is Wren!'"

I jolt. "What?" I turn to Mokov. "Don't put me in your moral lesson!"

He goes on without missing a beat, without pulling his gaze away from the canyon. "The other birds twittered and sang. How clever Wren was to stow away! Wren had soared to a height even greater than Eagle! They had a new leader!"

"Oh," I say, feeling embarrassed but . . . good. Wren is a bird in legends who's clever and outsmarts Eagle! Who knew?

But then Mokov goes and ruins everything. He says, "But when Wren returned to earth, the other birds' song began to change. Where Eagle was quiet, Wren was boastful, reminding all the others how clever he had been. At last Owl asked Wren, 'But who lifted you so high?' Wren cast aside the question and continued to boast, and soon the flock had had enough. It turned to Eagle and said, 'You are Leader, now and through time.'"

Suddenly I feel crushed and angry and . . . *tricked*. "I am not boastful!" I snap at Mokov. "Why did you tell me that story? I hate that story!"

He turns his ancient eyes on me and says, "You're not the Wren of this legend. But it's wise for all of us to respect the wings that beat hard to lift us."

I'm about to tell him to stop already with the lectures when I notice the way he's looking at the sky.

"Rain is coming," he says, then removes the knapsack and leaves it at my feet. "Let your heart open up like the skies."

I blink at the knapsack. Watch him walk away. Panic.

"That's it? You're leaving me *here*?"

I chase after him, but it's too late. He's already vanished.

52

It takes a few minutes for reality to sink in.

I'm alone.

Completely alone.

It flashes through my mind again that Mokov leaving me here by myself can't be legal, but what slaps that thought away is that it doesn't matter—there's no arguing my case in this desert courthouse. Out here, Mother Nature is my judge and jury, and objecting or redirecting or even being out of order won't help me escape. The only way to survive my sentence is to serve it.

It also flashes through my mind that maybe my mom and dad won't be grieving parents if I *don't* survive this. After reading my text history, they'll probably be more relieved than heartbroken.

I return to the knapsack and find that inside it is my food and water supply. I don't rummage through it, because the sky is a heavy gray and I know I need to set up camp. Shelter first, I tell myself, then firewood, then food.

I scan the area for a good place to string up my tarp but get distracted by the strangeness of where Mokov has left me. Over the last few weeks, I've hiked wherever I've been led. I haven't looked around much. I've just trudged along until we've been told to stop. But for all the *not* looking I've done, I know I haven't been anywhere like this before. I'm on a wide, red plateau with a big canyon in front of me and a towering wall behind me. It's like I've come up a secret back way to a giant notch in the earth. Looking across the canyon, I see that there are notches on the other side, too. Notches that go up the canyon like a staircase. Notches that lead to towers of red earth that look like chimneys. Notches that spill streams of black tears over the face of a sheer wall.

There are also places where the walls look scooped out like servings of orange sherbet. Some are shallow, some are almost cave-like, some are wide, some are small. And speckled up the canyon from the muddy river to the bases of the chimneys are shrubs and trees clawing onto ledges, clinging onto cliffs.

I feel like one of those shrubs on the other side—isolated, digging in, trying to survive. But taking time to *see* like this sets up a battle in my mind. Something's telling me it's important, but it also feels like I'm wasting time. Why am I looking at scenery, thinking how I'm like a bush, when I should be setting up camp? Rain is coming!

I turn away from the canyon and look around my little mesa. And it sinks in that where I'm standing is probably a lot like what I can see across the canyon. If I could fly over to the other side and look back, I'd probably see notched steps leading up to red-earth chimneys, sheer walls of rusty-red earth, and streaks of black tears.

In a flash of excitement, I realize that scoops of orange sherbet may be gouged out of my side of the canyon, too. So . . . maybe I won't need to set up a tent. Maybe I can be a cave dweller!

I grab the knapsack and set off away from the canyon, scanning the wall on my side for a cave I can sleep in. I see scoops, but they're either too high, too shallow, or just too small. I'm moving fast, passing by pinyons and junipers where I could string up my tarp tent, seeing dead wood that I could collect for building a fire, but I keep going, obsessed with finding a cave.

And then the rain starts.

I cuss because . . . why not? The consequences in the field are already happening, and besides, if a girl cusses in the desert and there's no one around to hear, did she actually cuss? "You're an idiot, Hollister Keegan," I shout into the air. "Of course it makes a sound!"

So now I'm talking to myself. In the rain. On a mesa in the middle of the desert. Alone. I yell, "THIS IS ABUSE! IT'S ILLEGAL! IF I DIE OUT HERE, YOU WILL PAY!"

My voice gets swept away by the wind, drowned out by the sky.

The Judge isn't backing down.

"Fine," I grumble. "I'll set up my stupid tarp."

And then I see it. About ten yards away. A scoop deep enough to be a cave, low enough for me to reach, and small enough to protect me from the wind and rain. I hurry over, toss in the knapsack, shove my backpack inside, and scramble into the cave. It's not very deep and not wide enough to lie down in, but it's perfect shelter. "HA!" I shout up at the clouds.

A streak of lightning shoots down into the canyon.

"You missed me!" I call out.

The sky answers with a long, low rumble of thunder.

"Quit grousing!" I shout, and laugh.

I've actually won a battle with the sky.

53

I enjoy being safe and dry in my cave for a little while, but then I start feeling panicked about the rain. Not because I worry about getting wet, not because a flash flood might sweep me away. No, I'm having a little freak-out because water is *getting away.*

It's more a low-flow showerhead kind of rain than one gushing from a fire hose. But the showerhead is the entire sky for as far and wide as I can see, and I'm not set up to catch any of it. If I was, I could drink it. Cook with it. Wash my hair or clothes with it. If there was a little gully, I could line it with my tarp and take a *bath.* But instead the most precious thing in the desert is just falling out of the sky and hitting the dirt.

It's not much, but I get my billypot and set it outside the cave to collect rain. Drops ping on the bottom and I feel like a beggar, thankful to the sky for tossing in a few coins.

I empty out the knapsack to see what I can eat while I'm

waiting for the rain to stop. The answer is . . . nothing. There's no energy bar, no trail mix, no dried fruit or *anything* I can eat without cooking it first. "Are you serious?" I cry at a big baking potato.

Reality stares at me through the cold, dead eyes of the potato. This is why Dvorka told me not to pack food. If I want to eat, I'm going to have to build a fire.

But why? *Why?* Do they really have to make it this hard?

My mind wanders to home, where there's always something in the freezer that I can zap in the microwave and just eat. But thinking about home reminds me of my parents reading my texts, and panic jolts through me like electricity. I don't want to think about that. Anything's better than thinking about that.

I look out at the sky hanging heavy and wet and try to figure out where the sun is. It's impossible to tell, but thinking back on the day and the hike with Mokov, I guesstimate that it's four-thirty or five. Each day has gotten a little longer as the weeks have gone by, with the sun now setting after eight o'clock. Which means—if my guesstimate is right—I've got about three hours of daylight left. If I was stuck in a class with Hollister Keegan, that would be an eternity. But out here, needing to find wood and start a fire, it's a scary short amount of time.

The lightning and thunder have stopped, but that doesn't mean it won't keep raining, and for who knows how long? And even though rain means drinking water and hair washing and cooking, if you have to go out in it, it also means getting wet. And without fire, wet means cold, especially at night.

So I'm tempted to wait it out, but the longer I sit watching the rain come down, the more I know I need to get out there and collect firewood. The wetter the wood gets, the harder it'll be to light and burn, and fire is important for more than just being warm and heating up dinner.

It also keeps animals away.

An image of hungry coyotes creeps into my mind. There's a pack of them coming for me, stealthy, hungry, determined . . . and they're not interested in my potato.

I force away the vision, open my backpack, put on my poncho, and go out into the rain.

Since it's not a hard rain and since it hasn't been going all that long, the upper branches of the pinyons and junipers have kept the area underneath them pretty dry. I go from one tree to the next, collecting any dead branches and kindling I can find, using the bottom part of my poncho like a sling to carry the wood and keep it dry.

After four poncho loads back to the cave, I've got a pretty good stash of firewood, but there's now a lot less room for me to sit. Especially with my backpack unlashed and spilling out. I try shoving stuff out of my way, try using my sleeping bag as a headrest, try telling myself to relax and wait out the rain. But no matter what I do, I feel claustrophobic, and I'm shocked to realize that I'd rather be outside *doing* something.

So I finish unbundling my pack, pull my tarp free, grab the cord, and go back out into the rain. I move fast, finding anchor rocks, setting up the tarp between two scrawny pinyons near the cave. The magic knot Michelle taught me slides tight and holds, making it so I can use low branches as a sort of back-door awning. The tent's up and trenched faster than I've ever done it, and I smile when I look inside. If I had ornaments, I could hang them on my back-porch Christmas tree.

I don't put anything inside the tent because I don't want to carry my sleeping bag and mat and ground liner through the rain if I don't have to. Instead, I ready a ring of rocks a few yards in front of my tent opening, thinking it will be a good idea to have a fire near me, but not so close it sends sparks into the tent.

That's about all I can do until it stops raining, so I crawl back into the cave, wait around, get bored, start thinking about my text messages and my parents, panic, leave the cave again, and go out for more firewood.

Anything's better than thinking about my parents.

This time I store the firewood inside the tent. I feel like a squirrel collecting nuts. How many nuts do squirrels collect? How do they know they have enough?

I check the trench around the tent, digging it out some more with a rock, extending the low spot to run farther away from the opening. I think about my brother and how he would love this. I wish he could be here, helping me dig. We hardly ever went to the beach, but the times we did, I built the castles and my brother dug the moats. He did great moats. Not great enough to stop the ocean for good, but still. Great moats.

My parents edge back into my mind as I dig. Water is running off my poncho hood. Water starts dripping from my eyes. The trench around the tent is plenty good enough, but I keep digging and dripping and wishing. For what I'm not sure. The impossible, probably.

Like moats that won't wash away in the tide.

54

I've been balled up in the cave thinking about hieroglyphics. Or, I guess, pictographs. On one of our day hikes last week, the jailers took us to a secret place where Native Americans had drawn things on a cave wall. It wasn't a scooped-out cave like mine, more a wedge area between rocks, with trees growing in front of the opening. I couldn't in a million years find it again, because after marching along for half the day, we were led to and from it blindfolded. Of course.

The pictographs were faded, barely even there, but John pointed them out, one by one. There was a circle, big X's, a bird, fire, a man with wavy arms, and raining clouds. John made up a story based on what the symbols might have meant, explaining that no one really knows because a circle could mean the sun or a shield or an eye or pretty much anything else that's round. He also explained that some wall art dated back to 7000 BC and said that we were in the presence of "America's earliest storytelling documents." He said the pictographs were painted by mixing natural minerals with plant and animal oils to make colored paints, which were then put on the walls with fingers or brushes made out of animal hair or yucca leaves.

I was more interested in when we'd finally sit down and have some lunch.

But in my own cave now, I look at the blank wall and wonder what I would draw. What symbols I would use. What story I would tell. I also wonder if the story John told was anything close to the *real* story that was painted on the wall.

I'm lost in thought about cave paintings when I notice how quiet it is, and when I look outside, the rain has stopped and the clouds are breaking up.

Yay!

There's still daylight, but it won't last long, so I scramble out of the cave with my bow-drill kit and the kindling and tinder bundle I got ready while I was waiting. I hurry to the tent, pull some firewood over to the fire ring, and get to work.

In the last few weeks I've gotten really good at busting out a fire. It's always hard, always intense, but I always volunteer to get the campfire started anyway, because I like the way it still feels like a genie rising out of the wood. When the spindle rubs back and forth in the fire board, it makes a puff of smoke, then a little stream of it rises, then the ember makes the bundle ignite, and *poof,* the fire genie grants three wishes—heat, light, and food.

Getting a fire going now is extra hard because everything's damp, but it would have been impossible if I hadn't gotten some wood out of the rain. When I've finally got a real flame burning, I'm tired and sweating and really hungry.

I retrieve my billypot of rainwater, a ration of freeze-dried meatball marinara, and a ziplock of spiral pasta noodles. Once I've got the water heating, I spread out my ground cloth inside the tarp tent, roll out the mat, and spread out my sleeping bag. Then I put my extra clothes inside the sleeping bag's stuff sack to make a pillow, hang my poncho on a pinyon branch, and lay the zip-off bottoms of my wet pants across fire-ring rocks to dry.

By the time dinner's ready, the cave is empty, the firewood is all stacked inside my tent so it's easy to reach and will stay dry if it rains again, and my stuff is organized and tidy.

At home Mom would cook pasta in gallons of water, then dump the water down the drain. Here, I've got hardly any extra water in the pot after the pasta's tender, so I just add the freeze-dried marinara sauce right into the cooked noodles, heat it some more, then eat straight out of the pot.

When I was little, being in the "clean-plate club" used to be linked to getting dessert, but we quit having to pay those dues after my brother was born. Leftovers got scraped off plates and went down the garbage disposal while the tap ran and ran and ran.

I never thought twice about it, but that's what I'm thinking about now as I'm wolfing down my food. There are no leftovers out here. If you don't eat everything you cook, you *will* go hungry. Maybe not today, but when your rations run out before resupply. Out here, everyone's in the clean-plate club, *especially* since there's usually no dessert.

As I'm scraping out my billypot with the wooden spoon Michelle helped me make, I realize how smooth the spoon has become over time. It seems normal, even comfortable, in my mouth, in my hand. I don't think of it as being a stick anymore. It's been my only utensil for four weeks. One spoon, one pot, one cup, one plate. I'm used to it now. I don't really need anything else.

My mind drifts to what the other girls are doing. I wonder if Mokov returned to camp, if he's telling the story about Eagle and Wren. I get mad at him all over again. Why tell me that story if he didn't think I was the Wren in the legend?

It's strange how you can hear other people's voices in your head. Not just their words, their *voices*. I've always thought it was spooky—like there's a ghost inside your brain, whispering, nudging, haunting. And right now, I hear Mokov's: *It's wise for all of us to respect the wings that beat hard to lift us.*

"Shut up," I say out loud. "You have no idea about the wings that have beat me *down*."

Now it's Tara's voice haunting me. *So tell me,* she whispers. *Let it out. Let it go. Stop poisoning yourself with hatred.*

"You can shut up too!" I shout. Then I rub out the billypot with sand to clean it, dump the sand into the fire, add a tight heap of new wood to the middle of the fire to keep it burning, and go to bed.

55

I wake up with a start. A nightmare about my parents, my texts, my brother hating me.

I don't know where I am at first. It's dark. My nose is freezing. There's something hard next to me. It feels like . . . bones?

I scream and jolt away.

And then remember.

Firewood. Tent. Quest.

I have no idea what time it is. I know that sunrise happens around six-thirty, but it feels nowhere near that. And it's so *quiet.* I look out at the fire ring to see if it's still burning. That would tell me *something.*

What I see instead is . . . snow?

Yes, snow!

It's drifting down from the sky, dusting the ground and the rocks of the fire ring, melting on the mound of ash.

I reach out to catch some, to *feel* it. It's so light, so silent, and it melts the instant it touches my hand. It feels more like a mirage than something real, so I stick my head out of the tent and catch flakes on my tongue. More flakes land in my hair than in my mouth, but it doesn't matter. I've tasted snow!

I try to make a mini-snowman from what's landed in front of the tent, but there isn't enough. And it makes my fingers as cold as my nose. I laugh at how surprised I am by that. Of course it's cold. It's snow!

Finally I dry off with my bandanna and snuggle deep inside my sleeping bag, grateful for its warmth. And as I watch the silent show outside, I giggle. I'm camping in snow! Wait 'til I tell Mowgli!

A sudden dose of reality douses me.

Mo.

I try not to let my mind go there, but it won't go anywhere else: My brother must know. How could he not? Kids talk. Parents "explain." Sisters narc.

And there's a swastika gouged in the piano.

My heart races. I can't breathe. Then I'm shivering and crying and just falling apart inside a cocoon of arctic insulation. How could I have gouged a swastika in my mother's piano?

I remind myself of my list of reasons.

My litany.

Everything that led up to that night.

I close my eyes and go over it and over it and over it like counting sheep until somehow I fall asleep. But when the sun wakes me in the morning, the snow has vanished, and what's running through my mind is the horrible truth.

I gouged a swastika in my mother's piano.

I force myself to get up, to get moving, to shake off the thought of the piano.

The air is chilly, but the sky is clear and the sun feels great on my face. I wonder if the snow was a dream, but then I see evidence of it. The upper steps of the staircase walls across the canyon are dusted with it. Powdered sugar on gingerbread.

I poke around the pile of ashes looking for an ember, a coal I can blow back to life like John does some mornings with the big campfire. But the fire is cold.

Dead.

For some reason, this makes me want to cry. I think about Michelle telling me that if I could start a fire out here, I could start one inside myself. That makes less sense to me now than it did then. I didn't need to start a fire inside me. I've been burning mad at everyone and everything for *years*. And at this point I've started *lots* of fires out here. So why does it feel like the fire inside me is going *out*? Why is the ember I could always fan into a raging flame with just a few puffs now lying there, still?

And why, after going through my whole list again and again and again, why do I have this throat-choking urge to tell my parents I'm sorry.

56

After breakfast, I sit in my tent with the notebook in my lap staring at a blank page, petrified. I can't make myself write "Dear Mom & Dad."

I just can't.

I also can't write to my brother.

It *hurts* to think about writing him.

I know I have to write my parents. I know I have to explain about the texts. I know that means I have to explain about other stuff, too. I know, I know, I know.

But facing this piece of paper is terrifying! It makes me want to hide. Lie. Deny.

It's worse, way worse, than starting a new school.

It's worse, way worse, than having no friends, no one to talk to.

It's worse, way worse, than not being seen. Even *I* don't want to look at me. I just want to disappear.

I think about the first time Meadow invited me to

"celebrate." It went against everything I'd been taught, everything my parents had warned us about. And it went against what *I* thought I should do.

But I caved.

Just like that, I caved.

What would have happened if I'd walked out of that bathroom instead? Where would I be if I'd been brave?

When I finally touch my pen to the page, what comes out is: *Please just listen.*

Writing that sentence feels like letting out a breath I've been holding in for years. Maybe because my parents' eyes aren't on me. Maybe because they can't interrupt me. Maybe because I don't have to defend myself against their words, or watch them turn oxygen into large dark clouds of disappointment.

I promise to tell you the truth, my shaking hand writes. *Please, just listen.*

And then I let it out. About the move. About feeling so alone. About Anabella and her having no time for me. About feeling lost in a new city, a big house. About losing the gears of our family. *We all spun off. Anabella had her new friends, Mo had after-school club, you guys work-work-worked, and I was alone in a corner, dying.*

Then I tell them about the day I met Meadow. How happy it made me to find a friend. How I didn't know how to say no.

Once I get started, it pours out. It's jumbled, and I know I put in too much drama, too many underlines, too many exclamation points, too many things that probably don't make sense, but I almost don't care. I just want it done. I want them to hear my side and know what's true and what's not. And once I've confessed about the weed and the whiskey, I tell them about delivering packages for Nico; how I didn't know what I was doing at first; how I feel sick about it now because of Hannah.

I really want to leave the heroin part out, but I have to tell them the whole truth so they'll believe that the texts to Meadow were not true; that I said those to get back at her for things she'd done to me.

All I can hope is that they do.

My letter winds up fourteen pages long. I don't cry a drop until I get to the end and write, *I'm sorry for so much, especially the piano. Please forgive me, Wren.*

I have fought those words for so long. Dug in hard against them. Battled them with all my might. It feels so strange to be saying them now.

And even stranger, that saying them is such gut-wrenching relief.

57

Most of my firewood is already gone. While I wander from camp to gather more, the sun grows sharp and hot, the air warm and windy. There are clouds, but they're white and puffy instead of blankets of cold steel. And it takes me quite a while to believe it, but there are no flies. Maybe the cold killed them off? I don't know. I don't care why. I'll take it.

I think about home. About my family. About Meadow. About Nico. One thing's for sure: I'm done with Meadow. It finally feels one hundred percent real. She's not my friend and has never been. Hannah has taught me that. Not just by the things she's said, but by the way she's *cared*.

Meadow never actually cared.

I can see that now.

An anger rises up when I think about Meadow and the things she's done. A good anger. One that makes me feel strong.

And Nico . . . ? I've felt a lot of things for him—the thrilling high of just being near him, the electricity of his look, his touch, even his voice. I've ached for him in a way that could only be love. And yet now . . .

Now I feel weirdly still inside about him. There's no churning. No racing heart. If anything, I feel a little nauseous.

Maybe that's also because of Hannah. She's tried to describe her addiction to me. How it sweeps back into her mind like a force she can't stop. How using heroin had become the focus of her entire day. How she's so glad, so relieved, to be clean now, but can feel this claw in her brain, shaking the bars of its cage, scheming for ways to get out.

She sounds scared when she talks about it. Like there's a boogeyman in her head all the time, not just under the bed at night. And even though she's clean now, even though she said it was torture to detox and she would rather die than go through that again, she's afraid of falling back into using. "If I slip up just once," she whispered last week when we were supposed to be doing curriculum, "it's over. I'm dead."

"So don't slip up," I whispered back.

"You don't understand!" Her eyes turned into oceans again. "It's in there! And it wants out!"

So thinking about Nico now, I don't picture his dimple or his smile, the style of his hair, or his smoky kiss. I think about being his delivery girl. I think about heroin. And I wonder how many people have a claw in their brain because of me.

Because of him.

I try to blame the way I'm feeling—the *guilt* I'm feeling—on Nico, on Meadow, on Anabella, on my parents. I try to fan the ember in me into rage against someone, *anyone*. But as I face into the wind and walk back to my camp with another armload of wood, what I see is me.

Guilty me.

I pushed myself on Nico. I was spineless around Meadow, and Anabella warned me about both of them. And my parents . . . my parents just believed my endless lies for way too long.

I dump the load of wood. Dirty, gnarled, ragged wood. And as it tumbles down, I realize there's another letter I need to write. One to Anabella.

I cook lunch, thinking about Anabella. Cursing how this wide-open place traps you inside your thoughts. Once there's wood and fire and food and shelter, you're left with your thoughts. Even when you're collecting wood and building fire and cooking food and making shelter, your body goes into autopilot while your head gets hijacked by your thoughts.

And even though Anabella is still on my hate list and the things I want to say to her have everything to do with how she abandoned me, other thoughts won't stay out of my head. Sentimental thoughts. About us as kids before the move. Thoughts about secret games of crazy eights after bedtime and her painting my fingernails before my seventh-birthday party. Thoughts about the way she held my hand when she walked me to my kindergarten classroom. Thoughts about piggybacks and popcorn parties and her teaching me to tie my shoes. "One rabbit ear, two rabbit ear, cross, tuck, pull!"

I try to push these thoughts out, but they keep wiggling back into my head, infiltrating my heart.

When I finally sit down to write her, the letter does start out angry. But it deteriorates into how hurt I am, and winds up talking about card games and kindergarten and how much I adored her when we were little.

It turns completely pathetic.

The whole thing hurts. It hurts to remember. It hurts to forget. I don't know what's better, blocking it out or bringing it up. But there it is now, down on paper—three years of hate and hurt and heartache.

I don't reread it. I don't rethink it. I just sign off: *One rabbit ear, two rabbit ear, cross, tuck, pull!*

Then I take a deep, choppy breath and cry my heart out.

58

By dinnertime I've collected enough wood for a bonfire. I was going to get by with what I'd already gathered, but after I finished Anabella's letter, I needed to walk around and clear my head, and while I was walking around, I found coyote poop. Or, as John wants us to call it, coyote *scat*.

I'd never even heard *scat* used that way, but for one of our "curriculum challenges" John took Mia, Shalayne, Hannah, and me on a full-day hike "scouting for scat." He promised it would count as a biology unit.

The whole idea seemed so gross, especially since John was weirdly into it. He was like a little kid on an Easter egg hunt. The rest of us were not, but what we did get into was joking about it. Shalayne started things off by calling John "Doo-doo Daddy," which made everyone—even John—laugh. So as we hiked along, we riffed on that, joking back and forth, laughing our heads off. John was cool enough to ignore the names that should definitely have had consequences in the field, and maybe it was him being cool that got us to back off and settle on our crew's final name: Deputy Dung and the Scat Trackers.

So we made it fun, but the day turned out to be interesting, too. John would take us off the trail and nose around until he found droppings. Most of them were pellety—round or longer and different in size and color, but definitely pellety. John could tell what animal the droppings came from— kangaroo rat, marmot, porcupine, prairie dog ... he even found some he said came from bighorn sheep.

We were all stunned.

"There's bighorn *sheep* out here?"

"Where?"

"Yeah, I'd like to see me some bighorn sheep!"

John laughed. "Well, one's been standing right here."

"Are you sure?" Shalayne asked.

He pointed to the pellets and grinned. "Positive."

We were at a wide spot after coming up a steep, rocky hill that had been more like mountain climbing than trail hiking. There weren't plants or water anywhere near us, and the sun was beating down hard. "Why would it come up here?" I asked, squinting around at the hot, barren rockiness.

John shrugged and moved on, saying, "Maybe the view? Great place to survey the surroundings."

We hiked and climbed and detoured all day, and every scat John showed us was some variation of generic pellet. Even with the joking around, scouting for scat got old after a while.

And then we came upon what looked like a mangled piece of furry gray rope sitting right in the middle of the trail. John put up a hand and got super excited. "Whoa, whoa, whoa! Here we go—coyote scat!" We circled around as John picked up a stick and started poking at it.

Mia frowned. "You're really doing this right now?"

"He's Deputy Dung," Shalayne said, and the rest of us snickered.

"See this?" John said, prying into it. "There's bones, fur . . . this is definitely coyote."

"Bones?" I asked.

"They eat everything, toe to tail," John said, and he seemed so pleased.

Mia snorted. "Pretty rude to plant it on the trail."

John stood and tossed the stick aside. "Coyotes do that on purpose to communicate."

We all stared at him. "To communicate?"

"It's a way to mark their territory. They want other predators to see it."

"Taggin' the trail with what comes out the tail," Shalayne said, and we all laughed.

I hadn't thought about being a Scat Tracker since that day, but when I was out trying to clear Anabella's letter from my head and came toe to turd with a big, gray, furry pile, I knew right away what it was, and it stopped me in my tracks.

The scat was fresh, and less than twenty yards from my tent. I scanned the whole area, looking for coyotes lurking behind the pinyons and junipers or rock formations, or in the shadows. I listened for footsteps, panting, the crunching of bones, anything!

All I heard was the wind.

So I started searching for something I could use to protect

myself. A spear. A club. Something that would ward off a pack of hungry coyotes looking to turn me into furry turds.

"HOW CAN THIS BE LEGAL?" I shouted up at the sky, but the sky just kept its burning eye on me and huffed in my face.

I found a pinyon with a dry branch still attached near the base of its trunk. I tried pulling it off but couldn't get it to budge, so I stepped on it like a ladder rung, held on to a higher branch, and jumped. I had to bash down on it over and over and *hard* before it finally cracked, then broke off enough so I could twist it from the trunk.

I snapped off all the little branches and used a sharp rock to smooth down a section where I could get a good grip to use it as a club or a battering ram. I liked the way it felt in my hands, and after I practiced swinging and jabbing, trying it out, I laid it in front of my tent like a threshold.

After that, I collected rocks that were big enough to hurt and small enough to throw and piled them up outside the tent. Then I went back to collecting firewood, because John's told us over and over that the best thing to protect you in the wild is fire.

So now I've got a huge heap of wood—I hope it's enough to burn all night. It takes way more than you'd think, but I just have to make it through one more night alone.

Maybe I'm worrying about nothing. I'm not even sure a pack of coyotes would try to take down a person, but there's not exactly someone here I can ask. And coyotes have teeth. And eat *bones*. If I had a choice, I'd trade the coyote problem for another night of rain like *that*. At least with rain I know what I'm dealing with and when it's happening. With coyotes, I'm looking over my shoulder all the time, wondering if they're out there stalking me, scheming up ways to take me down.

I've kept a small fire going all day so I don't have to start one from scratch again. The bonus is I've got coals that are now perfect for cooking my potato.

Boiling the potato is not an option. I've been good with my water, so I don't have to search for any more, but boiling the potato would just waste it. The best way to cook a potato out in the wild is to bake it.

We've done it a couple of times around the big campfire, and I've learned the hard way that good coals and patience are the way to make it edible. If you rush it or put the potato too close to the fire, you'll end up with something disgusting that you only choke down because you're starving and, hey, that's what's for dinner.

If you do it right, though, it is uber-delicious.

Doing it right means using a rock to dig out a divot near the fire, using a stick to rake in hot coals, putting the potato on top of the coals, and then covering the whole thing with more coals.

This works if you put a raw potato in the ground, but it works better if you oil the potato first and wrap it tight in aluminum foil, which is how the jailers taught us. And inside the knapsack Michelle handed off to Mokov is a large folded square of foil and a little plastic squirt bottle of oil, plus mini zip bags of salt and pepper and Michelle's favorite spice, cumin.

Once I start prepping the potato, I realize I'm starving. It takes about an hour to bake, so after I get it buried in coals, I make a package of vegetable soup in my billypot. When I'm done eating the soup, I turn the potato over, put fresh coals all around it, then grab my club and wander out toward the cliff, just to get my mind off how much I want that potato.

The sun's dipping down toward the cliffs on the other side of the canyon, and the canyon is already starting to fill in with shadows. I'm guessing that there's about an hour to sunset, which means it's around seven o'clock.

Seven o'clock.

Already.

Or finally. I'm not sure.

I think about what I've done today. The letters. The wood, the food, the arsenal. It's been a day full of surviving. Of trying to get through things.

Thinking about the letters makes me think about home. What would I be doing right now if I was at home?

The answer sweeps in clear and sure—I'd be on my phone.

Wow.

My phone.

I haven't thought about my phone in . . . weeks. I've thought about the texts and the mess they put me in, but I haven't reached for my phone, wished for my phone, even *missed* my phone in . . . weeks.

The wind comes up the canyon, strong and warm, lifting wisps of hair that are not anchored by my braid or bandanna. I stare down at the river, slipping slowly through the earth like a muddy snake, wearing down the sides of the canyon bit by bit, finding the low ground, looking for a way out.

For the first time, I see the changes. Inside the earth, inside me.

When did that happen?

How can I not even miss my phone?

But where does the river go after it turns that corner and disappears from view? To a lake? Underground? Does it join another river? Does it hit a plain of endless desert and just die out?

Fear swells up inside me. Am I like that? A muddy river, sinking slowly into the earth, finding the low ground, dying on the plains of an endless desert?

I turn away from the canyon, walk toward the fire.

No.

That's not who I want to be.

59

I've never even thought about *who* I want to be. The question has always been *What* do you want to be? You know . . . when you grow up?

I've never had an answer for that one either. Unlike Anabella, who wants to "join the legislature and make a difference"—whatever that means. And Mo, who's wanted to play baseball for the Giants since he was about three, even though we live in Angels country now.

Me? I have no idea.

But *who* do you want to be? Nobody ever asks that. The who just *is*. I'm Wren Clemmens, daughter of Morris and Lydia Clemmens. Middle kid, with a brother on one end and a sister on the other.

But . . . that's not *me*.

That's me as part of the mix of my family.

I thought I wanted to be mini-Anabella. That didn't work out so well. So I became a new me. An angry me. Only . . . I don't want to be her, either. I can barely stand the thought of her, carving the swastika, delivering heroin.

So . . . who, then?

Who do I want to be?

I dig up my potato, thinking this question. I unwrap the foil, cut the potato, inhale the steam, thinking this question. I drizzle some oil, sprinkle salt and pepper and cumin, thinking this question. And I eat the whole potato right down to the crispy skin, watch the sun go down and the sky turn dark, thinking this question.

On the one hand, it seems like a ridiculous question—one that would be fascinating if I was stoned, and then seem really stupid the next day.

But I'm not stoned.

And it *doesn't* seem stupid.

Actually, it seems like . . . *everything.*

Who do I want to be?

The question loops through my mind as I wipe down the used aluminum foil with a bandanna, then carefully fold it into a neat metal square, saving it for morning. There's pancake mix in the knapsack, and I know how to use sticks wrapped in foil to make a griddle. I'm excited, planning it out, smelling the pancakes in my mind, knowing I can do this.

And then suddenly, unexpectedly, tickling me from inside, I recognize a long-lost feeling. The one I looked for whenever I got stoned or drunk. The one I tried to corner by outsmarting Anabella, my parents, Meadow. The one that kept drifting past me, promising me I would find it right . . . over . . . there.

And here, now, tickling the pit of my stomach, pinging to life in my heart, the feeling has found *me?* I'm filthy, alone in the desert, making food in the dirt, and somehow, against everything I've said and thought and expected, it's found *me*?

I laugh out loud. It's so ironic.

But there it is.

Happiness.

Happiness from *inside*.

How is this even possible?

I rewind my thoughts and pause at the moment the feeling triggered inside me. It was knowing I could make a griddle out of nothing but sticks and trash. And right beside that thought is knowing I can build a fire with friction, I can cook pancakes over coals, bake potatoes in the ground. I can string up a tent, make my own shelter, outsmart the rain.

I can *do* stuff.

And knowing that—*owning* that—makes me feel . . . unstoppable.

Like I can do anything.

The ping gets louder inside me. It pushes me to my feet, makes me grab my club and hold it high above my head. Makes me shout, "Yo! Coyotes! If you wanna mess with me, I'm ready to take you on!"

I toss some more wood on the fire, sending sparks flying into the darkness.

This is who I want to be.

60

I start a list by the light of the fire. I title it *Who I Want to Be.*

It seems like a dumb list, but I don't care. No one's going to see it but me. I start each sentence with "I want to be someone who . . ." and then write down something that's important to me.

It takes a while, this list. I think about every single sentence. I think about them hard. Really try them on in my head and in my heart.

A lot of what I write down surprises me. I try to block out my sister's voice going, *Are you* serious? *Could have fooled me!* I try to block out my own voice going, *Who is this fabricated person?*

But this isn't a list of who I am or was.

It's a list of who I want to be.

I don't know how late it is when I stop adding to my list, because I don't know how to tell time by the moon. It's been up there, hanging with the stars, a little slice of crescent moving across the sky, but it's not like the sun. It shows up at different times. Or not at all. So I don't know how to track it or predict it.

I lean back a little and really look at it. The moon's just a crescent, and the sky is clear, black, and shot full of stars. And taking it in now, I realize it's the most beautiful sight I've ever seen. My breath catches.

Wow. Look at that sky.

I know that stars are suns, billions of miles away, but I've never been able to wrap my head around that. Besides, I want them to be *stars*. Things to wish upon. Things that make dreams come true. Things with magical powers on the ends of fairy wands.

I think of all the Disney stories I've read to my brother, and it brings me back to my list.

Who do I want to be?

I pick up my notebook.

I want to be someone my brother's not afraid of.

It hurts to write that down. It hurts to know he probably is. He's heard me yell and cuss and storm around the house. My raging made him hide in his closet. But I don't want to be those memories to him. I want him to remember the way we used to be. The way I used to hang out with him, read to him, play *Jungle Book* with him.

I want to be his friend when he gets older.

Someone he trusts with his secrets.

Someone he likes.

I used to think he was too young to understand, to see the things that were happening. But he's in fourth grade now. I remember fourth grade.

I could see.

I look back up at the sky, take in the stars again, the deep endless universe. With all the nights I've been out in the desert, why haven't I ever really looked up like this? There is nothing more beautiful than this sky.

Tears leak out the corners of my eyes, trickle back across my temples. I feel so bad about Mo. He must know. No one had to tell him. It was all there. Right where I laid it out for him to see.

"Star light, star bright," I whisper, wishing I could change things. But before the words have a chance to come out, a star shoots across the sky.

I gasp and wipe my eyes and sniff and laugh. And after I watch the universe twinkle at me a little more, I pick up my notebook and add to my list.

I want to be someone who remembers the stars, even in daylight.

I want to be someone who looks up.

61

I decide I need to say some things to Mo, so I add some more wood to the fire and write him a note telling him I know things have been nuts and that I'm sorry. I tell him he's the best brother ever and that I miss him. And then, because that all seems so heavy and serious and being nine years old shouldn't be heavy and serious, I write, *But I know what you really want to hear about is* . . . Then in big, block letters I write DESERT QUEST and beneath that I put *A Cross-My-Heart, Hope-to-NOT-Die True Story.*

Then I tell him about Mokov and the hike, turning it into a tale of looming danger. I tell him about the plateau and the canyon, the rain and the cave, the coyote scat and the fire and the stars and the moon. I draw pictures with bits of charcoal, illustrating as I go, and when the story is done, I sign off, *Good night, little brother. See you in another moon. Love, Cave Dweller*

It makes me feel good to tell him a story. It makes me want to build a bunk-bed fort and read *The Jungle Book* to him, beginning to end. It makes me wish he was here.

I'm glad he's not, though. The truth is, I've been putting off going to bed because I'm worried about getting eaten alive. The moon has moved across the sky, but there's still a lot of night left. I have no idea how much. I think about trying to stay up all night, but I'm really, really tired. I think about dragging my pad and sleeping bag into the cave, where the coyotes would have more trouble getting to me, but it's not near the fire and fire is my best defense.

So I add a lot of wood to the fire, spreading it out in a way that seems like it will take longer to burn. Then I tell myself that everything is going to be fine, and I crawl into bed.

My head spins as I put it down on my stuff-sack pillow, and I finally give in to how tired I am. If someone made me predict what I'll dream about, I'd say, "Nothing." You don't dream when you're this tired. You just sleep.

But I do dream. And it's not about my brother or my family or flying through space or even coyotes coming to get me.

I dream about Nico.

Nico and Biggy.

The three of us are in Nico's car—I'm in the back, alone. It's smoky and they're drinking, passing a bottle of Fireball back and forth. They're ignoring me, acting like I'm not even there.

I try to go out the back door, but it won't open. There's no unlock button. There's no handle. The window won't go down.

I look around frantically. I'm having trouble breathing. "Hey!" I shout. "Let me out!" but it's like there's cotton in my mouth and the words get choked off, trapped in my throat.

I grab the front headrests and shake the seats. I get no reaction. I shake harder, and Nico and Biggy finally look back at me.

Their eyes are strange. Frightening. Golden rings around big, black pupils. Nico laughs that laugh I hate, then starts to snicker. It's a soft, sinister snicker, through his nose.

Snick, snick, snick. Snick, snick, snick.

The joke's on me, but I don't know why. What have I done? Why have they trapped me?

I search again for a door handle, for a way out. I'm frantic, suffocating on cries for help.

Snick, snick, snick. Snick, snick, snick.

I see someone through the window. A woman walking by. I pound on the glass, scream "HELP!" but it never leaves my throat. The window's tinted, blacked out. The woman walks by without hearing, without seeing.

Sniff, sniff, sniff. Sniff, sniff, sniff.

Golden eyes narrow, move toward me between the seats.

I gasp awake, relieved to break out of the dream, then almost immediately choke back a real scream.

Sniff, sniff, sniff. Sniff, sniff, sniff.

Something's outside my tent.

I sit up, grab the club, my heart pounding, my whole body shaking. It sounds like there's water rushing through my ears.

There's not much light from the sky and only a little from the fire, which has burned down to coals. But I can see something moving along the side of my tent. Black on black. Shadow in darkness.

I watch the shadow move forward slowly, silently. I back up inside my tent, keeping what distance I can. Then the shadow turns and a face appears in the triangle opening of my tent.

A second face appears on the other side.

They have pointed ears, glistening eyes.

My heart stops.

Coyotes.

From somewhere inside me a voice shoots free. "HEY!" I shout, the sound exploding through the darkness. Suddenly I'm jabbing at the coyotes with my club, coming at them with a gust of power. "LEAVE ME ALONE!"

They scamper off, but just past the fire ring they stop and stand by, watching me.

"YOU THINK I'M GONNA LET YOU TAKE ME DOWN?" I yell at them.

My voice doesn't scare them, but the rocks do. I hurl them hard and fast and hear a yip when I connect. "GO!" I shout. "LEAVE ME ALONE!"

They disappear into the darkness, but I'm not sure they're really gone. So I lace up my boots, go out, look around, waiting, the club in my hand.

"STAY GONE!" I finally shout into the darkness. Then I add wood to the fire and fan it back to life.

I sit up the rest of the night, watching for coyotes, waiting for the darkness to lift. It's cold out, so I keep the fire burning big and bright, and I make my sticks-and-foil frying pan to keep my mind off coyotes.

My mind wanders. I think about the letters, my dream, what things will be like when I go back home, what it'll be like to face my family, to be back at school, to see Nico and Biggy and Meadow again. I think about all of it and ask myself what I *want* to have happen. Ask myself how in the world I'm going to face all of that.

Dawn sneaks up on me. It's like the whole sky gets a slow,

silent swipe of an eraser. Then another. And another. Suddenly I notice—it's daylight.

I'm so relieved to be able to see around me. So relieved to still be alive. I'm also *excited*.

I did it!

Michelle had told me that I'd be "escorted out" sometime this morning, so I get busy making breakfast. I level my sticks-and-foil pan on a square of rocks lined up around coals, squirt on some oil, and cook breakfast, one delicious pancake at a time.

At home I drowned my pancakes in syrup, but here I eat them right off the griddle and they taste amazing. Crispy around the edges, steamy warm in the middle. I wash them down with a cup of powdered milk. The milk isn't the best, but it's cold and wet, and that's good enough.

Then I clean up, and while I'm striking camp, I find a small gray-and-white feather on the ground. I pick it up and look around, wondering where the bird is that left it.

I've never really studied a feather before, so I'm surprised by how soft and clean it is. How intricate. How beautiful. "Thank you," I say to the phantom bird, because it feels like a gift. Then I go with the sudden urge to weave the feather into my braid. Maybe it's time to own my name, too.

I get back to striking camp, and I hustle because while I was waiting for daylight, I had an idea of something I want to do before I leave.

So when my pack's bundled, I take some charcoal from the fire—cooled chunks and sticks with blackened ends—and I head over to the cave where I escaped the rain my first night. I climb inside the cave, sit cross-legged facing a wall, and start drawing. From left to right I draw a cloud with rain, then fire, the moon and stars, a coyote, and a picture of me with my club.

It takes a while. The surface is rough and the drawings are crude. Simple lines and smudges of black against salmon-colored rock. The picture of me winds up looking like a crazy stick girl with a club, but that's okay. That's what I was.

I end my pictograph with the sun peeking up over a wall of rock. I look at the whole thing for a minute, then add the shape of a small bird inside a heart.

I know the charcoal won't last. I know it's like writing with a stick in the sand—wind and water will wash it away. So no one else may ever see this, and if they do, they'll interpret my pictures their own way, which may or may not come close to the story I'm telling. What they *won't* know is what the bird means.

That's okay, too.

Because I do.

62

I did come back different. And then everything *became* different. Over the next couple of weeks, Brooke and Kelsey finished the program; then Shalayne and Mia were gone, too.

Mia's leaving was sad. Not just because she was part of our group and we liked her and were going to miss her, but because no one came to get her.

At the end of your eight weeks, there's a "passage ritual"—someone from your family's supposed to come to Utah and camp out with you for a night. They set up a little side camp and Tara-the-Therapist is there to "facilitate the reunion."

With Brooke and Kelsey and Shalayne, people came. We could hear crying and raised voices over in the side camp, but people came. And the crying stopped and the voices went quiet and in the morning there seemed to be a truce. Even smiles.

Mia didn't get any of that. She packed up, came over to Hannah and me to say goodbye, then cried and said that we were her real family and that she didn't know what she'd do without us.

Hannah and I promised her that we'd stay in touch, that we'd start a private group online and talk each other through things.

And then she was gone, disappearing into the desert, hiking with Tara back to base camp, where someone would drive her to the airport and put her on a plane.

Which left no Falcons and Hannah and me as the Elks. The ones pulling the snow discs. The ones the new Rabbits and Coyotes watched and whispered about. It was feeling a lot like school—little cliques, eyeing each other, taking notes, gossiping—until I decided I'd had enough of that trap. Instead of steering clear, I started invading the Coyote circle to hang out or help out.

Brooke and Kelsey never did that, but you know what?

That's not who I want to be.

It's painful to hear new Rabbits freak out their first couple of nights. Painful to know what they're going through, but also painful to remember acting that way. Babies come into the world screaming and crying and gasping for air, and getting through Rabbit is a lot like that. And then there you are, in a new world, helpless and weak, needing to figure out how to survive.

The Grizzly Girls number has gone up and down, but there are seven of us again now. One Rabbit, four Coyotes, and Hannah and me. It's strange to feel like a leader, to show the others how to do stuff, to point out scat and plants and explain how to tell time by dividing up the sky.

It's also strange to hear them beg me to tell stories at night.

I'll never be Mokov, but I do like being the Grizzlies' story-teller in between his visits, and Mokov has definitely made me better at it. He's also helped me find the story behind the story, which is something I've really grown to love. Like a secret room with a wide-open sky.

Dvorka, Michelle, and John took turns going on leave for a week, sticking us with people who tried too hard to figure us out. The three of them are back now. Dvorka's hair is buzzed short again, John's face is clean-shaven, his man-bun is tidy, and Michelle looks exactly the same, only cleaner. I'm glad they're back. It's just easier to be around people who understand how to avoid certain buttons.

They also seemed to really miss us. I asked John about his regular life, and he gave me this little smile and said, "This *is* my life."

I snickered and said, "No, really."

He jabbed at the fire with a stick and said, "Well, let's just say it's everything I want my life to be." Then he smiled at me and changed the subject. "I heard there's been good mail."

I just looked down and shrugged, but it was true. I've gotten two batches of letters from home since the quest, and they . . . they've made me feel like . . . like things are going to be okay.

I was expecting arguments from my parents. Or shock and disappointment. Or for them to hit back. Or justify. Or explain how it was all my own doing. But for all the things I did, for all the lies I told, for all the damage I caused, they said they were sorry, too.

Even Anabella said she was sorry.

Actually, Anabella most of all.

I've read her letters, like, twenty times. Partly because I can't believe she's being so nice. I can't remember her ever acting this nice, even when we were little, and it kind of blows my mind. I keep rereading her letters to make sure the words are really there, to make sure there's not some hidden message I'm missing.

I also reread them because there's news about school. About Nico being expelled and in serious trouble because he's eighteen and officially an adult, about Meadow being taken in by Child Protective Services while she "awaits a hearing." I don't know what Child Protective Services is, exactly, or how long she won't be living with her parents, but it probably has to do with the stoner temple.

Whatever happens, I don't see Meadow changing. I'm pretty sure even the desert wouldn't change Meadow.

So I've spent a lot of time thinking about that, and also thinking about something my mother brought up. She said they're willing to look into sending me to a different school if I think it'll help. Tara-the-Therapist told me that the biggest problem with leaving the desert is falling back into the same bad habits; and she brought up again how a lot of teens go into transitional programs to try to ease back into the real world. But she also said that those programs are super expensive. So no. I'm definitely not doing that.

But going back to the same school—walking the same hallways, seeing the same people, facing the same teachers—I'd be lying if I said that doesn't scare me.

How's it going to be any different than it was before?

How am I going to make new friends?

Meadow may be living somewhere else, but Anabella said she still goes to school. Still looks the same. Still acts the same.

And what if Meadow blames me for what's happened to her? What if it *is* my fault? What if my parents took my letters to the police? To the school counselors? What if Biggy knows? What if everyone blames everything on *me*?

I panic inside, just thinking about it. Suddenly *leaving* the desert seems like something I might not survive.

I've got just over a week to figure it out.

What *am* I going to do?

63

The next morning, I do what I've done every morning since I was kidnapped.

I ink a tally mark on my pants.

Ten groups of five.

Day 50.

My birthday.

I mentioned my birthday to Hannah about a week ago, but I really didn't expect her to remember. She's getting ready for her passage ritual. Her dad's driving in from Kansas, and she's kind of freaked out about everything.

But when I return from doing my morning business, I find a present waiting for me at the opening of my tent. It's a folder not much bigger than my hand, woven out of long grasses. It has a braided loop wrapped around a little woven knot to keep it closed, and when I unhitch the loop, I find three yucca-leaf paintbrushes nestled in a little inside pouch. The brushes are different widths—about an eighth inch, a quarter inch, and a half inch—and flat.

Dvorka showed us how to make yucca-leaf paintbrushes during an art lesson weeks ago. We'd already spent days on making yucca cordage and yucca shampoo, so I was all about the yucca for giving me clean hair and a new bootlace. But as hard as I tried during the art lesson, my paintbrush came out awful. We tore a yucca leaf lengthwise, shortened it to brush length, then chewed on the ends to soften them until they were brushes. I hated the chewing part. Yucca leaves are tough. And bitter. And when I was done, my paintbrush was all jagged and stupid and I couldn't paint with it at all.

These brushes, though . . . these brushes are unbelievable. Their handles are straight, with the sharp edges buffed down so they're comfortable to hold, and the bristles are smooth across and *soft*. Like a real brush.

"You like?" Hannah asks, watching me from her tent.

"How did you do this?" I ask. "These are *amazing*." I tuck the brushes away and admire the case. "And this . . . this is incredible!"

I look at her, and it's like I've switched a light on inside her. "Thank you!" she beams. "It was so hard to keep it a surprise!" She scrambles over to my tent. "And guess what? Michelle said I could take you out painting today. She showed me a perfect spot. It's a bit of a hike, but the view is great."

"Just you and me?"

She nods. "It's your birthday, and the last day before my passage ritual, so I managed to twist her arm."

I laugh. "Besides, what are we going to do at this point, right? Run away?" I look at her present again. "Thank you so much."

Her voice goes soft. "I know you don't really *like* to paint, but—"

"That's because I'm terrible at it!"

"Today is going to be different."

I laugh. "Even if it's not, it'll be fun."

So after breakfast we head out with a knapsack full of painting supplies, lunch, and water. The day is warm and there's a lot of uphill, but it seems like nothing—I could hike like this all day. I find a feather to add to my growing collection. This one's small—only about two inches—and jet black. I can't find any sign of the bird that dropped it in my path, but I say "Thank you" anyway.

Hannah adds it to my hair, which she's been braiding for me the past week or so. "I wish you could actually see this," she says about my feathery braid. "It looks unbelievably cool."

We set off again, hiking along until we're inside a slot canyon where Hannah stops and says, "This is it."

I look around. The space is narrow, with walls on either side of us. I don't see anything to paint. "Here?" I ask.

She swings off the knapsack. "I was thinking about your list," she says.

"The list I made on my quest?" I showed it to her after she returned from her own quest, when we secretly compared notes.

She nods. "You told me about the stars, remember? And how you wanted to be someone who . . . ?"

She stares at me, waiting.

I blink at her, trying to fill in the blank.

Finally I look up.

Above us . . . way above us, two large trees are growing out of opposite sides of the slot-canyon walls. Their trunks poke out at right angles, then shoot straight up. They're like arrows aiming at the clouds breezing across the slice of blue sky above us. "Wow," I breathe out.

"Isn't that the most amazing thing you've ever seen?" she asks.

It's more than just the sight of them that gets me. It's the survival. Two doomed saplings from opposite sides of the canyon changed direction, reached for the sun, and became . . . that.

"It sure is," I choke out.

"So let's paint!" she says.

I'm still staring up. "I am never in a million years going to be able to paint *that*."

She laughs. "Well, right. We've only got blacks and grays to work with." She begins pulling supplies from the knapsack. "But I will teach you, and really, what matters is that it reminds you."

I'm not sure if she means that it should remind me of this place, of this day, of what a real friend is, or to look up.

And it doesn't matter.

However good or bad my painting turns out, it'll remind me of them all.

64

When Hannah and I return to camp, there's another surprise waiting.

Dutch oven birthday cake!

It smells delicious—warm and cinnamony, and it's drowning in powdered-sugar icing. I squeal like a little girl and dance around. "Can we, can we, can we?" I ask.

Dvorka laughs. "First, how'd it go? Can we see your paintings?"

"I made a lot of fire starter," I say with a laugh, because my first five tries are total trash. But I pull out my final piece—which isn't half bad—and show it around.

Hannah keeps hers—which is *amazing*—tucked away while the Coyotes make a fuss over mine. I show everyone the brushes Hannah made and explain how all the different lines and washes and shades of my painting come from coal and a paste of ash and water.

They look at both of us like we've just descended from heaven. "Can you teach us?" they ask.

Hannah saves me by saying, "Dvorka can. She's the one who taught me."

"Yeah, it's gonna have to be Dvorka," I tell them. "Because Hannah's leaving tomorrow, and I'm still, uh, learning." I smile around at them. "But I can teach you how to eat birthday cake!"

The Coyotes pump fists. "Yes!"

"Not so fast," John says, stepping in. He turns to the Coyotes. "Ready for the poetry slam?"

"What?" I ask, looking around. But the Coyotes are already spreading out around the campfire.

"Let's do this!" a Coyote named Glo cries. Then she turns to me and says, "It's not actually a slam, but you'll like it."

When all four Coyotes are in position, John starts a beatbox rhythm, and after everyone's in the groove, he points at Glo and the Coyotes throw down lines, fast and sure, like they've been practicing all day.

"She comes from Cali—"

"Her name's not Sally—"

"Don't dally, or rally—"

"She's not that kind."

"She's tough and buff—"

"A cool McGruff—"

"Don't doubt her spinnin' mind."

"A fire starter—"

" 'Push down harder!' "

" 'Watch the genie rise!' "

"She tells great stories—"

"They never bore ya—"

"Her Disney lullabies."

"So don't be messin'—"

"She's representin'—"

"That Grizzly Girls are fine!"

"She's cool and sure—"

"The birthday girl—"

"A red earth friend of mine!"

"HAPPY BIRTHDAY, WREN!"

I laugh and cry and wipe my eyes and clap and laugh and clap some more. Then John produces a pack of candles, and fifteen of them get jabbed into my giant cinnamon-bun birthday cake and lit.

I flash back to that early day in my tent when I realized I'd be spending my birthday in the desert, in the dirt. I remember how angry and devastated and hurt I was.

But now, as I take a deep breath and blow out my candles in one giant blast, I make a wish I would never have predicted.

That every birthday could be like this one.

65

Early the next morning, another surprise jolts me awake.

"Strike camp!"

In the tent next to mine, I hear Hannah groan, "Oh, you have got to be kidding."

But they're not. Michelle's already scattering fire-ring rocks, erasing our footprint, while John and Dvorka are making the rounds, slapping tarps, barking like drill sergeants. "Let's move it! Rise and shine!"

"Tell that to the sun," one of the Coyotes complains, because it's not up yet, which means it's not even six a.m.

Less than an hour later, we are stumbling in formation behind Michelle and John. Hannah and I are pulling snow discs, the Coyotes are behind us muscling the tarp stretcher, and Dvorka is bringing up the rear, dragging along a very ornery Rabbit.

"Why the rush to leave?" one of the Coyotes asks, but a couple of hours later, when we break for breakfast, the air's already dragon-breath hot, and the day will only get hotter. The flies are out, too, hovering around our sweaty heads.

"Wow," I pant, parking my disc and dropping my pack in the shade of a pinyon grove. "If this is springtime in the desert, I'd hate to be here in the summer."

"This is unusual," John offers. "Base camp gave us a heads-up."

"How much farther?" one of the Coyotes asks.

Hannah and I grin at each other, then turn to John, who delivers the usual answer. "Pace yourself, ration your water. We'll get there when we arrive."

Breakfast is trail mix, dried fruit, and as much of our own water as we dare to drink. Before we set off again, everyone zips off the bottoms of their pants, and some of us roll our shirtsleeves up to our shoulders and what's left of our pant legs up to midthigh.

Michelle passes sunblock around and then we set off again, slogging across the desert. It's too hot to sing. Too hot to talk. Too hot to do anything but escape from the heat by folding up inside your own head.

I think about home. About facing my family, facing school. After I get back, there'll be two weeks before summer break. How will this work? Am I flunking my freshman year? What about all the curriculum we've had to do out in the desert? What does it count for? Will I have to take summer school?

I think about what Mom offered—about going to another school. I wonder if I should. Maybe it would be better. Nico may be gone, but facing the gossip and glances and Meadow . . . it scares me. How can I fight all of that at once?

I'm pulled out of my thoughts by a sound in the distance.

A motor?

Yes, a motor.

And then, up ahead, Michelle unholsters her walkie-talkie.

I touch my ear, telling Hannah to listen. Then I point out Michelle and her walkie-talkie. "Resupply?" I mouth.

"I sure hope so," Hannah says. "This has been a horrible last day."

"But if you get to see Silver Hawk?"

She grins. "That would make it all better."

We cross a wide, dry arroyo, turn a bend, and suddenly there it is—the resupply truck.

"Wa-hoo!" Hannah shrieks, and she and I take off, our sleds bobbing and clanging behind us as we race to reach the truck. "He's mine!" Hannah calls over to me as Silver Hawk steps out of the truck.

"All yours," I call back. "I'm racing for water!"

She laughs, "Sure you are!" and sprints ahead of me.

I let her have him. Not that I don't soak him in. I mean, every time it's a brand-new wow. But I act cool. Or as cool as a girl fifty-one days in the desert can act around someone that gorgeous.

On my third time through the line for water, he opens the spigot only a little so the water comes out slowly. "I heard about the coyotes," he says, his voice low.

At first I don't know what he means. "The new ones?" I ask, thinking he's talking about campers.

He gives me a sly look as the water trickles into my cup. "No. The wild ones."

My mind clicks over to the fact that he's talking about the coyotes on my quest. The mini-wolves trying to kill me.

I want to ask how he heard about that, but something else suddenly clicks too. I came off the quest to a ceremony—to a yellow bead for my necklace and an immediate move up to Elk. It was a silent ceremony, with ash painted on my face. I wasn't allowed to tell my story to the group or the field staff, although I did finally spill it to Hannah.

But it was like the field staff already knew. I figured that was them understanding what a quest was. What it did. How there really is no explaining it, so it's best to keep its power inside you.

But now . . . now I get it.

"Your grandfather," I say to Silver Hawk, keeping my voice low. "He told you?"

His answer comes out slowly. Carefully. "The campers earn his affection and even his respect, but rarely his admiration." He locks his eyes on mine. "But you did."

"So he . . . he was there?"

"On a ledge above you." Silver Hawk turns off the water. "Our secret, okay?"

I nod.

"Swear?"

I nod again.

"He said you were ready to face the seasons."

"The seasons?"

"Whatever life throws at you." He grins. "High praise from Mokov." He glances behind him and cocks his head toward the cab of the truck. "Maybe you can influence him?"

"Who?"

He just cocks his head again, then says, "Back to work," and reaches for a waiting cup from the line that's formed behind me.

So I go around the truck and approach the cab. I don't notice anyone at first, but the windows are all rolled down, so I look inside and see someone half slumped in the backseat with his eyes closed. There's a loose blindfold dangling around his neck and a counselor on the far side sitting next to him. "Dax?" I half whisper.

His eyes flutter open. There are circles under them. Pain inside them. They look at me like they have no idea who I am.

"Wren, remember?" I tell him.

A little grin tries to take hold. "Wrenegade. How's it goin'?" He sits up a little. "Lookin' good, little bird." He sits up some more. "Whoa—check out those muscles!"

He reaches for my arm, but I edge away. "You're back."

"Back to square one!" He's in jive mode now. Like it's all a game.

"Try to stick it out this time, Dax."

"Oh, I will, I will," he says, but it oozes from him like an easy lie.

"No, really. We started this together, remember? You'd be on your last week if you hadn't run away."

He stares at me, computing what I've just said.

"You can do this, Dax."

"Right," he says. "Judge says it's my last chance, and I'm down with that. I'm good. It's all good."

But even as he's saying it, his focus is scattered. He's looking past my shoulder, looking out the windshield, looking out the back window.

Looking for a way to escape.

66

It was probably about three o'clock when we finally arrived at our new campsite. We were all wiped out from the heat, and the Rabbit had a complete meltdown setting up her tent. She actually jumped up and down on her tarp like she was trying to smash it into the ground.

Hannah's dad arrived with Tara shortly after we did. His face was red and dripping sweat, and it was super awkward seeing him give Hannah a hug. I'm not sure how it's going to go with the two of them, because they're basically strangers. But here he is. Which says a lot.

It's not even dark yet, but everyone's in for the night, exhausted. For the first time in ages, Hannah's tent is not next to mine. She's off in a separate area with her dad and Tara. I knew this was coming, but her being gone really hits home now. I wish I had thought about what it would be like to not have her tent, her midnight whispers, her soft snoring and morning rustlings right next to me. I miss her already, and she's just across camp.

Letters were delivered at resupply, but I didn't open mine. They're the last ones I'll get before I go home, and I've started really *liking* mail. I've never read a text or message more than once. I never *linger* over anything on my phone. Messages come in, go out. It's fast and . . . fleeting.

But my letters—the recent ones anyway—I've read again and again. I look at Mo's drawings, reread his big, underlined excitement. *That is so cool! I can't believe you went hunting for poop! My friend Trey says a coyote came into their backyard and snatched their dog! He says you sound like a warrior!*

How could I not read that again and again?

My brother's friend thinks I'm a warrior!

So I've been saving the two letters that were delivered at resupply because I don't know if I'll ever get letters again. Letters are so . . . medieval. But after just staring at the envelopes for a while, I dive in.

The first one is a birthday card, signed by everybody with little notes and promises to have a real celebration when I get home. I think about that a minute. I don't care about a "real celebration." Nothing could top my day with Hannah, or the poetry slam and the cinna-bun birthday cake. Now, if they want to do Disneyland, I won't argue. But if I had to choose between a birthday there and the birthday I had here, I'd stick with the one I had here.

The other envelope is from Mom. I pull out the letter, unfold it, and turn the page over and over in my hand. It's not in Lucida Handwriting. It's in Mom font, with ink from a pen.

Dear Wren, it starts. *Love, Mom,* it ends. The "L" is beautiful—like a ribbon floating on its side. The "M" swoops up and down, up and down like a graceful mountain range, and the "W" on the opposite side is like its reflection. And all the letters in between flow together, connecting letters into words, words into thoughts, thoughts into love.

I can just feel it, coming off the page.

I don't know why seeing a letter from my mom in her own handwriting means so much to me, but it does. Maybe because it comes from her hand, not a machine. Maybe it's because I feel like she touched the page, didn't just press print. Maybe because it means she listened.

I finally read the letter and discover that she's also been thinking. Like, a lot. She talks about wanting to help me find things that make me excited to get up in the morning, that make me look forward to the day and my life and my future. And after lots of explaining how she's not trying to direct my life, but there were deadlines and she had to pull a few strings, she says she really, really hopes I don't mind that she's signed me up to be a youth counselor at Camp Takaneo, starting right after school lets out for summer break.

It's for kids in 3rd, 4th, and 5th, she writes, *and your brother is very excited that you might do this, since he and his friends have all enrolled. (He's done nothing but brag to them about your wilderness skills, and his friends keep asking him if he's got another installment of your Hope-to-NOT-Die True Stories.) (Please tell me they're fiction!)*

Then she goes on with some alternate suggestions and asks again if I think I might want to transfer to a different school.

Her other suggestions don't do much for me, but the thought of being a camp counselor? I sit there thinking about it, picturing it, feeling so wrapped-up happy at the thought of doing crafts and activities and camping stuff with kids.

So I write her back. Right away, and fast. I tell her YES

to being a counselor and thank her for thinking of it and enrolling me. And in a flash of certainty I tell her NO to a new school. I don't explain, but the truth is, seeing Dax again made me realize something: it wouldn't help to run away. I know it's not going to be easy to go back, but "fearless" is on my list of who I want to be, and hiding from what scares me is not being fearless. It helps to think of going back as being like facing coyotes. I know I can stand up to them. I know I can chase them off.

And the reality is, all schools have coyotes.

67

It's been lonesome without Hannah. We both cried a lot when it was time for her to go, and we promised each other the same things we promised Mia. As soon as she was gone, though, I went off to a shady spot by myself and wrote her a letter. I told her that we should do all the things we talked about—messaging and texting and all that—but that we should also write each other old-fashioned letters; that they'd be good to pull out in the middle of the night to remind us that we were forever friends, even if we lived half a continent apart.

And suddenly it's my turn. Someone from my family is showing up today. I'm on Falcon now, and part of the transition ceremony mentioned guiding others and "achieving confidence." I was so proud when Dvorka strung the orange bead on my necklace. Like I'd really earned the right to wear it.

Now I feel like I should give the bead back. I *don't* feel confident. I've been getting more and more nervous every day. I don't know who's coming, and I don't know what to expect. I keep telling myself that it's going to be okay, but I'm feeling so frayed about everything. Part of me doesn't want to go home, like, *ever,* and part of me can't wait to get out of here. Fifty-eight days in the desert? I want a real bath!

I'm hoping it's my mom who shows up today, though it'll probably be my dad. Dad said he likes camping. Mom, I know, does not. All Michelle would tell me is that Tara would be arriving with my "family member" later today.

Michelle showed me where our side camp will be, so I've spent the day collecting firewood, putting together a fire ring, digging a latrine, and wondering how far apart I should put the tents. Or if we'll even need tents. It's hot today. So hot I've got my pant legs zipped off and rolled up, and my sleeves rolled up too. It looks like it'll be a good night to sleep under the stars.

But . . . maybe it'll be better to have tents. Little wedges where we can escape from each other. After all, what am I going to say to my dad? I haven't really talked to him in *years.*

It's midafternoon when I finally hear Tara's voice. I can't see her, but I can hear her calling, "You can do it—it's right up here!"

I feel a wash of relief. It must be my mom, because my dad wouldn't need coaxing. But when Tara comes into view, the person right behind her *is* my father.

He doesn't see me, so I start toward them, only he and Tara turn and look back the way they've come, and suddenly there's my mom.

My parents are both hot and sweaty, but Mom looks like she's walked across Hell.

I can't help grinning.

Welcome to camp.

But they're both here, which is amazing, so I grab my canteen and head toward them. And then I see them both looking back the way they've come.

I stop and hold my breath, and then there's my brother, dragging himself in.

"Mowgli!" I squeal, and go charging toward him.

He dumps off the sleeping bag strapped to his back and hugs me hard. "It was so far," he tells me. I hand him the canteen and then see that my mom is crying. "Hey!" I say, standing up. "Sorry! I'm happy to see you, too!"

"No, it's not that. . . ." She holds my shoulders. "*Look* at you!"

Then my dad says, "Wren?" like he barely recognizes me.

"Is it that scary?" I ask, and I'm starting to feel defensive. "It's not like there's mirrors out here, you know."

Mom says, "No, it's—"

But then my Dad calls, "Over here! Anabella—we're up here!"

I look at my mom. "You're kidding, right?"

Dad gives me a quick hug and says, "We thought it would be good for us all to be here."

Anabella comes dragging in, dumps her pack, flops on top of it face-first, and groans. It looks horribly uncomfortable, but I guess it feels better than standing up.

I turn to Tara. "How far did you make them hike?"

She shrugs. "Maybe a mile and a half?"

I snicker. "Going easy on them, huh?"

"Shut *up*," Anabella cries, her face buried in her pack.

"Hello to you, too."

I can feel my parents tense up. Like, oh no. Trouble already. But I don't feel like there's trouble. I feel like . . . it's good. She's here. Not many sisters would do this. "Relax," I tell them. "I'm really glad she's here."

Anabella sits up and scowls at me. "So I can experience the torture?" But before I can say anything, her eyes go buggy and her mouth drops open and she gasps, "*Look* at you."

"I know I'm gross," I snap, and that old anger toward her is right back. "You would be, too, if you'd been out here fifty-eight days!"

"No!" she says. "What I mean is, you look like . . . like . . ." She stands up and starts circling me.

"Like what?" I snap.

"Like a warrior," my brother says.

"Exactly," Anabella breathes. She touches my arms, touches my feathered braid, looks me up and down. "I want that," she says to my mom when she's gone full circle. Like it's something you can go to the store and buy.

My mom gives my dad a helpless look, Dad rolls his eyes, and my brother puts things in perspective by saying, "The toilet's a hole in the ground. You know that, right?"

Anabella's face scrunches in disgust, and Tara comes to the rescue, motioning us to move along to our side camp. "Let's just get through tonight, shall we?"

On the walk over, my mom puts her arm around me and says, "I am so incredibly proud of you. But what I was wondering on the drive over was—"

"You *drove* here?"

"Well, we all wanted to come, and it was the only affordable way."

I look down. "Sorry. I know this was expensive."

"No. I don't care about that. I care that . . . that you've found this new you. What I want to *know* is what changed things? Was there a moment? An event?"

I think back, shake my head, think some more. And what's amazing is she lets me. She doesn't interrupt or fill in my blanks. She just waits while we walk and I think back. Which tells me that she's different now, too.

Finally I look at her and say, "It might have been my first fire."

"How's that?"

"Starting a bow-drill fire is hard to do. It's really frustrating. But it's the point when you're sure it won't light that you need to bear down and keep going. It's the point when you feel so frustrated that you want to kick everything as far away as you can get it that you need to lean in and not let go."

Mom nods thoughtfully, and then Mo calls out, "Hey!" because the two of us have lagged way behind.

Mom gives me a hug, then joins Dad and Anabella. And as they survey the campsite and talk to Tara, I stay back because it's really sinking in now.

This is my last day.

I look around, taking in the junipers and pinyons, the sharp shadows cutting across red dirt, the jutting walls of sandstone in the distance. I think about parched earth and hidden water, about unexpected fields of flowers and trees reaching for sunlight from the shadows of canyons. I remember the miles I've walked, the buckets I've sweated, the blisters I've endured, and the tears I've cried to get here. And I realize for the first time how grateful I am to have tripped, stumbled, and collapsed into the arms of the desert.

"Wren?" my brother asks, shaking me from my thoughts. "Are we going to bake a potato? Can we make a griddle out of sticks? Do you think there'll be coyotes? What are we doing? I'm starving!"

I laugh and sling an arm around his shoulders. "First things first," I tell him.

"So what's that?"

My mind flashes with the things I've learned out here. Not just the things I learned to survive in the desert, but also the things I learned to survive myself. I think about how all of it, everything really, comes down to learning how to lean in and not let go.

So I know what's first.

What has to be first.

"Come on," I say, pulling him forward. "Let's go start a fire."